Acclaim for Alix Ohlin and

Babylon and Other Stories

"Ohlin's talent isn't just her ability to intrigue us. Once we're hooked she doesn't let us go. . . . Her work is funny, sad, sweet and terrifying all at once: quite an accomplishment."
—*Austin American-Statesman*

"Elegant, disquieting. . . . Ohlin finds all the acute angles in these intersecting lives, and she sharpens them to a cutting edge; her voice rings clear and true through every story."
—*The Seattle Times*

"Ohlin's stories stay grounded with their complex characters and sparkling moments of insight. She's great at probing the moments that can change everything."   —*Time Out New York*

"Via a process all the more impressive for its apparent effortlessness, Ohlin puts readers down in a place quite different from where she picks them up. This is a beguiling and very impressive collection."   —*The Gazette* (Montreal)

"Engaging and intelligent, ironic and heartfelt, all at once."
—*Variety*

Alix Ohlin

Babylon and Other Stories

Alix Ohlin was born in Montreal, graduated from Harvard University, and studied at the Michener Center for Writers in Austin, Texas. Her fiction, which has appeared in *One Story* and *Shenandoah*, among other periodicals, has been selected for both *Best New American Voices 2004* and *Best American Short Stories 2005*. She has received awards and fellowships from *The Atlantic Monthly*, the MacDowell Colony, *The Kenyon Review*'s Writers Workshop, the Sewanee Writers' Conference, and Yaddo. She lives in Easton, Pennsylvania, and teaches at Lafayette College.

ALSO BY ALIX OHLIN

The Missing Person

Babylon and Other Stories

Babylon

and Other Stories

Alix Ohlin

Vintage Contemporaries

Vintage Books

A Division of Random House, Inc.

New York

FIRST VINTAGE CONTEMPORARIES EDITION, JUNE 2007

Grateful acknowledgment is made to Alfred Publishing Co., Inc., for permission to reprint an excerpt from the song lyric "Facts of Life," words and music by Alan Thicke, Gloria Loring, and Al Burton. Copyright © 1981 by EMI Belfast Music Inc., EMI Worldtrax Music, Inc., and Thickovit Music. All rights reserved. Reprinted by permission of Alfred Publishing Co., Inc.

These stories originally appeared in the following publications: "The King of Kohlrabi" in *Five Points*; "Transcription" in *Best New American Voices 2004* (Harcourt/Harvest); "Simple Exercises for the Beginning Student" in *Swink* and subsequently in *Best American Short Stories 2005* (Houghton Mifflin); "You Are Here" in *Bellingham Review*; "A Theory of Entropy" in *Prism International*; "Edgewater" in *The Ex-Files* (Context Books); "Wonders Never Cease" in *Colorado Review*; "I Love to Dance at Weddings" in *XConnect*; "Land of the Midnight Sun" in *Shenandoah;* "Meeting Uncle Bob" in *The Cincinnati Review*; "Babylon" in *Salt Hill*; "Local News" in *Backwards City Review*; "The Swanger Blood" in *Southwest Review*; "In Trouble with the Dutchman" in *The Massachusetts Review*; "The Tennis Partner" in *One Story*.

The Library of Congress has cataloged the Knopf edition as follows:
Ohlin, Alix.
Babylon and other stories / Alix Ohlin.—1st ed.
p. cm.
I. Title
PS3615.H57B33 2006
813'.6—dc22
2006040985

Vintage ISBN: 978-1-4000-3139-9

Book design by Wesley Gott

www.vintagebooks.com

Printed in the United States of America
10 9 8 7 6 5 4 3 2 1

to my parents

Contents

Babylon and Other Stories

The King of Kohlrabi

It was a summer of disasters. I was sixteen and just starting to relax fully into my vacation when my father took my mother and me out to dinner at the New Chinatown and told us over the Kung Pao chicken that he'd fallen in love with his law partner, Margaret, and the two of them were "going away for a while" to "sort things out." While he was talking, he twisted a corner of the tablecloth into a ring in his right hand. My mother, leaning back in the corner of the booth, said, "Oh, for crying out loud." She sounded annoyed. She was drinking a Mai Tai, as usual, and had given me the umbrella, also as usual. Tonight's was blue and I twirled it between my fingers. I was always pleasantly surprised that it really opened and closed, just like a real umbrella. I stuck it into a piece of my chicken and moved some baby carrots and water chestnuts into an arrangement around it, like small, edible patio furniture. No one said anything. I stared at the couple at the table next to us, who were sharing a Volcano, holding hands over the blue flame in the center of it. They saw me looking and loosed their hands as if they were embarrassed.

"You know how much I love you both," said my dad. My mother and I didn't say anything to this. Margaret had been at our house for Christmas that year. She was a quiet, large-boned woman with a wide, dark mouth and I'd always thought she was a lesbian.

"I thought she was a lesbian," I said.

"Well, she's not," said my dad.

I drove home from the New Chinatown. I had just gotten my driver's license but my parents wouldn't let me take the car anywhere without them. My mom always sat in the front passenger seat, making a big show out of white-knuckling the armrest and covering her eyes when she thought I was being reckless. My father sat in the back seat and whistled. He was a good whistler, and that night he did an up-tempo rendition of "I Get a Kick Out of You."

I looked at him in the rearview mirror and wondered if he was so happy with Margaret the lesbian that he couldn't stop being happy, even for just a few minutes, even for us. Then a guy came out of nowhere in a red Toyota Corolla, turning in front of me off a side street with a stop sign. I don't know what he was thinking.

"Aggie!" yelled my mother, gripping the dashboard.

"It's not my fault," I said quickly, and braked hard, too hard I guess, and the car skidded to the left; the right front fender of our car collided with the side of the Toyota. The driver, steam pouring from under his hood, got out and started walking around the dark street, clutching his arm and howling. Next to me my mother began to cry in a dry, sharp way, jaggedly inhaling. These two noises, my mother's and the driver's, were the only two sounds, the night otherwise quiet. We all sat there breathing. My father whistled the first few notes of "Be Careful, It's My Heart."

This was the second disaster.

The next day my father packed a suitcase and left for Santa Fe, where he and Margaret had sublet an apartment for the summer.

She came to pick him up in her Saab and they drove away together, leaving our crumpled Honda in the driveway. I watched from the bedroom window but didn't say good-bye. As soon as they were out of sight, my mother walked into my room without knocking and plopped herself down on the bed.

"Things are going to be different around here now that your father's gone, Aggie," she said severely. "You'll be giving up your pampered life of leisure."

"What?" I said. I had planned to spend the summer learning to play the bass guitar so I could start an all-girl punk band—and it was a good plan, except I didn't own a bass guitar and had no money to buy one—but Mom said I'd have to get a job instead. I wasn't thrilled by this idea. My two best friends were waitressing, and they kept calling, in the middle of their shifts, asking me to remind them never to do it again.

"No, seriously," said my friend Karen, calling from the pay phone at Shoney's. "I'm going to have a bruise the size of a quarter where this guy pinched my butt. I mean, you should see him, Aggie. His fingers are like *cigars*."

Lucy, my other friend, was working as a hostess at a place where she had to dress up as a pirate, with an eye patch and everything. When people from school drove by the restaurant she ducked behind the counter, whether there was a customer there or not. If anybody got upset she'd say, "Sorry! It's that peg leg of mine acting up again."

I put off the job search for as long as possible, but it wasn't easy. Every night, before she fixed dinner, my mother would fling the cupboard doors wide open and sigh dramatically. "I guess I can eke something out of the meager supplies I have here."

"We aren't going to starve, Mom."

She'd shake her head. "I don't know, Aggie. You know what I

make." She was a substitute teacher. She made next to nothing during the school year and exactly nothing in summer. "I mean, who knows if we'll ever see your father again."

"Mom, he's an hour away. It's not like he absconded to Mexico."

"So far as you know."

She'd send me to the grocery store with twenty dollars and tell me to get enough food for the week. While I was gone, she hung around the living room building tall houses out of the L.A. IS FOR LOVERS cards I'd brought back from our last family vacation, three or four levels high, stretching across the whole dining room table. When I got back she'd blow on the structure and say, "See? Everything just collapsed like a house of cards." This was her favorite joke.

"Mom, I feel like you're not handling this very well."

"Well, thank you for your honesty, Aggie."

"Why don't you get out of the house or something? See your friends?"

"Sure I will! I'll invite everyone out for a fancy dinner! And what I'll do is, I can use the money you've made in your new job."

At this point we usually declared a truce and ordered out for pizza.

One night at Smith's I was weighing two pounds of potatoes— "It worked for the Irish," my mom had said, "and it can work for us. Just pray there's no famine, Aggie"—when a man came up to me and said, "Excuse me, miss, what do you think of this kohlrabi?"

"I don't work here, sorry," I said.

He shook his head quickly. He was a short man, probably around five-three or five-four, with longish gray hair and tanned, stocky arms. "I know you don't," he said. "I'm asking you as a consumer. I need an impartial opinion. My wife wants me to bring home some kohlrabi, and it has to be perfect. If you knew her you'd know what I mean. The way she cooks it is so succulent, it's just wonderful. She's the Queen of the Kohlrabi. You should come by and meet her sometime. Anyway, if I don't get the good kohlrabi I'm a dead man. So please, what do you think?"

The vegetable he was holding up looked like some kind of alien spaceship, with four or five long stems shooting out from a little pod in the middle. At the ends of the stems were green leaves that trembled gently in his hands.

"I've never eaten kohlrabi," I said. I'd never seen it before, either. "So I have no basis for comparison."

"You don't eat kohlrabi? Why? Do you have something against it? Is there something I should know?"

"Look, I'm young, I just haven't gotten around to it yet," I said, and started edging away from the produce section.

He followed me. "I'm sorry, I'm sorry, I didn't mean to offend you." He seemed sincere, if slightly insane. "Look, a fresh eye is good. It doesn't matter if you've never eaten any. Just look at it and tell me what you think."

I picked it out of his hand and felt it briefly, cupping the pod in my palm like a baseball. The whole thing was a little strange and I glanced over at the canned-goods aisle, mapping an escape route in case it turned ugly. "Well, I'm no expert," I finally said, "but this one seems a little . . . limp."

"Limp?"

"Just a little."

"Oh my God, you're right," he said, taking the kohlrabi back and staring at it. "You are just exactly right. Thank you so much. Really, you'll never know what you've done for me tonight."

"Okay," I said.

We shook hands, and I wheeled my cart away. I didn't even know what kohlrabi tasted like or how you cooked it—this was the kind of thing I would've asked my dad, if he were around to ask. But he wasn't. I finished up the shopping and was standing in the express line when the man came up behind me. I didn't have many items in my cart, and nothing fancy. His was full of kohlrabi and gourmet cheeses.

"This is very crisp," he whispered. "I think she's going to be happy, my wife."

"Good," I said.

"You eat very plainly," he said.

"We live in an age of austerity," I told him.

He looked surprised. "We do?"

"Well, my mother and I do," I said. She told me this all the time. I started putting the groceries on the conveyor belt. It was what my mom called peasant food, or life's necessities. I couldn't help staring at the decadent foods, like Pop Tarts and Ruffles, that other people had in their carts.

He nodded. I looked over at him and saw that his gray T-shirt and jeans were neatly ironed.

"I'm Mr. Dejun," he said.

"Aggie."

We shook hands and shuffled forward in line.

He unloaded his kohlrabi behind my stuff. "So what do you do with yourself when you aren't coming to the aid of strangers in grocery stores, Aggie?"

"Well, right now, I'm supposed to be looking for a job."

"Is that right?" said Mr. Dejun. "What kind of job? Can you type?"

I didn't see why not. "I guess so."

"I'd like to hire you, Aggie," he said. "I could use someone with your outgoing personality and discriminating eye for produce. Come see me tomorrow." He pulled a business card out of his jeans, and I put it in my pocket, then we shook on the deal.

I was at his office by nine the next morning. His company, Dejun Enterprises, Inc., was a private environmental testing firm. They tested just about everything you could think of—water, soil, air, machinery, fabrics, textiles, even once, he confided, condoms. As soon as I got there Mr. Dejun took me on a tour of the place, through all the labs where technicians in white coats hovered over long orange counters covered with Bunsen burners and petri dishes and test tubes, just like the labs at school.

"Listen, if you can think of something that needs to be tested, we'll test it for you. That's our attitude here at Dejun Enterprises, Inc. We test things that have never been tested before, and we test 'em cheaper than anybody else. Never turn a job down. Listen, Aggie, I've been in business for a long time, and one thing I've learned is that you *always* have to be willing to take the customer's money. Got it?"

"Got it," I said.

He led me down hallways and into the employee lounge. I was completely disoriented, but somehow we wound up back in the reception area. There was a frowning, wrinkled woman sitting at the desk wearing a headset, apparently to leave her hands free for smoking. Her ashtray was full of cigarette butts. Next to the desk was a free-standing fishtank. Its water looked alarmingly gray, and I wasn't sure whether there were fish in it or not.

"Sophia, you're free," said Mr. Dejun. "The cavalry is here."

"Yippee," said Sophia, not moving.

"She loves me," Mr. Dejun told me.

"She's a young one, isn't she," said Sophia.

"Hi, I'm Aggie," I said, and shook her hand. She didn't really shake back.

Mr. Dejun said, "Sophia is actually not the receptionist, she's our accounts payable czaress. She is the Diva of Debts, aren't you, darling?"

"Sure," said Sophia.

"She loves me. The point being, Aggie, that she's just filling in because we had to, ah, part with the receptionist. But now we have you for the summer and we don't have to hire a new receptionist until fall. Isn't it great, Sophia?"

"Good morning, Dejun Enterprises," said Sophia. She lit a cigarette and blew the smoke at Mr. Dejun.

"What happened to the receptionist?" I said. I caught a movement out of the corner of my eye and saw some fish emerging from behind the plastic plants of the tank. They looked okay in spite of the secondhand smoke.

"She was a terrible liar. Are you a good liar?"

"Pretty good, I guess," I said.

"Only pretty good?"

"Actually, I'm an excellent liar. The 'pretty good' part was a lie."

Mr. Dejun tilted back his head and laughed. His long gray hair was stiff and bristly and maintained its shape when it moved, like a cloud formation. I could see the backs of his teeth.

"You know, I'm really starting to get a kick out of you, young Aggie. Now listen. We get a lot of calls here, a *lot* of calls. And we can't always take them, right? We're only human, and there are only so many hours in a day. So sometimes we'll come to you and say, 'If so-and-so calls, I don't want to talk to him, tell him I'm in a meeting.' Now if I were to say that to you, what would you do?"

"Tell him you're in a meeting."

"Excellent! That is exactly the right answer. You're brilliant, Aggie. You are really terrific."

"What did the old receptionist say?"

"It turned out that she was a very devout woman who refused to lie. She'd say, 'Yes, he's here, but he doesn't want to talk to you right now.' Nothing about meetings. You've got to respect her integrity, but man-oh-man did we have a lot of pissed-off people on the phone."

Sophia gave me five minutes of training and then left me on my own, carrying her big ashtray with her down the hallway. The reception area was separated from the rest of the building by almost-walls that stopped about a foot from the ceiling. I was alone. Mr. Dejun was right—the phone rang all the time. Mainly I had to find out what it was they wanted tested and transfer them to the appropriate lab. There were labs for textiles, for chemical compounds, for river water and for drinking water. Besides transferring calls, mainly what I did was lie. I hadn't even been up there for an hour before people started coming up front to introduce themselves, saying things like, "If that jerk from San Miguel Water calls, tell him I'm out working in the field today." Everyone who worked at Dejun seemed to be ducking somebody—clients, spouses, or accountants. Reports and results and bills were always overdue. This was how I got to know most of the people who worked at Dejun, through all the lies I told on their behalf. I did it all the time, fluently and convincingly. It was kind of exhilarating. I told Lucy and Karen it was creative work.

Within days, life settled into a routine. I rarely saw Mr. Dejun, and then only when he was striding out the front door to meet a client for lunch, wearing small, beautiful gray suits. I wondered if he had to get them custom-made, since he was so short. Or maybe they were hemmed for him by the Queen of Kohlrabi. I punched a time clock and ate my lunch in the smoky employee lounge with the lab techs and accounting clerks and got paid every second Friday. I wore hose. It was like a game of real life. At five I'd head home and collapse on the couch, refusing to speak to my mother except in nods and hand gestures.

"I talk all day," I'd whisper exhaustedly, hand to my forehead. "Please, no more."

"Oh, you poor working stiff," my mother would say. "Get changed and let's watch the game."

Lucy and Karen were working nights during the week, so Mom and I spent the evenings slumped on the couch, watching TV and drinking beer. I'd never drunk beer in front of my mom before, but it didn't seem like a big deal. After all the stuff that had gone wrong, who could worry about a minor issue like the legal drinking age? We didn't hear anything from my father or Margaret. Apparently they were still sorting out whatever needed to be sorted. Mom and I didn't talk about him much. Mostly we talked about the Dodgers.

My father tried to get me to follow baseball the whole time I was growing up, and I was never interested until the summer he went away. There was something about the games that was perfect for those nights, the lazy pace of long games, the commentators' voices hushed and reverent and excited at the same time. By the middle of July I could trade statistics with the guys in the employee lounge. They treated me like some kind of child prodigy just for knowing division standings in the National League. They'd come up front just to ask me what I thought of the game.

"The whole bullpen is pathetic! We'd have won it if that guy hadn't blown it in the bottom of the fifth. Dejun Enterprises, good morning."

Then one morning in July I woke up in so much pain I couldn't breathe or speak. I just lay there in bed until my mother came to tell me I was late for work. She'd taken to wearing her housecoat most of the day and night, with anything she might ever need stuffed into its pockets: nail polish, a deck of cards, rubber bands, gardening tools. She was starting to look like some kind of crazy building superintendent.

"What's the matter with you, sailor?" she said, fishing a bottle of Tylenol out of her pocket and offering it to me. "Too much fun on the town last night?"

"Guh," I said.

"Aggie, you know what? I think your whole face is swollen."

"Guh."

"Is that the only word you can say, or just some new kind of teenage slang?"

"Guh."

She drove me to the emergency room, where they told us that my wisdom teeth were impacted, causing an infection in my mouth, and would have to be removed immediately. I was in no condition to argue.

"You're going to be fine, honey," said my mom. "Here, drink some water."

"Has it been tested?" I mumbled.

When I regained consciousness, I had four fewer teeth and no memory at all of their extraction. I didn't even know what day it was. I woke up in my own bed, with a bowl of red Jell-O sparkling on the bedside table. I was starving and dug right in.

"The princess awakes," said my mother, striding into the room. She fluffed my pillows and stood back. She was wearing a suit and lipstick and looked like a million dollars. For a couple of seconds I wasn't even sure it was really her.

"Guh?" I said, not from pain but shock. Some Jell-O worked itself out of my mouth and dribbled down my chin.

"Not this again," Mom said. "Is that all you can say after being unconscious for two days? Can't you find the will to add just a few more consonants?"

"You wook nice," I said.

"Thank you," she said, pulling the curtains open to let in the sun. I winced. "I've been filling in for you at work. You don't get sick days, you know. So when I told them you wouldn't be in for the rest of the week, they asked me to substitute. Or I offered. Whatever, we agreed."

I leaned up on my elbows in bed. My head felt like a hot-air balloon, something large and heavy floating over the rest of my body. "No way," I said.

"There's no need to be rude," she said primly. "I am a substitute, you know."

"Teacher."

She shrugged. I hadn't seen her this alert in ages.

"Same difference. Look, I have to go, I'm late. There's more Jell-O in the fridge if you want it, and some soup."

"You can't really be doing this," I said.

She put her hands on her hips and said, "Oh, be quiet. You sound just like your father."

I sat up and started struggling with the bedcovers. In my weakened state it was like wrestling a bunch of monkeys. My own mother stood there and laughed at me.

"Honey, come look at yourself," she said. She led me by the hand to the bathroom mirror, and I gasped in horror. My face was about three feet wide.

"Now, you just relax today. Frank says to take it easy and get healthy, which is the most important thing."

"Okay." I was back under the covers before I remembered to ask who Frank was.

"I mean, Mr. Dejun," she said. And that probably would've worried me had I not immediately lost consciousness again. When I woke up throughout the day, it was only to eat more Jell-O and leaf through the sports section my mother had left by the bed. The Dodgers were still having a lot of trouble in the bullpen, which was really depressing.

I was out for a week. After a couple of days I was well enough to get out of bed, but I didn't. My face was still swollen and I was afraid that by venturing outside I'd frighten young children and dogs. Karen and Lucy came by between waitressing shifts to keep me company. Lucy had some rum she'd gotten from the pirate restaurant, and she and Karen used it to make some alcoholic Jell-O. We sat around in my room eating it with our fingers. None of us was having the summer we'd thought we would.

"So where's your mom, anyway, Ag?"

"She's doing my job."

"At Dejun Enterprises, good morning?"

"Yeah."

"Your own mother replaced you in the workforce? Man," said Karen, "that is just so typical of our generation. We have no control over anything."

"Yeah, man, you're not a person, you're a statistic," said Lucy.

"Thanks a lot, Peg Leg," I said.

"Oh, I'm sorry," she said. "Here, you can wear my eye patch if you want."

"Cool," I said, putting it on. Karen and Lucy burst out laughing. "Ahoy, mateys," I told them from between my puffy lips.

After the swelling had mostly gone down, I went back to work and my mother stayed home, but nothing was quite the same at Dejun; it was just too weird that Mom and I had done the same job and everyone there had met her. The textile-testing guys came up front and said, "Hey, Ag, your mom's cool. And now we know how come you know so much about baseball."

Now, this was unfair. Everything she knew about baseball she'd learned from me just that summer. "Actually, no," I started to say, but then I had to answer the phone.

"Dejun Enterprises, good morning." I was a little out of practice, and my mouth felt sore and dry. The hours dragged past until I went home and sank into the couch to watch the news. This was when I realized that disaster had struck yet again.

What happened was this: a truck carrying chemical material tested by Dejun Enterprises overturned on the interstate in Tijeras Canyon and spilled. Dejun had tested the stuff, inspected the storage containers, and declared it safe to transport, but environmentalists at the scene were saying it wasn't safe at all, and the truck should never have been allowed on the road. Police sealed off the entire area with a roadblock, causing massive delays. The road was contaminated, the soil was contaminated, everything was contaminated. I had never heard of the chemical and I didn't know what it looked like, but I pictured it as a fluorescent green ooze spreading like a living thing across the ground. The reporter, her stiff black hair barely flapping in the canyon wind, said there was some question whether Dejun had even looked at this material before issuing its report. Camera crews shot Mr. Dejun going into his house, saying "no comment," over and over again, his scowl barely visible under a sport coat he draped over his head. "Allegedly" was a word the reporter on the scene used a lot. In the darkness of the canyon behind her, groggy families evacuated their homes, children asleep in their parents' arms.

From the moment I punched my time card the next morning, everything was chaos. All the techs were gathered in the hallways outside the labs, whispering chemical terms like crazy. I got to the front desk and all fifteen lines were blinking. I took a deep breath and dug in. "Dejun Enterprises, good morning. I'm sorry, Mr. Dejun is not in, would you like to leave a message? I'm sorry, I don't know anything about that. Dejun Enterprises, good morning."

The next time I looked up it was ten o'clock. Mr. Dejun came thundering in, wearing a dark blue double-breasted suit with gold buttons.

"Don't talk to the press, young Aggie!" he said, grabbing a fistful of While You Were Out slips. "Don't let anyone here talk to the press, either. Just don't talk to them, whatever you do!"

"But I'm the receptionist," I said. "I have to talk."

"This is no time for secretarial humor," said Mr. Dejun sternly. "Now listen, I'm out to everybody except my lawyer."

"Dejun Enterprises, good morning," I answered. All fifteen lines rang constantly. All the newspapers and radio stations and TV stations in town called. It was weird to talk to people I usually watched on TV at night. It wasn't just the press on the phone, though, it was people who'd driven through the area around the time the spill had taken place. I took down all their names and numbers. Pink messages piled up around me like leaves. My voice cracked and went dry. No one came to the front to see me, or talk ball, or tell me what was going on. For all I knew, I was the only one there.

"Listen," a man on the phone said. "I have a young child who was exposed to this stuff. He's four years old, my son. Please, isn't there anything you can tell me?"

"Hold on, please," I said. I picked up another line and hung up on the person to free it up, then called Sophia's extension and asked her what I should say to people with young children who'd been exposed.

"Take a message, for chrissake," said Sophia.

I could hear her exhaling smoke. "But what about his kid?"

"Take a message," she said, and I did.

"Is someone really going to call me back?" he asked.

"Of course they will," I told him convincingly, knowing it was a lie. Then I took off the headset and walked outside and caught the bus home. There was no one at the house. I walked around the living room. I looked at the pictures on the mantel—my grandparents, my parents' wedding picture, me on vacation in L.A., me graduating from junior high school, me and Mom and Dad sitting on the living room couch. There were more pictures of me than of anything else. I picked up the phone and called work. Sophia answered, and I hung up. I went upstairs and crawled into bed.

I woke up at night and lay there for a while, trying to decide whether to just keep on sleeping. I could hear the rhythmic sounds of the ball game. I was hungry, so I went downstairs. Mr. Dejun was sitting on the couch in the TV room, watching the game with Mom. He was still wearing his navy blue suit, minus the tie and the jacket, which were folded neatly over one of the armchairs. He'd taken his shoes off and had his feet up on the table.

"Hi, Frank," I said.

"Aggie," said my mom. Sitting on the couch, Mr. Dejun came

up to her shoulder, which was bare and pale. Ordinarily, by this time in the summer she'd have freckles there, from mornings spent outside gardening. But not this year. She was wearing a sundress and her eyes were shiny.

"I was worried about you, young Aggie," said Mr. Dejun. "I thought I'd come by and see how you're doing."

"Fantastic," I said. I didn't think he was a very good liar, or would be a decent receptionist. I went into the kitchen and got a beer. I was sort of expecting someone to follow me in there, but nobody did. I went out the back door and sat on the steps, sipping my beer and looking at the stars. It was a nice, clear night. The phone rang, three times, so I sighed and got up. If there was one thing I couldn't stand hearing that summer, it was the sound of a ringing phone.

"Dejun Enterprises. I mean, hello. Shit."

"Aggie, it's me," said my dad.

I couldn't think of anything to say and so I didn't. Instead, I carried the phone back outside with me. "Ahoy, matey," I finally said.

"What?"

"Never mind. How's Margaret?"

"How are *you,* Ag? Are you all right?"

"Who wants to know?" I said.

"I understand you're upset," Dad said. "I understand you're mad. I'm sorry I haven't called. I've had some things to work out, do you know what I mean?"

There was silence on the line. I was listening for the game, trying to get the score and the inning, but couldn't hear it anymore. I drank some of my beer, gulping it noisily down my throat.

"Ag, sometimes adults and kids get the same sorts of feelings about their lives—you know, um, powerlessness, feeling trapped and that kind of thing."

"Are you speaking hypothetically?" I said.

He took a deep breath and let it out. I imagined Margaret in the background, giving him big, encouraging nods with her big, wide head.

"What I mean is, sometimes adults don't know what to do, like kids don't always know what to do. Do you understand what I mean?"

I looked up. The stars blurred in my vision and I shook my head a little bit to clear it. "Sure I do," I said. "I just have one question—who's the kid in this scenario, you or me?"

"You're so sarcastic," he said in a soft voice. "You sound just like your mother."

"It's not my fault," I said.

"I know," he said. "I know. Okay, listen." Suddenly he was all business. "I hear you had a bad day at work. Do you want to talk about it?"

"Who told you that?"

"Your mother called and told me."

"Oh," I said. I didn't even know she knew how to get in touch with him. Tears slid down the receiver and collected in the base of it, cool against my cheek, sliding into the little holes.

"Ag, your mother knows, and I hope you know too, that I love you more than anything. That's one thing we see eye-to-eye on, and that'll never change, no matter what else happens."

I felt like this was the worst thing I'd ever heard. The King of Kohlrabi was in my living room drinking a beer in his socks, and I had to talk to my dad on the phone with a lesbian who wasn't a lesbian listening in the background. Somewhere in the desert, green slime was oozing toward families as they slept. What else was happening all around me, all the time, and I couldn't do anything to stop it or even slow it down.

"Dad," I told him, "Mom's inside watching baseball with Mr. Dejun."

He said, "Oh? So how's the game?"

I sighed, and then the sigh turned into a hiccup.

"You like the Dodgers this year?" he asked.

"Their bullpen's a disaster," I said.

"You've really been following? Aggie, there might be hope for you yet."

"Maybe," I said. "Are you coming back?"

"I don't know," my dad said. "I just don't know."

"Okay." I stood up and looked at the night sky, the sound of cicadas throbbing around me. "I have to go now," I said.

"Listen, Aggie, take down my number, okay? Take it down so you can call me whenever you want. Do you have a pen?"

"Sure," I said. I didn't. But I closed my eyes and listened carefully to his voice in my ear, as if I were taking the most urgent message. As he told me the numbers I traced them, small and invisible, in the air in front of me, then let them go out into the night.

This is a preliminary report for a 65-year-old Caucasian man who entered complaining of shortness of breath.

Walter was coughing again. He sat up in bed, his red face hanging over his chest like a heavy bloom, coughing. He didn't try to speak or even wheeze, instead dedicating himself to the fit with single-minded concentration. Carl watched the oxygen threads quiver across his cheeks. The cough ran down like an engine, slowing to sputters, then ended. Carl handed his uncle a glass of water, and he drank.

"Thanks," Walter said. He pressed one of his large hands against his sunken chest, passed the glass back and took a few breaths.

"How do you feel?"

"I feel fine." He grabbed his handkerchief from the bedside table, hacked up some phlegm, looked at it, and then put the cloth back on the table, folded.

"Do you want something to eat?"

"No. " Walter looked at his watch and his features brightened. "Time for my beauty routine."

Carl fetched the towel and the electric razor. Walter took off the oxygen and offered his face, eyes closed. He didn't have much facial hair, but he always insisted on being shaved before a visit from his girlfriend, Marguerite. His skin was cool and pale and evenly colored, like clay or a smooth beach stone. While shaving him, Carl thought about how Walter's face had looked when he was a kid—swarthy and stubbled, deeply tanned by cigarette smoke—and how different it was now, the skin so papery and light, as if in transition to becoming some entirely different substance. The bedroom was quiet except for the mosquito buzz of the razor and the hiss and pump of the oxygen machine. Every once in a while Walter drew a labored breath. When he was done, Carl dabbed Aqua Velva on his face; Walter was, and always would be, an Aqua Velva man.

Walter ran his right hand over his cheeks and down under his chin, then frowned. "You missed a spot," he said.

He reinserted the oxygen in his nostrils and walked downstairs slowly and purposefully, carrying the oxygen line raised behind him like a king with his robe. Adding to this effect, his wispy hair stood up and waved, crownlike, above his balding head. By the time Marguerite showed up he was installed in the living room in his favorite armchair, his thick, veiny ankles visible between the cuffs of his brown pants and his brown socks.

"Hi, handsome," Marguerite said.

She was wearing a flowing green pantsuit with gold buttons and smelled like roses. She and Walter had been dating for years. They'd met in the home, and Walter's moving back into his house, when Carl came to live with him, had given him the reputation among the residents there as a heartbreaker. But Marguerite came to see him faithfully—taking a taxi—every Tuesday and Thursday, and they drank weak coffee that Carl made, and played gin. Marguerite looked better than Walter did, in spite of being older, but she was delicate and getting a bit, as Walter put it, soft in the head. Sometimes she'd smile at Carl and say, "Oh, dear, my mind is going. If you see it anywhere, could you tell it to come back?" Other times she'd forget words and Carl, walking past the living room, would see her sitting on the couch with her hands up in the air like an agitated bird, saying, "I'm so stupid— what's the word I want?" Walter could never guess.

Carl put out the coffee, went downstairs to his office, turned on the computer, put on the headset, and listened.

GENERAL APPEARANCE: patient exhibits pedal edema. Earlier this evening patient was found by a relative who brought him in for examination.

He had started working from home a year ago, when he moved back in with Walter, in this house where he'd grown up. Walter didn't say anything to him about the first heart attack, just checked in to the convalescent home and then called to announce the change of address. Carl understood that this was Walter's dignity in action: the refusal, at all costs, to be a burden. But when he went and saw the place he felt sick. The fecal smell, the dim light, the wan, shrunken people like some alien and unfortunate race, all this had frightened Carl and pissed him off. He resolved to do whatever was required—including quitting his job, moving back home, and taking care of Walter himself—to get Walter free of it. While he was sitting in Walter's room, a man passed by the open door in a wheelchair, then back in the other direction, then again, and again. When he noticed Carl watching him, the man bared his gums and laughed.

"Walter," Carl said, "we're getting out of here."

"Don't trouble yourself, son," Walter said, but he was clearly pleased.

Before setting up his own business, Carl was employed by a

transcription service at a hospital, and he didn't realize how much he hated going to work every day until he no longer had to do it. Everything about it—the commute, the workplace banter, the fluorescent lighting and bad coffee—had filed him down into points. Carl had no ear for gossip, didn't tell jokes, was uneasy with the siege-like camaraderie of the office. He was not a people person. And now, away from those things, he was a great deal happier. He worked only with voices he turned into reports.

Transcription was a habit that could be mastered and even internalized. When he was watching television with his uncle or shopping for groceries, he would hear people's voices and almost unconsciously transcribe them, his foot tapping as if he were working the foot pedals. In medieval monasteries there was a room called a scriptorium where certain monks labored all day long transcribing the world into text, and it seemed to him there was an equivalent purity to the work he did in this bare basement room. Correct spelling and grammar, the unadorned finality of the perfect text, these had an astringency that pleased him.

VITAL SIGNS: steady and strong
TEMPERATURE: 99.6 degrees
RESPIRATORY RATE: 20

Carl worked for exactly one hour. It took him forever to get through reports by Dr. Sabatini, who was his least favorite of all the doctors. Here was the height of rudeness: he ate while dictating. Chomps and smacks between words, slurps and molars grinding. It was disgusting and necessitated guesswork on the part of the transcriptionist, which Carl hated; but it was either that or ask him to clarify every other word. Sabatini sounded like a jerk, too, his syllables impatient and clipped. For some reason that Carl couldn't specify, he also sounded bald. This suspicion hadn't been confirmed, though, since they'd never met.

Carl avoided the hospital as much as possible, which was very nearly completely. The world of technology made this miracle happen.

Most days he stayed downstairs until five, at which time he and Walter ate dinner while watching *Jeopardy*. Between the two of them they always did better than the contestants. If they could go on as one person, Walter sometimes said, pretending they were Siamese twins or with one of them hidden behind the other, well, they'd clean up. Walter was a game-show fanatic. The first summer Carl had come to live with Walter, when he was eleven, there was a guy on *Tic Tac Dough* who had a summer-long winning streak, and at the time, through childish superstition, he felt that as long as that guy could keep winning, as long as Walter cheered him on, then everything would be OK. He and Walter watched every day, and the tension was almost unbearable. This was years ago, of course, after Carl's mother died of what Walter liked to call "the rock-and-roll lifestyle." In the stairwell there was a picture of her, Jane, from high school, smiling broadly, even crazily, as if she were drugged—a glimpse of the future, maybe. And there was a picture of Marie, as well, even though she and Walter had only been married five years before she left him for an army man and went to live on a base in Germany. She was still there, and every year she sent Walter a Christmas card. On the inside she crossed out the German words and wrote "Merry Christmas!" instead.

SKIN: unremarkable
HEAD: Atraumatic
CHEST: There are coarse mid-inspiratory crackles heard at the right lung.
FACTOR CONTRIBUTORY TO CONGESTIVE HEART FAILURE: smoking 30 years

At the end of the hour he went back upstairs. The television was on, sound turned up loud, and both Marguerite and Walter were dozing, their cards still spread on the table. Marguerite had gin. Carl stood behind the couch and coughed softly. Marguerite made a kind of low moan and her face sagged terribly in the second before she pulled herself into her usual cheery expression.

She glanced at Walter and then at Carl. "I guess I'd better be off," she said.

"I'll call your cab."

"Thank you, dear. You're a . . ." She looked down and turned the loose gold rings on her fingers, then said, as if to the jewelry, "What's the word I want?"

"Blessing?" Carl said, since this was what she usually called him.

Marguerite beamed. "Just so," she said.

After he'd called, he took her elbow and they began the slow, careful walk out of the house and down the driveway. She leaned against him and clutched herself closely around the waist. They stood at the end of the driveway, waiting. Marguerite swayed a bit in the wind. "You know, dear," she said, "he doesn't look too good."

"Walter?"

"Dear," she said, "of course Walter."

"Well, he's sick," Carl said.

"Has he been making his weekly visits?"

Carl began to tap his foot. "You know I take him, Marguerite."

"I know you do, dear." She looked at him, then took a tissue from her white handbag and dabbed a bit at her nose. "It's just . . . well." She sighed. "At the home we get excellent round-the-clock care."

"Walter hates the home," Carl said flatly. Marguerite took a deep breath, drew herself up to her full height, which wasn't very high, and said, "It isn't anybody's first choice, dear." The taxi appeared around the corner and crept toward them.

"He's fine," Carl said.

When the taxi pulled up, he lowered Marguerite's fragile bones onto the ripped upholstery of the backseat. As the car pulled away he felt a flash of guilt and called, ridiculously, "Thanks for coming!" He could see the white blur of her tissue in the window as she waved good-bye.

Patient has been prescribed

Walter was awake and watching *Matlock,* drinking a cup of coffee that by now must have been quite cold.

"Faking, Uncle Walter?"

"If I pretend to fall asleep, she falls asleep too," Walter said, and slurped.

"That's not very polite," Carl said.

"Well, Jesus. You know I think the world of Marguerite. But if I have to hear one more word about her grandchildren in Boca Raton, I'll fall asleep and never wake up."

"She thinks you should go back into the convalescent home."

"Convalescent home, my ass," Walter said. His eyelids were heavy and he held his coffee cup loosely on the arm of his chair. "You keep convalescing and then you're dead. What day is it, son?"

"Thursday."

"Thursday's bingo night in the home. I won once. Jar of cold cream."

"They gave you a jar of cold cream?"

"That was the prize." Walter put the coffee cup down on the

table, leaned back, and closed his eyes. "I gave it to Marguerite. That's how the two of us got started."

"Oh."

"Yeah," Walter said. "Don't worry. I'm fine."

HISTORY:

That night Walter fell out of bed. What woke Carl up from a restless, dream-drenched sleep (since he never knew the people whose illnesses or accidents were described in the reports, and never saw the doctors who dictated them, his periodic nightmares were filled with faceless strangers undergoing unidentifiable medical procedures while Carl watched, helplessly) must have been the thud of Walter's body hitting the floor. He sat up in bed, not knowing why he was awake, and heard a ragged, whispery gasp from the other side of the hall. When he got to the bedroom, Walter was looking up expectantly from the floor.

"I fell out of bed!" he whispered.

"I can see that," Carl said.

"I feel okay, though."

"We should probably go to the hospital."

"I said I feel all right."

"I heard what you said," Carl said. He knelt down and slipped one arm under Walter's back and pulled him to a sitting position. His uncle's back felt meaty and solid through his T-shirt. But he was unsteady on his feet, and in the car he closed his eyes and didn't seem to feel well enough to talk.

At the emergency room they put him under observation, since they couldn't decide exactly what had happened to him. At the foot of the bed, Carl stood facing the digital flickering of the medical instruments. He felt calm. It wasn't the first time they'd been to the ER and in all likelihood wouldn't be the last. He examined the screen and thought of all the tests he'd seen, the signals from inside Walter's body: the CT scans, X rays, EKG. How many people ever saw that deep inside anybody else? He was proud of it somehow.

"Sometimes people just fall out of bed," the intern told him.

"Is that your actual diagnosis?" Carl said. "I want to see the chart."

"I can't give you the chart."

"I want to see the chart," he said, and grabbed it from the intern's hand.

Walter grinned at the intern from his bed. "He knows everything."

"You need to rest," the intern said.

Carl took the chart out to the hall and sat down with it. The jangling noise of the hospital, even at three o'clock in the morning, and the spasmodic blinking of the fluorescent lights and the bad-smelling, recirculated air were making him claustrophobic and irritable. He rubbed his eyes and looked at the chart, the scrawlings of medications and symptoms. Everything about his uncle was here, Walter on paper, his body reconstituted as a record of its processes and ills. This, he thought, is a body of information, and there arose before him a brief image of Walter's naked body, made not of flesh and blood but of a shell of data like tattoos in the air. In this image the body was as fine and translucent as a moth, numbers running down the arms and separating into five fingers, diagrams banded across the chest: statistical, eternal.

"Mr. Mehussen?"

Carl looked up at a woman extending her hand.

"I'm Dr. Newman," she said. "I'd like to talk to you about your uncle. And I'd like to have his chart back, please."

Patient appears fragile but in good spirits. Is able to communicate symptoms and receive information.

Dr. Newman had straight, thin, slightly greasy blond hair that swung as she talked. Under her white coat she wore khakis and sensible brown shoes. She was in the middle of saying that falling out of bed, while a traumatic event, might not have meaningful consequences for Walter's condition when he realized who she was. He glanced at her sharply.

"Do you have a question?"

"I just—you're Dr. Newman."

She ran a hand wearily through her hair and nodded.

"Dr. Amanda Newman."

"Yes, that's me."

"I do your tapes," he said.

"My tapes?"

"Transcription," he said. He watched her nod again, and smile politely, and then recalibrate her manner to the one she used while dealing with people employed, however tangentially, in the medical profession. She took a deep breath, moved her shoulder closer to his, and became at once friendlier and more professional.

"You have excellent diction," he told her.

She raised her eyebrows. "Thanks," she said.

Walter spent the night under observation. Carl spent the night in the hallway, drinking bad coffee from a paper cup. They were running some tests and awaiting results. Dr. Newman was still on duty, and at times he could hear her cool, clear voice giving orders and asking questions, and the sound of it was oddly soothing to him, reminding him of his office and his work. He closed his eyes to focus on it. Other people waited near him, flipping through magazines or whispering softly together. They were all quiet, dazed-seeming. A woman came through and began searching around all the seats, saying, "My bag. I know I left it around here somewhere." Then a man came and put his arms around her and led her away, glancing back guiltily over her shoulder as if the bag were a shameful or deeply personal subject, not to be discussed. He heard one of the nurses say, "Dr. Newman!" and Dr. Newman say, "In a minute!"

Walter was asleep, wheezing rhythmically. The other patient in the room was groaning in pain, a sound as distant and constant as traffic. It didn't seem to be keeping Walter up. Carl wasn't sleepy, but he slipped into a kind of a trance in the hallway, slouched in his seat. He didn't know what to do except sit and not sleep, sit and be vigilant. Whatever happened, he would be awake and present for it. He thought about when his mother died, and someone—a teacher—came and said to him, "Your mother is dead," and it seemed like because it had happened off stage, out of his sight, that it could not be real or true. He tried to feel sad but couldn't. He kept trying to grasp the fact of it, and would sometimes repeat to himself, "My mother is dead," and though the words would make him cry, he still didn't really feel it. The fact was too big. It defeated him. The days around the funeral passed in a blur of dark mystery, adults wearing black, speaking in whispers, the sense of being pressed in by crowds, the smell of unfamiliar food. Instead of grief he developed a sense of irritation and injustice, of being unfairly put upon. More than anything he wanted to find someone to complain to, maybe a teacher or someone else at school. He wanted to say that if only he'd been given more information, more evidence, more time, then he would have been better prepared.

PROCEDURE: patient will be informed as to the likely future developments in his condition.

Early in the morning the shifts changed and new nurses came on, pouring themselves cups of coffee and bustling around the station. He was looking down at the floor when he saw Dr. Newman's brown shoes.

She sat down beside him. "You should have gone home and slept," she said.

"Why?" he said.

She laughed shortly, on the exhale. "Because you look tired."

"So do you," he said, and she did. The skin under her eyes had turned bluish and looked wrinkled and taut. She had pulled her hair back in an elastic band, but a few strands had escaped it here and there. He noticed that she was carrying a chart, and knew it must be Walter's.

She cocked her head in the direction of his room. "Let's go talk to your uncle." She took a step, but when he didn't follow she paused and looked at him, waiting.

"Please," he said. Meaning, Please be a good doctor; meaning, Help him. Dr. Amanda Newman stepped back and put her hand briefly on his arm, and the touch of it was shocking to him—though not as shocking as when, in the days to come, she began to say his name at the beginning of her tapes: "Hello, Carl. This is a preliminary report on . . ." and he would listen, fascinated, to this part, the intimacy of these four letters spoken by her clear voice, *his name,* for minutes at a time, before he could move on.

"Let's go," she said.

He followed her to Walter's room and they went inside, and Walter looked first to her and then to Carl, who saw his uncle's worried eyes go tranquil because he was there.

"Hi, Walter," he said.

" 'Lo," Walter said, and coughed with the effort. He lay stolid and unmoving, his arms exposed above the sheet. The skin there was blotched and veiny. The other patient thrashed uncomfortably in his bed while his visitor, a younger woman, tried in vain to quiet him. Dr. Newman began to explain that Walter could go home, that there would be observation and additional medication.

As she spoke, Carl saw the cool black letters of her report unfurling in his mind.

ASSESSMENT: the heart labors.

He stood still with the revealed truth of it—that in the end, the real end, Walter was not going to be fine—and a pain bloomed hotly in his chest, as if his body were offering Walter's sympathy of its own kind. The tape in his head clicked and rewound, whirred all the way back to childhood. What he heard then was Walter's voice, smoke-tinged and hearty; what he smelled was Aqua Velva and tobacco and sweat. They were standing in the doorway of the living room, looking in at it, Walter behind him. He felt Walter's big hands pressing a bit too hard on his shoulders, the weight of them forcing him to slouch, and he was eleven and his heart flew up when Walter said, "From now on, son, this will be your home."

Simple Exercises for the
Beginning Student

He did not have friends. He was silent much of the time. He picked his nose, and when told to stop he would remove his finger slowly and stare at the snot, seemingly hypnotized, then put his hand in his pocket without wiping it. He had bad dreams: for one whole year he woke, white and crying, from nightmares about snakes. The next year it was clouds. He couldn't explain why the clouds frightened him and just shook his head, trembling and sweaty under the covers. Although his mother, Rachel, made an effort to find the nicest clothes she could within the budget, the same clothes that other kids were wearing, as soon as he put them on they drooped and sagged, changing from their store-rack normalcy into something disheveled, misshapen, patchlike.

Sometimes his eyes looked blurry and unfocused, but when Rachel took him to the eye doctor, his vision tested fine.

For his eighth birthday, he asked for piano lessons. Rachel and Brian, the father, looked at each other, then back at him. The three of them lived in a two-bedroom apartment. They had one bedroom, and he had the other. In the kitchen there was only enough room to stand up, and so in the living room, cramped together, were the dining table and chairs, the couch and the TV.

Rachel and Brian both worked but, between credit-card debt and car payments, were barely making the rent. And there was something else. Rachel was pregnant; she was the only one who knew. She'd been pregnant once before, since Kevin, but didn't keep it. This time would be different. At night, with her eyes closed, she breathed in deeply, and at the innermost point of her breath she felt the baby, tight and insistent and coiled. It wanted to be born.

"Kevin," she said, "since when do you want to play the piano?"

"Since now."

"Listen, buddy," Brian said. He motioned Kevin over the couch, and he stood between his father's legs. "I don't know if you've noticed, but we don't have a piano."

"The teacher does."

"But you have to practice," Brian said. "That's part of taking lessons—you spend like an hour a week at the teacher's or whatever, then you go home, and you have to practice. Like homework."

Kevin looked up at him, his eyes both wary and blank. Rachel saw that he hadn't thought of this. Where did he get the idea for piano lessons in the first place, if he didn't even know that practicing was part of it? It was a mystery. Her son came to her and, wordlessly, placed his hand on her knee.

"It's okay," she said. "We just have to think about this." She felt Brian staring at her. She knew what he wanted: for Kevin to play hockey, stickball in the street, be more of a boy, be more like other boys. But somehow, she knew, it was already too late.

On the day of the first lesson Kevin wore a blue sweater and brown cords and smoothed his hair across his forehead with his fingers. He was excited. Bright images flickered through his mind, just out of visible reach: a grand piano, a stone castle, people dancing.

Rachel called, "Are you ready?"

"Coming." He walked out of his room, hearing the beats of his own tread, his socks hitting the carpet, dum dum dum dum. His mother stood in the hallway with her boots on, holding his coat. When he put it on, she handed him his hat, then picked up her coat.

"I want to go alone," he said.

She put her hands on her hips. "Well, you can't."

"Why?"

She ticked off the reasons on her hand. "Because it's the first day. Because you don't know where it is. Because I need to meet the teacher." The teacher was a friend of a friend of a friend. She'd just moved into the neighborhood and was charging low rates.

"Tell me where it is," Kevin said, "and I'll find it. You told Dad I could walk there."

"I meant later."

"Now," he said.

"Kevin, come on."

"I'll only go if I can go alone," he said.

"You have to go. I made the appointment."

"I know," he said, and held up his hands for his mitts.

Rachel gave them to him and they stared at each other for a long moment. Their eyes were the same color, very pale blue, although what was watery in Kevin's face looked tired and opaque in Rachel's. Then Rachel sighed and he knew that he'd won. She bent down, told him carefully how to go, and watched him walk down the street, his arms sticking stiffly out from the coat, his mitts drooping down from the wrists.

They lived in an apartment building next to a small park with brown grass splotched with snow. He was supposed to go halfway around the park to the exact other side from home. Then left, then right on Oakhill. The house where he was going was 1330 Oakhill. He had to look for the left part of it, which would say *A,* for Anita. The teacher's name was Anita Tanizaki. In his mind's eye his mother's handwriting rose up from a piece of paper: Mrs. Anita Tanizaki. A-ni-ta. I-need-a Tanizaki, he said to himself. Get me a Tanizaki this instant! I will now perform the famous Tanizaki maneuver. It has never been done in this country before.

He skirted the park, kicking the iced crusts of snow with his boots. From the big street a few blocks away he could hear a siren, maybe a fire engine's, bubbling and boiling. It came closer. He closed his eyes and listened: a note falling through the air like skiing downhill. With his eyelids shut, the sound was the color red splashed over the sky. Next it faded to pink, and then was gone.

He opened his eyes and started walking again. A car passed by, but nobody else was walking around. It was Saturday morning. He went left, then right. Inside his mitts his fingers closed against his palms, making warm sweat. He found the house without any problem. There was ice on the steps, and he slipped a little and almost lost his balance. He stamped his feet on the ice to steady himself, then pressed his finger against the doorbell, ding-dong. No sound came from the house, no music, no movement, and for a moment the world wavered and threatened to collapse. Nothing was the way he planned it. Then he heard a rustle behind the door, and it opened.

"Come in," said Mrs. Anita Tanizaki.

He stepped inside and took his boots off on the mat and hung up his coat. She waited for him at the end of the hallway, not smiling. Her short dark hair had waves all over her head, like frosting on a cake. The house seemed very dark and its smell reminded him of a restaurant, with all the food cooked and eaten hours before.

"So, come in," she said again.

He followed her into the living room, where she gestured to the piano. He had never seen one up close before. It was smaller than he had thought it would be, and blacker. All of a sudden he was frightened: it just stood there, its wood body staunch and foreign, looking back at him like an animal. Mrs. Tanizaki sat down on the bench and patted the spot next to her and he joined her. They both looked down at the piano's keys as if the thing might start playing itself. Then Mrs. Tanizaki reached down and stroked a white key with her finger, from the top to the bottom, holding it down. The note resounded, pure and direct, resembling nothing except itself. She hit another key, then a black one, then another white.

"I'm going to be honest with you, Kevin," Mrs. Tanizaki said. "This is my first lesson. Your first lesson, and mine too. We're going to be learning together. Here's what I can tell you right away. I love the piano. I love the touch of it"—here she made more strokes with the one finger, from the top to the bottom, the pad of her fingertip sliding—"and the sound"—adding another note, with the left hand, and Kevin flinched when her elbow touched him, but she either didn't notice or pretended not to—"and the way it looks. I can't teach you to love the piano, but I can teach you some basic things about it. So, now we'll start."

She took his finger and pressed it down on a key. "C," she said.

"Okay."

"Not like, Do you see. I mean middle C. This note is the middle of everything. It's the center of the piano. Look down, don't look at me, it doesn't matter what I look like. Press it again."

"C," he said.

When Kevin got home he was in a daze. He waited at the table without speaking while Rachel heated up some vegetable soup and cheese toast. His eyes were misted as if he were staring into the distance, even though he wasn't. Actually, he looked stoned. That's what my son looks like when he's happy, she thought, with a glow like pride.

To pay for the lessons, they gave up cable TV. But then Brian started watching hockey and basketball games in bars, drinking with his friend Steve, so it wasn't clear how well this worked out, budget-wise.

Mrs. Tanizaki had a son named Lawrence. He was fifteen. The next time Kevin had a piano lesson, Lawrence crept into the room behind them. Kevin could feel him there.

Mrs. Tanizaki, who was guiding the fingers of Kevin's right hand up a scale from middle C, stopped at the top. "This is Lawrence," she said. "Lawrence, this is Kevin."

Lawrence didn't nod or anything. His black hair flopped over his glasses. He was gangly in the arms and legs and fat in the middle. "I'm hungry, Mom," he said.

She sighed. "Excuse me, Kevin. Lawrence, make yourself a sandwich."

"Don't want a sandwich."

"Then you can wait until we're done here, and I'll make lunch. There will be no lunch until I'm done teaching. Do you understand?"

Lawrence left the room. Kevin and Mrs. Tanizaki returned intently to the scale, and the song they were singing with it: do re mi fa sol la ti do. C D E F G A B C. After E you tucked your thumb under the rest of your hand and started over. Kevin didn't understand why the notes of the song had different names from the notes, but maybe one was for singing and one was for playing. When Mrs. Tanizaki sang, her voice was hollow and slightly rough. It was not at all clear like the piano. She made him sing too, and his voice was so ugly and unrecognizable that he tried to sing as softly as possible, hearing one set of notes but not the other, while his fingers moved thickly up the keys.

"Now you do it by yourself," she told him.

Kevin swallowed. "Do re mi fa," he sang, trailing off. Behind him he could hear a wet, chewing sound. Lawrence was back in the room, eating a sandwich.

"Excuse me, Kevin," Mrs. Tanizaki said. "Lawrence, either close your mouth when you chew or leave the room. Or maybe you could do both."

Kevin looked down at the keyboard while Lawrence shuffled out of the room. He was learning to memorize the shape of the keys, their color and configuration, the scuffmarks on some of them, the way they added up to a whole entity like a person's face. In his bedroom now, or at school, his fingers skimmed along surfaces, over the blanket or the desk, as if divining for sound. Inseparable from the keys was the smell of Mrs. Tanizaki's house, a spicy, sour smell of leftover dinner, and her smell too, different from his mother's but distantly related to it, an older-woman smell, and the darkness of the room, and the one lamp that pooled light over the piano. He was drawn inside all of this. Still, at times, he woke up at night and remembered the visions he'd had about the dancing and the castle, a piece of color at the edge of his sight like a scarf fluttering in the wind, and he knew that as piercing as the notes were, as clearly as they answered to his fingers on the white and black keys, still they were only notes, they weren't the music.

———

Rachel told Brian about the baby.

"I think it's a girl," she said. "I just have a feeling."

They lay side by side in bed.

"I want to keep it, Bri," she said, then waited a moment. "I know it's going to be hard, but we won't regret it. I promise. It'll be worth it."

He said, "If that's what you want."

He put his arm around her and went to sleep, and Rachel stayed awake for hours, watching shadows and streetlights weave through the window. She waited for something else to happen, but nothing did.

She went to the doctor. Everything looked fine. She heard the baby's heart beating along with the pulse of her own blood. Brian acted kind yet impartial; when she talked about the baby, he listened. He said nothing against the baby, about the money or the apartment or how or whether they could live on just his paycheck. Rachel also avoided these subjects, knowing they were knotty, inviting danger. She kept her worries to herself. She tried to maintain the certainty she'd held in the pit of her stomach, the push of the extra life inside her, but somehow the energy of these feelings seeped away from her, more and more quickly, each day. In the mornings she felt nauseous, in the afternoons she felt great, and at night she was exhausted and went to sleep right after dinner.

One Saturday, at lunch, she asked Kevin if he understood what the word pregnant meant, and he said yes. She told him that he was going to have a little brother or sister.

He put down his forkful of macaroni and cheese and appraised her. "You don't look pregnant," he said, and gestured a bulge over his stomach.

"It doesn't show yet. But it will soon."

"Okay," he said.

He started eating again, and Rachel felt herself plummet down into empty space. But then he said, with his mouth full, "Mrs. Tanizaki has a son."

"She does?"

"He's fifteen," Kevin said, and swallowed.

"Is he your friend?" Rachel said, not understanding.

He shook his head. "No. He sits in the room and eats sandwiches during my lessons."

"Oh."

"Lawrence is fifteen and I'm eight," Kevin said. "When the baby's eight, I'll be sixteen."

"Yes, that's right."

"Sixteen," he repeated. "I'll really play piano by then. I'll play for the baby."

Rachel smiled. "That's right," she said.

Mrs. Tanizaki loaned Kevin a book called *Simple Exercises for the Beginning Student*. When she presented it to him, the moment took on the aspect of a ceremony. Lawrence was not in the room, and it was very quiet.

Mrs. Tanizaki stood up, took the book off the top of the piano, and put it in Kevin's hands. "I'm going to lend this book to you, Kevin," she said. "It's my book, and I want it back eventually. But you can use it for now. I'm going to assign you exercises from it each week, and you'll practice them. Every day."

Kevin nodded and held the book loosely, afraid of damaging or marking the short, wide book with yellow pages, its cover already dog-eared and bent. He opened the cover and saw penciled handwriting on the inside: *Anita Osaka*. I-need-a, I-need-a, he said to himself, then looked at her.

"That was my name before I married Mr. Tanizaki," she said. "I've had this book for a long time. That's why you have to be careful with it, and give it back."

"Okay."

"I trust you, Kevin. I know you'll take good care of the book, and practice every day."

"Okay."

"Do you understand? Say yes, Kevin, not this 'okay' all the time."

"Yes," he whispered. He was close to desperation. He had not told Mrs. Tanizaki that he had no piano to practice on, and was scared to tell her because she might say he couldn't take lessons anymore. Every two weeks his mother gave him an envelope with a check in it for Mrs. Tanizaki, and he brought it and laid it on the piano. It stayed there, undiscussed, until he left. They never talked about his family, or where he lived, or anything. The piano was their only shared element. Now he didn't know what to do. The book was ancient and valuable; he shouldn't have it. In his hands, as if by themselves, the pages flipped open, and he saw the long black lines stretching across the pages, notes rising and falling in small streams. As he looked, the notes wrapped themselves around him like ribbons of seaweed. He could not tell her.

He took the book home and laid it on his bed. Then he took his school notebook and ripped out three pages and fastened them side-to-side with Scotch tape. He took a pencil and drew middle C in the center of one page. It looked lopsided and thick and the bottom right side spread downward like something that had been left out in the sun and was starting to melt. He thought of Mrs. Tanizaki's face and Lawrence's chewing and the smell of food that laid itself over all his lessons, and he was angry then and ripped up the pages and threw them in the garbage can.

But the next day he started over and drew eight white notes and five black ones, enough for a scale and the simple exercises for the right hand, and in the bedroom he practiced from the book, his fingers rustling and tapping against the paper. Before figuring out that he needed to put the paper over a book from school, he broke through it twice and ruined it. Eventually he drew the best, longest-lasting one.

Rachel, cleaning out the garbage can a week later, found all his failed attempts. By this time she was showing, and although she wasn't too ungainly just yet, the consciousness of weight invaded all her actions, including the way she bent to pick up the garbage can or sat down on the couch to examine the piano pages. When Brian came home from work and turned on the news, she brought him a beer.

"Brian," she said, "we need to get Kevin a piano, so he can practice. Maybe we can find him one of those—what are they, like a synthesizer? Those little flat things that shouldn't be too expensive?"

He looked at her, but not in the face. Lately she'd noticed he wouldn't meet her eyes; instead, he looked at her stomach or his gaze seemed to fasten on her neck, not quite making it any higher, as if seized by that weight she carried, her additional gravity.

"You want to buy a goddamn piano?" he said.

"Not a real piano," she said. "Just something for him to practice on. He loves it, Brian. It's really amazing. He could turn out to be a genius, I mean who knows?"

"Yeah," he said.

"Or maybe if we gave Mrs. Tanizaki a little extra money, she'd let him go over there and practice on her piano. She can't use it all the time, can she? I bet she'd do that. I think she would."

Brian put down his beer and held her hand and looked at her

lap. When he spoke, his voice was tender and soft. "Rachel, I don't know how to tell you this, but I want you to listen to me. I think you're losing it. I think you really are."

The next morning she got a call from Brian's boss asking if he was sick, which he wasn't. When he didn't come home after work, she didn't call Steve or his parents. She wasn't going to ask anybody else where her own husband was, not in this lifetime.

A month passed and Brian didn't come back. Kevin practiced daily on the paper piano. He could play "Twinkle, Twinkle, Little Star" and "Au clair de la lune." On paper the melodies whispered and tapped, but on the piano, in three dimensions, the sound burst out so strong and plain that he was shocked. A lot of times, when he touched the wrong notes it wasn't because he didn't practice but because the keys were higher and farther apart than in his drawing of them. If Mrs. Tanizaki noticed his surprise or his fumbling readjustments, she didn't say anything.

"Good, Kevin," she said softly. "Wrists up. Fingers bent. Don't look at me, it doesn't matter what I look like. Keep going. That's good."

Sometimes she rapped against the piano with a little stick, to help him keep time, and this made him feel sick to his stomach. Other times, while he was playing, she disappeared behind him, even leaving the room. He hadn't seen Lawrence for a while, and wondered if Mrs. Tanizaki had to go make Lawrence his sandwiches in the kitchen. These days Rachel wasn't making Kevin lunch anymore. When he got home he'd make it himself in the microwave and eat it alone at the table, the taps of Mrs. Tanizaki's stick still beating inside his ears. His mother would be sitting on the couch, looking out the window at the park, there and not there at the same time. He thought the baby in her stomach was dragging her down; it was round like a bowling ball and maybe that heavy.

Rachel had decisions to make, had to figure out what to do—about her job, the rent, the future. The words *what to do* ran together in her mind until they lost meaning and became a chant instead, *whattodowhattodowhattodo.* At times she felt like she was drowning in air—too thick, it bore down until she couldn't move or breathe. The baby was due in two months. This much she knew: she was going to name the baby Jennifer, she was going to put little barrettes in her hair, she could practically feel the silky skin of the baby's cheek against hers. One day a fifty-dollar bill came in the mail, in an envelope with no return address. She was waiting to find the strength inside her, waiting for it and building it up. In the meantime she rested, and Kevin played piano in his room.

It was summer and Kevin did not have school. He stayed in his room playing the piano. The apartment was hot and dense. He played "Pop Goes the Weasel." Rachel was lying down in the bedroom. Then the doorbell rang, and he answered it. It was his father. Kevin looked at him. Rachel had said that Brian was away on a trip, but he hadn't believed her. Maybe it was true.

"Hey, buddy," Brian said, "how's it going?"

"Okay."

"Just okay? Not good, not great?"

"Good."

"Good," Brian said, holding out a plastic bag. "Here, I brought you something."

Kevin took it and looked inside. It was a toy truck.

"Can I come in?"

Kevin stepped aside, and Brian walked in. Rachel was standing in the living room, rubbing the sleep from her eyes. Each time she went to sleep she seemed to fall deeper and deeper, and it took her forever to wake up. Even the sight of her husband couldn't shake her into action; she stood there blinking.

"Hey," Brian said. "I came to see how you guys are doing."

Rachel rubbed her stomach. "It's a girl," she said. "Jennifer."

When Kevin closed the door, the sound of it made Brian turn around. He smiled at Kevin. Rachel and Brian sat on the couch, and he did all the talking. It was like he'd been storing up words all the time he'd been away, and when he got home and opened his mouth they tumbled out on top of one another, falling and falling. But the things he was talking about had nothing to do with his trip—baseball scores, stories about his job, jokes he'd heard. Kevin sat down next to him, on the other side of Rachel, and put his hand next to Brian's knee. He could feel the weight of his father's leg on the couch. A while later Rachel went into the kitchen to make dinner and Brian stood there in the doorway, still talking. After dinner, Kevin went to his room and could hear his parents' voices rumbling in a steady rhythm through the walls. With a book and the paper piano on his lap, he turned this rhythm into a song, making it the bass clef to a melody he made up as he went, a tap-tap beat up and down and around the scale.

In the middle of the night he thought he heard a scream and jumped up out of bed. Standing outside their door, listening, he heard his mother sob. Was it the baby? So heavy that it dropped out of her, ripping her open? "Mom?" he said.

"Go to sleep, Kev," Brian said. "Everything's fine."

Kevin looked at the closed door. "Mom?" he said.

Finally she called, "It's okay."

He was still standing there, and Brian said, "Did you hear her, bud? Go back to bed."

In the morning, they were still asleep when he left for his piano lesson. He drank a glass of juice and ate some toast and walked around the park, green and weedy now. He rang the doorbell at Mrs. Tanizaki's.

"Come in, Kevin," she said. "Today I've got a surprise for you."

He followed her into the house. Lawrence stood in the kitchen doorway, chewing. When Kevin passed by, he opened his mouth wide and showed him the pile of chewed-up food on his tongue. Kevin stared.

"When you're finished eating," Mrs. Tanizaki called, "we'll be waiting for you, Lawrence."

Lawrence smiled at him with his mouth still open and his tongue covered with food. His eyes were barely visible behind his glasses and his hair. Kevin sped past him.

"Sit over here, Kevin," Mrs. Tanizaki said, pointing to the chair at the back of his room, where Lawrence used to sit chewing his sandwiches. "Where is your book?"

He opened his backpack and took it out.

"Open to the last page," she said. "I want you to learn this piece. This section in your book is just a small part of the piece. But Lawrence knows the whole piece and plays it very well, so I asked him to play it for you. And I want you to listen to it very carefully."

"Okay."

"Lawrence, are you ready?"

Lawrence came into the room with his mouth closed and sat down on the piano bench. Kevin looked at his slouching back. All he could think about was bits of food falling out of his mouth and landing on the white and black keys, and when Lawrence started playing he could barely hear the music. He was thinking about the food, and the notes were wooden and dull. He closed his eyes. Lawrence's fingers moved over the piano without ceasing, and he pictured them and made them into his own fingers, and then he was playing and finally he could hear the piano. He heard it without Lawrence in it. And there it was. The notes lined up, partnered and separated and circled, moving swiftly through a clear, empty hall; there were no smells in this place, just a pale and pure background, like water. Then he thought, This is the castle. These are the dancers.

A cascade, a chord, a castle.

The music stopped, and he opened his eyes. Mrs. Tanizaki smiled down at him, not at his face but at his hands, and he looked and saw they were balled into fists. Lawrence made a snorting sound.

"Thank you, Lawrence," Mrs. Tanizaki said. "Kevin, would you like to thank Lawrence for his performance?"

"Okay."

"Kevin," she said.

"I mean thank you," he said.

"No big deal. Can I go now, Mom?"

"Yes, Lawrence."

He slipped heavily off the bench and disappeared into the kitchen, where Kevin could hear him opening and closing the refrigerator door, then took his place at the piano.

"Now, you try," Mrs. Tanizaki said, opening the book.

Kevin's fingers moved thickly, sluggishly through the first bars, and it sounded nothing like what he had just heard. He thought about his paper piano and his mother and his father there or not there and his fingers making empty sounds on a flat surface and he bit down, hard, on the inside of his cheek. His fingers stopped.

"It's all right, Kevin," Mrs. Tanizaki said. "It takes practice. If you go home and practice, you'll be able to play the piece, I guarantee it."

He looked at her dark eyes. She was the teacher. He bent his head over the keys.

When he got home his father was not there. His mother looked dazed, and kept moving her hands over her swollen stomach, from top to bottom, over and over.

"I don't think he's coming back this time," she said. "He packed a bag."

Kevin set his own backpack down, as if it incriminated him, and put his hands in his pockets.

"The duffel bag," Rachel said. "He took the duffel bag this time." She looked at Kevin, his thin arms poking out of his T-shirt. "Sit down at the table," she said. "He's not coming back, okay? But we're going to be fine. I'm going to make lunch."

She heated up some soup in the microwave, then brought it to the table and poured him a glass of milk. She sat down opposite him and crossed her arms. "How was your lesson?"

"I'm not going back," Kevin said.

"What do you mean? You love the piano."

He shook his head. He picked up his spoon and slurped down some soup. Even though he'd had his eyes closed during Lawrence's performance, he couldn't stop picturing his hands moving quickly, unhesitatingly, over the keys, gathering the notes into perfect strands, as Mrs. Tanizaki watched. The two of them sat together at the piano under the pool of light. It was their world, and he did not belong in it. He saw himself walking slowly toward them, a sheet of paper in his hand, and Mrs. Tanizaki didn't hear him; but Lawrence turned and saw Kevin and he was laughing, his head flung back.

"I hate her." He couldn't say her name. "I'm not going back."

"You really don't want to? You don't like the piano anymore?"

"I'm not going there anymore."

"Come here," she said. "Stop eating and come here."

He obeyed, walking around the table and standing next to her. They looked into each other's pale blue eyes. Then his lower lip, still orange with soup, trembled, and tears slipped down his cheeks. Rachel felt her blood pump in her veins—moving through her, waking her up—and she put her hands on the slight, slack muscles of his upper arms.

"I won't let you stop," she said, and her fingers sent strength into his skin. Her voice was the world's warmest sound. It pulled and pulled him until he found himself leaning close against her, and he pressed his forehead to her neck.

You Are Here

There were three days left of life in the suburbs; afterwards, it would all vanish. From her bedroom window, Iz could already see it starting to disappear, color bleeding from the edges of parks and elementary schools, asphalt thinning in driveways. This was in August, and all the neighborhood came out at dusk to walk their dogs in the park across the street. When Iz was in her room painting she kept the window open and could hear them calling their pets, names echoing in the twilight, like those of lost children. All the dogs ignored their owners. Off leashes, they danced and spun in the center of the park, barking and biting, threatening to bring or, again like children, come to harm.

Iz was leaving. School started Tuesday, and then she would not look back; she would never come back, either, except possibly in the very distant future, when she was either rich or an aristocrat. But until Tuesday she had to wait and, today, had to go shopping with her mother. In order to survive their trip to the mall, she was treating it as a sociological expedition, a journey into the heart of America. Also, she was pretending to be French. She would address silent queries to her mother: *Please, could you tell me what ees Orange Julius? Eet ees not in my dictionary.* Seen through this lens, American culture was fascinating.

"Izzy, are you ready? Is that what you're wearing to go shopping?" Her mother stood on the landing outside Iz's room, adjusting the straps of her purse and wearing a light blue seersucker dress. She was of a generation that did not choose to leave the house in slacks. She was of a generation that used the word *slacks.*

"It's hot, Mom. I'm wearing shorts." *Please, what ees the difference between slacks and trousers?*

Her mother, who didn't know she was French, who thought Iz was from Newton, Massachusetts, sighed and shook her head. "Well, you're all grown up now, so do whatever you want," she said, in a tone that meant just the opposite. Iz's wearing shorts to a public place and going off to study art against her father's wishes—he thought she should major in business or computer science or both—were to her equally incomprehensible actions. She always sighed and shook her head. And it drove Iz crazy, this failure to discriminate between tragedies.

Her mother was in her element in the shopping mall; she responded to the filtered light and Muzak like some kind of specialized plant. At home she was mostly quiet and withdrawn, obeying Iz's father's barked, alcoholic commands; she spent a lot of time sitting in armchairs, reading thrillers under isolated pools of light. But once they got inside the mall she drew herself up to her fullest height and took a deep breath. Iz lagged behind, watching packs of teenaged boys pick up teenaged girls. The boys, white kids from Chestnut Hill, were wearing huge, baggy jeans and hundred-dollar sneakers. The girls' hair was sculpted up above their foreheads like a wall of defense.

"Excuse me, but isn't your name Samantha?" one of the boys said, lying in wait outside of the Gap.

"No."

"Oh. Well, what *is* your name?"

At the black map of stores, Iz's mother hummed and pointed. She was wearing a shade of nail polish called One Perfect Coral. Iz had no nails to speak of; shards of oil paint were visible beneath what was left.

"Now, let's see," breathed her mother. "We are . . . here." She pointed to the red dot labeled YOU ARE HERE. *Vous êtes ici,* said Iz to herself.

"And we want to go . . . here, I think. Is that all right, Izzy?"

"Whatever, Mom. I don't really have an opinion."

"Oh, don't be ridiculous," said her mother. "Of course you do."

By the time she left for school, Iz owned three color-coordinated outfits she would never wear: angora sweaters and corduroy skirts, Shetlands and kilts, clothes her mother must have seen on the front of New England college brochures. At school she wore jeans and a man's button-down shirt every day and slept whenever she could in the studio. Her roommate was a girl from Houston who wanted to be an accountant or else marry one. She was the daughter Iz's parents should've had. She wanted to stay up late and make brownies and talk about life; she wanted them to gain the freshman fifteen together. Her name was Shirelle, like the all-girl group. *Excusez-moi, could you tell me please, what ees a Shirelle? Eet sounds like a kind of, how do you say, mushroom. But eet ees not a mushroom, ees eet?*

Iz was now Izabel and she was still from France. She had toned down the accent and was telling people that although she was American she'd grown up in Europe, and would ask them to explain simple things. *What ees mac-and-cheese, please? What ees gangsta rap? Ah, oui, le rap des gangsters.* It had become a game that gave so much protection she couldn't let go of it. She was mightily disappointed to discover that the people she met at school were from backgrounds just like hers, from indistinguishable suburbs all over the country. They sat around talking about TV shows they all remembered from childhood, as if this represented some kind of shockingly universal human condition, and held contests to see who could remember the most theme songs, or even the most lines from *The Facts of Life.* "You take the good you take the bad you take them both and there you have the facts of life, the facts of life." *Please, who ees Mrs. Garrett?*

She escaped to the studio and stayed there whether she was painting or not. Sometimes she just sat around reading books about Greek mythology. She was fascinated by the stories of gods and women, of rapes and transformations. Zeus came to Leda in the form of a swan. Apollo turned Daphne into a tree. She was sketching out a whole series of paintings where the women turned around and began lustfully attacking the gods, who promptly ran away, terrified by the women's desire. The men, meanwhile, were turned into objects from the modern world of America, Kit-Kat bars and McDonald's golden arches. Apollo became the Lone Ranger, and Zeus became a 1970s Corvette, his head sticking out in front, like a hood ornament. Her fellow artists thought this was a real critique.

Only one of them, Wade, thought it was bullshit. Short, dark, wiry, and intense, he was very hairy and always had five o'clock shadow, and he walked around the communal studio dropping art terms into casual conversation, *contraposto, chiaroscuro.* He was from New Jersey but said he was from New York. Supposedly his parents owned a gallery.

"Well, I mean, look, I like it, I do, I think it's clever, I certainly think it's very glib, very facile. I just think it's possibly a little bit too self-conscious, you know, the self-flagellating American artist?" This was what he said of Izabel's sketches, standing with one hand holding the other elbow, motioning with his thin, hairy fingers.

"Excuse me please, what ees self-flatulating?"

"Flagellating," said Wade.

"Oh," Izabel said, smiling apologetically. *"Excusez-moi."*

In class discussion, Wade's remarks were articulate and penetrating and difficult for her to follow. Sometimes the professor, a short, rotund man with a plummy, not-quite-British accent like Cary Grant's, would abandon the pretense of speaking to the whole class and converse with Wade for a few minutes, both men serious and collegial, holding certain things to be understood between them. The classroom was dark, windowless, and hot, and Izabel frequently fell asleep during their discussions. Nevertheless she liked the dense, enclosed air and felt she continued to learn even when asleep, through osmosis, the art slides imprinting themselves on her brain, translucent and colored, like stained glass.

Wade drove around the ivy-walled campus in an old Toyota that had been crumpled in some accident and was missing all the windows on the left side. The whole left side of the car, in fact, was wrapped up in plastic and taped together. It looked like somebody's refrigerated leftovers. He asked Izabel to a movie and drove there talking the entire time, his thin fingers jerking and pointing. The art world was like the Roman Empire near the end, he told her, in that it had stopped responding to the world and responded only to itself, speaking its own decadent language. When he asked her if the situation was different in France, Izabel shrugged.

"I get it. I get it," said Wade, grinning, and tapping his fingers against the steering wheel. "The true artist cannot be moved by these considerations. Okay, I see, the artist creates outside of the institutions that sponsor him—or her, as the case may be. Well, okay, fair enough. I mean, I understand there's a certain legitimacy to that point of view, but personally I think it's sort of naïve in this day and age. I mean after the eighties you can't really think the art world exists outside of a context of politics and commerce, can you? I don't think anybody can, not even you."

"Not even me?" Izabel couldn't tell if he was being sarcastic. Feeling out of her depth, she turned to look out through the cloudy plastic. "Don't people in America fix their cars?"

After the movie they drank coffee while Wade continued to talk. He held passionate views on many subjects, and Izabel was amazed by the sheer number of things he found to say. As he spoke he leaned very far over at the table and pressed his hand against his forehead, as if trying to contain all the furious activity inside his brain. After a while she became convinced that this was, in fact, what he was doing. Whenever he asked for her opinion, which wasn't often, she shrugged. The shrug, she decided, was her best weapon. She couldn't really follow all that he was saying, not because it was necessarily so difficult, but mostly because it was so rapid and exhausting. Her mind wandered. She looked at Wade's hand pressed up against his head and started thinking about one of the Barbie dolls she'd had as a child. Ballerina Barbie came with a crown sticking out of her blond hair like a tumorous silver growth. It looked all right when she was dancing, but when she was just hanging out it seemed ridiculous. Izabel had once tried to remove the crown with a pocket knife, but it wouldn't come off and eventually the doll was hospitalized in a shoebox. She never recovered. She had a hard life compared to regular Barbie and Ken, whom Iz kept together in another shoebox and who engaged constantly in passionate, violent love-making. They did nothing else, had no other hobbies or jobs. *Oh, Ken. Oh, Barbie.* After the ballerina's operation, Ken and Barbie came to visit, sighing condolences, but then rapidly stole away to squirm and bash their plastic bodies against each other. They only ever had one thing on their plastic minds. While Wade spoke to Iz, she decided to work on a series of paintings in which Ken and Barbie reenacted the romances of Greek mythology. She would tell the class, *I call thees one "Ken Appears to Barbie in the Form of Campbell's Chicken Noodle Soup."*

That night it turned out that Wade, too, only had one thing on his plastic mind. Back at the studio, they looked at some of his canvases, which were enormous, geometric and monochromatic. Izabel had no idea what they were supposed to be about.

"It's a post-Rothko thing," Wade said, and put his hand on her breast. His eyes were hazel, his expression as intense as a side-show hypnotist's. Izabel couldn't help laughing, but to her surprise this didn't make him stop or even blush. He kept his hand there and started moving it around, and then she quit laughing, and they stayed together in a dark corner of the studio, behind a stack of stretched-out canvases. *Oh, Ken. Oh, Barbie.*

In class they were studying eroticism in art. Everyone was working on being mature about it. They were looking at fairy tales and oil paintings, woodcuts, each detail laced with meaning, the importance of flowers and the angles of wrists. Professor Edelman was isolating the elements of the erotic, cataloging them with his plummy voice and his red laser. He had a dry wit and parchment skin to match it, and Izabel wondered if he could even imagine the physical realities, as opposed to their artistic representations: herself and Wade each night in the studio after everyone else had left, the messiness of their fluids and sounds. The professor pointed in the dark at women facing sideways, huge breasts projecting outward like crescent moons, their nipples like rocks. These breasts weren't just breasts, they represented the fertility of the earth. This was art, where layers of meaning were contained beneath the obvious. It was its own language, just like Wade said. *Zee language of love.*

By October, Wade would not leave her alone. He stood behind her and talked to her while she painted. She was trying to find the exact fake-flesh color for Barbie's breasts. Barbie was trapped in a prison, locked inside, but the prison was the regular kitchen of a suburban American home, with a red-checkered tablecloth on the table. Ken's head was vaporously visible in the steam rising from her bowl of chicken noodle soup. Her breasts leaned toward him precipitously, and tiny chunks of chicken hung from the non-separated strands of his hair. Barbie was looking at him with a complex swirl of emotions—shock, confusion, a terrified desire—that Izabel was trying to convey within the limited range of expression afforded by the trademark Barbie smile.

Shirelle had moved down the hall and was now rooming with a girl named Kelly. When Izabel went back to the dorm, to change clothes, she sometimes saw them in Kelly's room, the door open, watching movies under a poster of a Georgia O'Keeffe flower, eating microwave popcorn and giggling. Wade was following her back to the room by now. Professor Edelman had come to regard them as a couple and had given them to understand that he approved. A favored pair, they'd been over to his house for dinner and called him by his first name, Marius. After class, they'd routinely have coffee or a drink in his office, the two of them slouching in front of his desk he sat behind, surrounded by shelves of papers and books and incunabula, pictures tacked up everywhere, a scholarly collage. He and Wade would discuss personalities of the art world while she stared at a pornographic Mesopotamian piece directly behind Marius's head. It had dawned on her that Wade and Marius were the same person, just a few years apart: Wade was what Marius had been as a young man, and Marius was what Wade would become. In either case they were equivalent; it was a transitive property of men. She could see Wade at forty and at sixty, still intense and thin and profusely hairy, though his hair would turn salt-and-peppery and start sprouting out of his nose; he would still gesture with thin fingers in support of his many points.

While she painted, Wade would put his hands on her shoulders, or his arms would encircle her from behind. His body temperature was always high, as if to match his mental energy. He was in love with Izabel, he said, and he brought her gifts, including paints, books, cups of coffee. She didn't know when he found the time to paint, but his canvases grew daily, a huge seven-by-ten wall of color. Her paintings looked like watercolors by comparison, little washed-out sagas of women and men. While she painted, he whispered a stream of plans for their future together and memories of their past, to him already richly detailed. Their relationship was like a painting he was building on canvas, blocking it out section by section, adding layers and color; it had its own internal references and symbols, flowers and the angles of wrists, an iconography of past and future, things that stood for love.

On the phone Iz's mother wanted to know when she was coming home, her voice plaintive and distant. She was preparing a turkey for Thanksgiving, and making a special dressing. In the background Iz's father growled about the rising costs of college tuition. Iz imagined the clean, silent house, where all her old toys lay trapped in liquor boxes stored in the basement, Ken and Barbie forever silent and entwined, like Baucus and Philemon, who grew into a tree. Ken and Barbie could never become a tree, except maybe a plastic one, and perhaps this could be another painting in the series: *Ken and Barbie Grow Together into a Fake Potted Plant.*

Iz's mother said, "Your father wants to know if you're taking any accounting classes."

"Mom, I'm not taking accounting. I'm taking English, math, history, and Visions of the Erotic in Art. Do you remember me, Izzy, I'm an art major? Does he? Does he even remember who I am?"

Her mother sighed into the receiver, low and loose, a sound like flatulence: self-flatulating. Her father's voice rumbled darkly in the background. He had been like this all her life, a shadowy, angry figure, rarely present, issuing proxy commands, whose wrath must be avoided at all costs.

"Your father," translated her mother, "wants me to tell you that you should take economics or computer science. Otherwise he won't pay for next semester. It's a practical thing, Izzy. It's about your future."

Iz said, "Well, since this is my last semester of school, I might as well stay here for Thanksgiving. I guess I'd better get the most of it while I can."

Her mother sighed again and said, "Your father and I only want the best for you."

In France we do not celebrate Thanksgiving, said Izabel. *Please, what ees sweet potato pie?* Out of loyalty to her and her foreignness—"An exile in your own country," he said, "but aren't artists always exiles?"—Wade decided to stay on campus, too. The college saved on heating costs over the long weekend and the two of them shuffled morosely around the studio in winter coats, breathing clouds of smoke. Feeling like an orphan, Izabel caught cold and began to sniffle and cough. She did not paint. The canvas around Ken and Barbie was murky and indistinct, featureless and gloomy, like the November weather. This, she decided, was the landscape of the suburbs, so she kept it that way. Wade brought her chicken noodle soup and covered her with blankets on the mattress they kept in the corner.

Remote with fever, Izabel slept. She slipped into a dream that felt like church, floating under stained-glass lights; men murmured, first a drone and then a hum. Wade was on top of her, a solid, hairy weight, and she couldn't breathe. This was not a dream. She pushed him away, but this didn't stop him, any more than her laughter had stopped him the first time. *Oh, Izabel.* To him it was ecstasy, it was a frenzy of joining. She didn't need to see his face to know this. He was unstoppable as Zeus, but didn't need any disguise. The pain was the color red, and the sheets were red, and the sounds he was making were also red. The world was a canvas splotched with red, and she was the paint; she thinned and spread.

When she woke up, Wade was gone. She sat up and then, pain shooting, lay down again.

Wade came back and lay beside her, stroking her hair. "Are you all right? Do you feel okay?"

"*Oui, ça va.*"

"Do you want any more soup?" The hair on his chin hurt her skin.

He held her in his arms. He still did not stop talking; he was incapable of silence. She closed her eyes and dreamt of men: young gods who spoke little, yet eloquently, in heavily accented English. A French trapeze artist, wearing tights, beckoned to her. *Come away with me, Isabelle. I beg it of you.* They would join *le cirque* and perform gravity-defying feats together, catching each other without fail midair. Or perhaps she'd had enough of French, and instead would meet a German, a nobleman, and they would leave America together, travel to the Old Country, and live in the Black Forest, eating Black Forest cake. Dreaming again, she was now her own mother, walking through a church that was also a shopping mall but still beautiful, like a shopping mall in France or ancient Greece. In its high, domed ceilings, angels hung from the rafters singing songs of purchase, sweet hymns of sales reductions on ladies' wear and pantyhose, the sun shafting through the skylights down to the foodcourt and the altar. It was so beautiful, so warm and light, that she wanted to get closer, but she couldn't figure out how to. She couldn't move at all. She was in a world so beautiful that it didn't require signs or maps. All she needed was a red dot with an arrow labeled *You are here.* The angels swooped down toward her, singing *You are here,* holding red sheets open between them like a banner. *Where is here?* she asked, but the angels wouldn't stop to answer the question. They flew off, these pale, singing cherubs, toward a shoe store where everything was 40% Off.

After Thanksgiving, Izabel was sick for a long time. She moved back into her dorm room and stayed in her bed, sickness a haven she didn't want to leave. Shirelle came back to take care of her, clucking in a gratified, motherly way, and making her tea with molasses, which in Shirelle's family counted as a special treat. As Izabel moved in and out of fever, Shirelle sent Wade away every time he came to the door. Izabel had papers and tests, but did none of them, Shirelle writing notes for her and forging doctors' signatures. The college granted her extensions on everything: everything, they said, could wait. They were so kind that Izabel didn't have the heart to tell them she wouldn't be back. She was going to freeze in her bed and waste away like Echo, disappearing into sound. Shirelle wouldn't hear of this and brought her Rocky Road ice cream to eat in bed. Wade left a twenty-five-page letter in a manila envelope outside her door; it looked like a term paper, double-spaced, in a ten-point font, complete with footnotes and an index of lists. In it various issues of importance to their relationship were exhaustively explained, all the scholarly evidence marshaled in favor of Wade's argument. *Dear Izabel, I have been doing a lot of thinking and have come to certain conclusions, which are elaborated in the following pages. We can be friends, can't we? We have so much in common. For example . . .* he wrote, and then gave five pages of examples. He reproduced entire conversations. *In conclusion, even if you don't love me anymore, we can be friends. Please be my friend. Be my best friend.*

"No," said Iz out loud, sitting in bed. "No."

Shirelle said, "You should call the police."

"He loves me."

"So fucking what," said Shirelle, in her Texan accent.

Izabel looked at her with new appreciation.

"Please come home for Christmas, Izzy," said her mother on the phone, silence in the background.

Iz could picture it, the snowdrifts on roofs and swing sets, the lights spiraling around trees. Christmas in the suburbs. In the mall children climbed reluctantly onto the hot polyester fabric of Santa's lap, doubtful, afraid, but willing to risk it for the reward of presents. She remembered what that was like.

———

On a Wednesday afternoon in the second week of December, when Shirelle was taking her math final, Wade came in. Shirelle had left the door unlocked and he just walked right in and stood there, breathing a little heavily, as if he'd crashed through some immense barrier instead of simply turning a doorknob. Izabel was sitting in bed with a child's coloring book. This was as much art as she could handle these days; she was happy to stay inside of the big black lines. He was wearing a ski sweater and no jacket, and his cheeks were red from the cold. The rest of his face was wan, though, and there were dark circles under his eyes. Izabel was not afraid of him; in fact she felt nothing, and was vaguely surprised. She'd heard that love and hate were two sides of the same coin, that people could feel both at the same time, that this was how they came to kill those they loved the most. But she hadn't known it was possible to feel love, hate, and indifference simultaneously, with the last overlaying everything else, like new paint on a twice-used canvas.

"*Bonjour,* Izabel," said Wade.

"What?" she said. "I mean, *pardonnez-moi*?"

"I've been learning French in the language lab," he said, his breath still labored. "I thought that it would be great if we could communicate in French, you know, so we could be closer. I mean, I know sometimes I talk a lot, and sort of dominate the conversation a little. My parents are always telling me to slow down and listen instead of talking so much, they've been telling me that ever since I was a little kid, but you know me, Izabel, I get so wound up. I mean, nobody knows me as well as you do, Izabel."

"Wade," said Iz.

"I was thinking maybe you and I could go to France this summer—wait, hold on. *'On peut aller à la France ensemble.'*

What do you think? You could show me some places where you grew up, maybe, wouldn't that be great? And we could both paint, and talk, and—"

"Wade, I'm not French. I've never even been to France. I'm from Newton, Mass."

He stood frozen in the center of the room. Izabel watched from the bed and waited for him to grow into a monster, a thunderbolt or a bull, but he just threw back his head and laughed.

"Well, that's pretty goddamn clever, I have to say. Pretty goddamn hilarious, Izabel, if that is your real name. That is your real name, isn't it?"

She nodded.

He came and sat down next to her on the bed and stroked her hand, which she pulled away. His voice softened and thickened, like Shirelle's molasses dissolving in tea. "It's so great you shared that with me," he whispered. "Now we're in this together. *Izabel, je t'aime.*"

"Wade, it's over."

"No! *Non.* Seriously, I mean it." He began to work a corner of her bedspread, folding it and refolding it. "You love me," he said, "and I love you. If we love each other, that's all that matters, right? And nothing can come between us." He bent over and kissed her hard on the mouth.

She leaned back and hit her head against the wall. It made an inanimate-sounding clunk, like the head of a Barbie doll. She scrunched up her legs to try to get away from him, but he was strong. His hand twisted up the fabric of her shirt, but he was weirdly clumsy and didn't seem to know exactly what he wanted to do. Pushing against him, Izabel felt incredibly dizzy, as if the blood were flowing from her head. All the blood was flowing away. She grabbed a fistful of his hair and pulled.

"Ow!" Wade sat back, rubbing his head and looking puzzled. "You hurt me. What are you, crazy?"

Izabel, gulping air, began to laugh.

"I'm leaving," he said. "I can't handle this. I love you, Izabel, but you're crazy, I mean, seriously, I don't want to sit in judgment of you or anything, that's the last thing I'd want to do, and I know some people think there's a correlation between artistic genius and mental illness. But seriously, you might want to consider getting some help."

"Okay," she said. "Maybe you should go."

"Maybe I should. I'm sorry, Izabel. I really am." His hand reached up to stroke her hair gently, twice, then he got up and left, closing the door behind him with a quiet, considerate click.

Shirelle invited Izabel home for Christmas. Her family lived in the country on a ranch, and she promised hay rides and dances. She had four older brothers and made life at her house sound like an episode of *The Waltons*.

"It'll be a nice, traditional American Christmas," she said. "We leave milk and cookies out for Santa."

"Really?" said Izabel in her French accent. "Are zey not wasted? Santa does not eat zem, does he?"

"Izabel," Shirelle said patiently, "Santa is my dad."

"*Ah, mais non!* Zen you are very lucky. You must get zee most presents of anyone in zee world."

"Girl," said Shirelle, "sometimes I think you're putting me on."

But Izabel did not go to Texas for Christmas. Her mother called, her voice trembling with the accomplishment, to say that she had brokered a peace with Iz's father, who had agreed to a double major of economics and art, so Iz could continue her classes. She didn't mention to her mother that she hadn't yet finished the first semester. There were presents waiting for her under the tree, if she would only come home to claim them.

"I went to the mall, Izzy," said her mother, "and it was so beautiful!" Her voice was firm and happy. "All the decorations and the music, you just have to see it."

Izabel could see it. She could see her mother moving alone through their house like some sad, ancient heroine, Demeter in Newton, decorating the tree, wrapping gifts. She could see her calling her daughter on the phone, picking out a tie for her husband at the mall, each day an act of small bravery. Izabel could see everything. She could see it because it was all inside her, hanging on to her like snow dissolving over their roof into a border of icicles. She could see it as clearly as she could see the children of the neighborhood bringing their toboggans to the park, where Iz would paint them over the holidays, watching from her bedroom window as they climbed through the snow, spots of color bundled thickly by their mothers into snowsuits, dragging their heavy loads behind them.

A Theory of Entropy

What could reach them here was the mail, and Claire took the boat across the lake to Bob's store to pick it up. The first of the summer people were in, browsing through the aisles, stocking up on canned goods and batteries. From behind the counter Bob nodded and passed her a rubberbanded stack, her bills and Carson's heavy magazines—*Science, Journal of Organic Chemistry*—saying, as he did each time, "A little light reading for you, Claire?"

"Puts me to sleep," she said. Around her children tugged their parents' sleeves, begging for candy and to be taken fishing.

"Hold on a minute. Something for you in the back," Bob said. He came back with a bundle in his arms, a padded envelope nearly as square as a box. She didn't have to look at the return address to know that it was Carson's book.

She piled the bills and magazines on top, then slid it off the counter and pressed it to her chest for balance. Bob was frowning at a boy handling a box of fishing lures with larcenous fingers; when she left, he raised his hand briefly without looking away from the boy.

The dock was not ten yards from the store. She threw a tarp over the mail and, gunning the engine, glanced back at it.

She never opened his mail, although he sometimes asked her to, and anyway he opened it in front of her, showed or told her everything—he had no secrets, he always said. But these were her scruples. The boat skittered a little as she maneuvered around driftwood. On the other side of the lake a motorboat roared and circled. Underneath it and closer in, a smaller sound almost evaporated as it reached her: the hoot of a loon.

Carson came into the kitchen, where she was snapping beans. He dipped his hand into the bowl and sat down at the table with a handful. "She wants to come here," he said.

"Here? Why?"

"Because she knows I won't go to the city."

She turned. His legs under the table stretched the length of it: he was over six feet tall, strong-shouldered, rangy. Long fingers with thick knuckles, like knots on wood. To relax he built furniture, including this table.

"To work on the book," he said.

"I thought she already did." Claire set the bowl in the sink and ran water over the beans. "Isn't that what came today, the edits?"

"She says we have a lot more to do. That the book isn't quite coming across. She thinks a few days of hammering it out in person could do it. So, can she come?"

"You're asking me?"

"It's your place," he said.

She looked at him. She loosed a clove of garlic from its paper and set it, along with an onion, on the table for him to chop.

Carson studied entropy. Claire didn't understand his work and had given up trying. It was entirely theoretical, divorced from the data sets and experimental designs on which he had built his early career in chemistry. He produced it, as far as she could tell, whole and unprecedented, a rabbit from the black hat of his mind. Sitting in his office at the back of the cottage, he wrote page after page of thoughts with a blue marker on lined yellow pads. What she knew of entropy came from a college textbook that she'd bought, in a vain effort to educate herself, after they met. Entropy is a thermodynamic function measuring the disorder of a system. The greater the disorder of a system, the higher its entropy. Disorder equals randomness.

Or it used to, until Carson came along. He developed a new way of looking at entropy, of evaluating the whole idea of order and equilibrium. He charted the paths of molecules through systems and began to wonder if entropy veered toward simplicity, if there was order within disorder, whether disorder had a quality of inevitability to it and was, in fact, the lawful tendency of a non-equilibrial universe. Possibly, Claire thought, entropy was a scientific term for fate. But she never said so to Carson, who would tell her gently that science was science, not metaphor.

At the beginning, in the city, he'd tried to explain the model to her, defining its basic elements, then moving on and almost immediately losing her, his logic twisting along a corridor she could not follow. He drew outlines, equations, the universe in boxes and arrows. The blanker she looked, the faster he talked, reaching into his brain for examples to teach her by, striving to share his clarity. He stretched his hands wide, carving the air: his words a map to show her where he was. Claire was no scientist at all—simply a freelance designer who'd failed math in high school. Instead of listening to his words she became distracted by the passion in his voice, the shaking timbre of it, by how he peered under the surface of things to discover some elusive knowledge of the world. She forgot to pay attention, and attraction overruled. Eventually, they both gave up on explanations.

She had known Carson for a year when he published the first diagram of his model in *Science* and was suddenly acclaimed in the nonscientific press. Scientists made pilgrimages to his office at the university, besieged him with letters, never stopped calling. Some of the letters and calls came from Jocelyn Gates, who acquired manuscripts for a popular publisher. She wanted him to write an account of his work for the general reader, which she said could be the biggest scientific best-seller since the *Origin of Species.*

The other members of his department assumed that he signed this contract for the usual reasons, the temptations of money and self-inflation. But he had been seduced, Claire thought, by different riches, the only treasure he really craved: time away from the university, from grant writing and the company of difficult colleagues, from the obligations to students and administrators. Time to think. He could take leave from the university, write the manuscript, and meanwhile chase the magnets of his own ideas. In interviews he always said, "There is so much left to be done."

When he decided to write the book, Claire offered him her cottage on the lake, and her presence with it. They had been here two years.

Even in May, the nights were cold. Under the blankets she moved closer to Carson, whose body gave off heat constantly, no matter the season, as if it were electric. She turned her back to him and brought his arm around her. From where she was lying she could see out the window to a clutch of birches on a rise behind the house, the bark silver in the light from stars.

"How old is this woman?" she asked.

"Claire," he said, his tone a reminder that he hated any sign of insecurity. Carson was generally even-tempered, but frustration sometimes sparked from him in angry fits. What he liked best about her, she knew, was the idea he had of her strength. He liked being indebted to her for the favor of this house, and it was important for him to think she didn't need him.

"Old?" she said. "Or young?"

"She's not much younger than you are. Twenty-nine."

"How do you know? I mean so specifically."

"She told me. She took one of my classes at one point, apparently, and mentioned what year she graduated." His hand twining hers began to sweat, and he unclasped and moved it to her shoulder. His cheek scratched her face. "Don't be jealous," he said in her ear. "I hate it."

She flipped onto her back and looked at him. His eyes were open, colorlessly glinting in the darkness. "All right," she said.

Jocelyn Gates arrived on the noon bus. She wasn't what Claire was expecting, although she hadn't realized she'd been expecting anything at all. Her long, wavy hair had been dyed an unnatural brownish red that looked like dried blood. Behind thick brown frames her eyes were blue. When she stepped off the bus she flung her backpack over her shoulder, like a student, and her eyes found Claire's immediately.

"Are you Claire Tremble?" she said. "I'm Jocelyn."

Claire stepped forward and shook her hand. "Is that all you have?" she said, nodding at the backpack.

"Dear God, no," Jocelyn said as the bus driver lugged a large suitcase in their direction.

Claire looked at it.

"It's mostly manuscripts, I swear," Jocelyn said. "Carson said there'd be a boat. There is a boat, isn't there?"

"That's the boat," Claire said, pointing.

"Oh. Should I—"

"It's fine. But you might have to sit on it, that's all."

"I can do that," Jocelyn said.

Claire reached for the suitcase, but Jocelyn shook her head firmly, hefted it up, and gestured for Claire to walk on ahead. When they reached the boat, Jocelyn lowered the case down on its side then got in and straddled it. With the extra weight they sat heavily in the water, but Claire judged it would be all right. Jocelyn sat precariously, her white hands clutching the gunwale, spray from the lake misting her glasses. After a minute or so the boat seemed to adjust itself and moved slowly but smoothly through the branches of spruce trees clearly mirrored in the water.

Jocelyn leaned over to trail her fingers through their rippling needles. "It's beautiful here," she said.

"I know."

"What a wonderful place to write a book," she said, and inhaled with deep satisfaction, as if catching the scent of unborn books in the wind. She caught Claire's eye. "Thank you for letting me come."

Carson was waiting for them on the dock, a surprise, since he regularly worked every day until five and would brook no interruption, which habit had led Claire to offer to pick up the girl in the first place. Yet here he was, reaching out a long arm to catch the prow and rope it to the dock. Then he grabbed Jocelyn Gates's hand and pulled her up. The two of them laughed and moved from handclasp to shake. Jocelyn would not permit her suitcase to be carried for her, so she trudged after Carson up the hill to the house. Halfway there she paused to readjust her grip and said again to Claire, who was behind her, "It's so beautiful here."

"Yes."

"A refuge," she said, her eyes glowing, blue coals. "I hope I won't disturb your peace."

"Don't mention it," Claire said.

Because the desk in Carson's office was small, the two of them settled on the kitchen table, where they could spread the manuscript out in stacks. Claire shut the door to her office and tried to work, but on a trip to the washroom she heard them already arguing. She couldn't make out the specific words, only the general grievance in Carson's voice, and from this tone she suddenly heard her own name rising and realized he was calling her.

She stood in the doorway.

"This woman," Carson sputtered. His face was flushed but Jocelyn's was not. "She wants me to tell my story. She wants me to sell the material. Would you tell her, please, that science is not a *story*? Will you please agree with me on this so I'll know I'm not insane?"

Claire looked at Jocelyn, who smiled politely.

"I think I'm the wrong person to ask," Claire said, and Carson groaned. "I mean, you know I'm no scientist."

"So? You still know that a scientific theory is a model, not some fairy tale."

"Well, yes, and I'm not saying that it's fiction. But I do kind of think—sorry, Carson—that science is a story we tell ourselves about the world. In a way."

Carson said, tight-lipped, "It's not just any story."

"The important thing here, Carson," Jocelyn said, "is that we tell it well."

Over the next three days Carson and Jocelyn worked on the book. They fought often and loudly while Claire, in her office, didn't even pretend to work and just listened. For some time it seemed they couldn't even agree on terms or the meanings of words. She heard Carson's voice, strained and hoarse through the walls. "Order and disorder are only categories. They don't hold up, statistically." Jocelyn's voice flowed quietly under his. She was trying to simplify Carson's theories, to put his arguments into the plainest terms. They could be expanded later, she told him. The book was a pyramid requiring a foundation, a wide and basic layer.

Claire thought of the phrase Carson, quoting Jocelyn, had used to describe this process: hammering it out. This was certainly what it sounded like, voices striking hard as metal, Carson's strident, hers relentless, pounding his science into flatness like nails into wood. Claire was afraid for him to see his work— so famously abstract—popularized and, inevitably, reduced. Moreover, for him to cooperate in the reduction. And she was surprised by Jocelyn's persistence, her conviction that his ideas could be explained to the average reader. She kept on hammering.

"So all things tend naturally toward a simpler state," Claire heard her say.

"Where do you get this *naturally*?" Carson sounded anguished by her lack of precision. "Where? You're creating some kind of animism that isn't inherent in the work." Claire pictured him spreading his palms, trying to explain. "There is no *naturally*. Things can only happen according to the physical laws of the universe."

"So explain those laws to me."

"Look, miss, I didn't realize that you came up here for a scientific education. I thought you came here to work on my book."

"I'm your reader," Jocelyn said without a pause. "Explain it to me."

"Maybe you're not my reader," he said. "Maybe I have no readers. The kind of people you're talking about don't want to know about my work. Couldn't understand it even if they did."

"They want to."

Other times, as Claire passed through the kitchen, she saw them working smoothly, heads together, one nodding, the other speaking, in a low and constant and rhythmic tone, like two birds on a branch. In the evenings she and Carson cooked dinner for their guest. By tacit agreement they all three avoided the subject of science, instead discussing politics or weather, the natural beauty of the region, the improvements Claire and Carson had made to the cottage in order to live in it year-round. Conversation stayed polite and almost distant, with none of the contention or excitement that echoed through the rooms during the day.

Claire took the boat across to Bob's, and Jocelyn asked to go with her. She needed to use the phone to check in at the office.

"Although I'd rather not," she said at the dock, hands on her hips, looking out at the water. "The office seems a bit unreal at this point."

"It'll seem real enough once you get back," Claire said.

She raised an eyebrow. "I guess," she said.

"Whenever I go back to the city," Claire said, "I feel like I could take up my old life again in a minute, and this is the place that seems unreal."

Jocelyn nodded. "Do you ever miss it there?" she asked.

Claire wasn't sure whether this question was sincere or merely conversational. Possibly it was an editor's technique, a way of seducing writers, giving them the sense that she was curious about them, or about the knowledge they could provide. Claire took a breath and looked out over the lake. A string of starlings lassoed themselves into a circle, twisted, formed into a symbol that looked, for a second, like infinity. "Sometimes," she said.

"You grew up here?"

"In the city. This was our summer place."

Jocelyn reached over and touched the water. "Can you get across the lake in the winter?"

"Usually," Claire said. "If not, well, we have a lot of food stored."

"Must be a long winter." When Claire didn't answer, Jocelyn added, "But beautiful."

Inwardly, Claire rolled her eyes. Of course it was beautiful, but beauty had little to do with it. She had come here not just to be with Carson but to prove she could live here. Putting up food, trying to get Bob and the rest of the village not to look at her as one of the "summer people," insulating the cottage, chopping wood, all the other chores—the chores had everything to do with it. "My parents built the house," she finally said. "We were always working on it. They never intended it to be lived in year-round. But Carson needed a quiet place to work. And I can work from anywhere."

"Lucky for him," Jocelyn said.

"Not lucky. Just something I was able to do," Claire said. She felt Jocelyn's gaze on her. "I was glad to be able to offer it." She was speaking unwillingly but couldn't stop, the words being reeled from her as if the other woman held a line. She felt she had to explain, to give Jocelyn the correct impression of her life, the necessity of it bearing down on her with a pressure like physical weight. "This isn't a sacrifice for me," she said. "I like living here. I don't just see to Carson's needs. It's not like he's the, you know, reclusive man of genius and I'm the handmaiden."

"The handmaiden?" Jocelyn started to laugh, shaking her

head, then clamped her hand over her mouth. "I'm sorry. I'm not making fun of you. I've just never heard anybody use that word in conversation before."

"Oh, God," Claire said, "you're right." Her tension cracked and she could feel laughter breaking the surface of her skin, bubbling up through it as if it were water. "I don't know where that came from."

At the store Bob handed her the mail.

"Got a visitor with you, eh?" he said, looking at Jocelyn, who stood at the pay phone frowning at an open engagement book and making notes in it.

"That's summer for you," Claire said, and shrugged. She bought a chicken and some bread, then crossed the street to the vegetable stand. When she came back Jocelyn was still standing next to the phone, no longer talking, just standing, her face tilted to the sky. She had removed her glasses, and her pale skin, exposed to the sun, seemed doubly naked.

As if she'd recognized Claire's steps, she opened her eyes with a smile already present in them. "Ready to go, handmaiden?" she said.

"You stop," said Claire.

They took the boat back in silence. It was late afternoon, the sky changing to gray, and the water they passed through was planed in shadow, alternately clear and opaque, plants rising up from the deep into occasional visibility. As she docked, Claire looked up and saw Carson moving past a window, his silhouette dark in the light, the line of his neck, the curve of his shoulders. For one instant she didn't recognize him, didn't feel the familiar jolt of his presence. A blankness swept inside her. When she met him she memorized those outlines, raptured by the shape of him, a desire she could not ignore. Now she stood on the dock and looked at him and some emotion drained from her in a trickle like grains of sand marking the passage of time. Jocelyn walked up the hill in front of her, and Claire thought of the woman's questions and her own answers. Whatever she'd said to Jocelyn, she had changed her life because of him, her drastic desire for him. It wasn't possible—or was it?—that after making such a change, the feeling could dissipate, could disappear.

It made her wonder if she knew just what that feeling was. From the moment she met Carson she knew there was a part of him that she could never reach, the part devoted to an abstraction she would never touch. And then the move to the cottage, the distance and isolation and cold. She hadn't been coerced into anything. But what she had chosen was difficult, in fact was chosen for its difficulty. If she'd made a mistake, it was to believe that things struggled for—the cottage, Carson, their life here—had to contain more value than things fallen into with the simple force of the inevitable. A belief engineered by pride.

That night she lay awake, Carson breathing heavily beside her, Jocelyn inaudible in the guest room. She tried to remember as much as she could about his work, her thoughts circulating in a dull frenzy, as they would the night before an exam. All she could think of were the examples from the textbook. Dye dissolving into a glass of water; a dense red drop issuing a cloud of pink. Picture a truck crashing into a wall, she remembered. This is the world in spontaneous action, growing in disorder. Picture a mirror shattering on the floor.

They were almost finished, Jocelyn and Carson, with the final chapter, framing the conclusion. Claire could feel their exhilaration. She made a pot of coffee and joined them at the table with a cup.

"I think that we have an opportunity to extrapolate here,"

Jocelyn said. "From the level of chemical processes, the ones you've established, to larger ones."

Carson shuffled the papers of the manuscript on the table, then ran his hands over his face up to his forehead. From repetition of this gesture his eyebrows had risen into unruly tufts, adding to his look of worry. "I'd like to resist leaping to unwarranted conclusions," he said.

Jocelyn exchanged a smile with Claire. "I appreciate your caution," she said, "but this isn't a scientific paper. You don't have to worry about peer review. This is the time for you to make wild claims about the potential of your model to explain biology, economic and social phenomena, the very nature of human existence. Say that the second law of thermodynamics has been forever broken. You can be speculative. Be sexy."

"Listen," he said. "You must know by now that physical laws can't be broken. I only uncovered them a little further. They were always there."

"Come on, Carson," Claire urged. "Have a little fun with it."

"Claire."

"What?"

"I'm a scientist, not a comedian," he said, sounding stricken. This made both women laugh, and Jocelyn wiped a tear from her eye. Carson shook his head. "You two," he said. "Ganging up on me."

She remembered when, in a bar near the university, a colleague of Carson's, an older man, wheezy and red-faced and drunk, rambled on about great discoveries in science, the leaps and bounds of thought. This was a popular subject among scientists, Claire had noticed, as if by discussing the personality of genius they could associate themselves more closely with it. This man said there were two kinds of thinkers, those who led—who thought the new, the fully original—and those who followed in the existing tracks. The searchers and the followers, he called them.

Carson had snapped, "It's true there are two types of thinkers: people stupid enough to believe there are two types of anything, then everybody else."

"Sore subject, Carson?" his colleague said.

They finished the final edit at seven o'clock, so Claire fixed a late dinner. She lit candles and set a bouquet of wildflowers in a jelly jar on the table.

Carson lifted his wineglass and declared a toast. "As Claire and many undergraduates can attest, I've never been successful in spreading my ideas outside of a narrow group of scientists," he said to Jocelyn. "I know it's been like pulling teeth to get this book out of me, and I thank you for it. And I'm very glad it's over."

Though he was smiling, Claire sensed how strongly his relief tugged him: that tomorrow Jocelyn would leave, silence would return, and he would retire to his office with three months left of his leave from school. Three months completely devoted to real work. He lapsed into quiet, and a general exhaustion seemed to spread from him across the table. By nine the candles had burned low and the talk had dribbled to nothing.

At midnight, rising to go to the washroom, Claire passed the guest room, saw light through the door, and, without thinking, knocked. Jocelyn sat up in bed surrounded by sheets of paper, one pencil stuck in her hair, another in her hand.

"Don't you ever stop working?"

"I couldn't sleep." She waved for Claire to come in.

Claire sat down at the foot of the bed, on a folded quilt her mother had made. She traced the line of a square with her thumb. The pieces came from blankets, rags, and old clothes that her mother had stitched together on rainy summer days, having collected the scraps through the year in a box in the kitchen. Something to pass the time, she called it.

"What are you working on?"

"Paleontology," Jocelyn said. She put down her pencil and stretched, her neck's tendons visible and strong. When she reached up, the sleeves of her T-shirt fell back, showing the very smooth skin at the underside of her arms. "It's a new theory of dinosaur life. Dinosaurs are very big sellers."

"I don't know how you do it," Claire said. "Understand all these things."

Jocelyn rubbed her eye. "Well," she said, and smiled, "they're still dinosaurs, right? They still disappeared."

"I guess that's true."

"And anyway, I don't have to completely understand it."

"You don't?"

"Not at all. I just get it as clear as I can, then I move on to the next book."

Claire looked at the manuscript on Jocelyn's lap. Neat penciled notations lined the margins. Suddenly she was horribly conscious of having interrupted her work. She felt herself flush. "I'm sorry for intruding," she said, getting up and walking to the door.

Jocelyn gathered up the pages and moved them aside. "No," she said. "You didn't."

She practically missed the bus. In the morning she came out of her room with her bags packed, but at the last moment Claire couldn't find her. She went out the back door and saw Jocelyn crouched in a clearing behind the house, staring at a trillium, its single white flower nodding in the grass like some reminder of snow.

"Jocelyn, we really should leave."

Jocelyn stood and turned around. The slope of her shoulders was outlined in gold by the sun as it arrowed through the pine branches. Her blue eyes looked jeweled. In the sharpness of the light Claire could see the fine down of hair on her cheek. Silence swooned between them.

"I'm sorry to go," Jocelyn said.

Carson's book appeared the following spring. There was no preface, no page of acknowledgments. The book launched itself into being from the first page, his voice transposed into type: *I begin by stating that we live in a non-equilibrial universe, and that the state of disorder we know as entropy is itself an order of the universe that we have not, up to now, been able to recognize.* Claire could hear him saying it, picture his palms spread wide. In the bookstore she flipped through the pages, ran the tips of her fingers over the glossy jacket. *This new model of entropy could change the way we look at the organization of the universe, the way we think about its future and ours.* She turned to the back flap and touched the black-and-white picture of his face, her fingertip leaving a print behind.

Then she put the book back on the shelf, tapped it into place, and walked quickly to the front of the store, where, because, Jocelyn was waiting for her.

Edgewater

When Luz was a baby she used to be afraid of the water, but she wasn't anymore, or said she wasn't. In winter, the water in Lake St. Louis was still and pale, ice-crusted, as gray as the surface of the moon, though in summer it took on a deeper, more alive tinge that she liked better. What she didn't like, even now that she wasn't scared anymore, was how the water slapping against the rocks at the shore turned them green with algae—a slippery, scary mold, akin to pictures of plaque on teeth—and how slippery her hand felt, too, when she dipped it in. Luz had an idea of what water should be like—she'd seen a picture of an ocean once, an endless, clean, turquoise one, with a white beach and pink sunset—and Lake St. Louis was a disappointment to her because of the many ways it didn't conform to this idea.

But she was getting used to it this summer, owing to all the time she spent down by the water with Marie-Claire. Although she wasn't with Marie-Claire so much as within shouting distance of her. While Luz played down by the rocks at the water's edge, Marie-Claire wandered around the park looking for secluded places to smoke a joint. Luz knew about this. She'd seen a joint at home, inside a tin box her father kept in the bottom drawer of his nightstand, and she knew what it smelled like when he smoked it, even in the middle of the night with the windows open. One thing she didn't know was whether her father knew about Marie-Claire. She hoped he didn't, because she was liking spending the summer out here, just thinking and looking out over the lake and pretending that the dim blue land opposite wasn't the south shore of Montreal but China or Mexico or France. She liked to picture the people over there, foreigners wearing strange hats and riding bicycles through foreign streets, never knowing they were being watched. This was a lot better than spending the summer at summer school or at the YMCA or in her backyard playing "imagination games" with her dolls, which was what her last babysitter, Maureen, used to make her do. Maureen would always say, "Let's see you use your imagination," and then she would stand back, nodding, waiting for Luz's imagination to make an appearance. "Be creative," she'd urge. Maureen was old, older than Luz's father, and had gone back to school to get her degree in early-childhood education. While Luz played she could feel Maureen's eyes fixed on her, memorizing her every move.

Marie-Claire was calmer; she had her own imagination games to play. When Luz looked back over the grass, Marie-Claire was sitting on a rock, a small black figure (Marie-Claire wore black every day) resting her chin on her knees. They waved at each other and went back to their own business. It was early Wednesday afternoon and not many other people were around. Beyond Marie-Claire, cars went by on Lakeshore Drive, taking the curves too fast. A mom with two babies in a stroller crossed the street toward the lake. Seagulls circled and squawked. Luz turned around and concentrated on watching a couple of boats on the water, sails dipping lazy and graceful and white. She believed that to a certain, impossible-to-prove extent her watching kept the boats and the people in them safe from overturning, and she took the responsibility seriously. She didn't want the people to land in the slippery, gunky water or to have to touch any of the green slime that hovered on the rocks under the surface. You could see how polluted the water was down at the shore: by Luz's feet, scattered over the rocks, were Coke cans and beer bottles and other pieces of disintegrating trash she tried to identify by poking them with a stick. She saw a shoe. A worn-out bicycle tire. She saw Popsicle wrappers and plastic bags and lots of cigarette butts.

Later, when she thought about what she saw next, she would picture it as something small, something that could have come off one of her dolls, and she would think about putting it in her pocket and taking it home and keeping it for herself forever, secret and safe. But in reality it was much too big to fit in her pocket. It was bigger than Luz's whole arm, and it was a weird light brown, almost pink, and it was batting against the rocks like an animal trying to escape a cage: a plastic leg.

On the next block over from the park was the Edgewater Bar & Grill. Inside, there was only one window from which you could actually see the water, and only one table at that window. This was Kelly's table, and had been for ten years. She first started coming to the Edgewater when she was underage, heavily made up, treading carefully in high heels, flirting with older men before retreating to the safety of her friends at the table. By the time she was eighteen she knew the jukebox, such as it was, by heart. She celebrated her birthdays here and was tearfully consoled here after breakups, threw up in the bathroom a few times, tried cocaine in the bathroom once and then twice, came here after classes and instead of them. When she started university she also started waitressing at the Edge a few nights a week to make extra money. She told Manny, the owner, that she spent so much time there, she might as well get paid for it. Then she stopped going to school, but she didn't stop working.

She met the first man she ever slept with here, as well as the last. The last one being almost a year ago, just before she took her chastity vow. Which she also did at the Edgewater. Quitting was easier than she thought, a hell of a lot easier than quitting smoking. It wasn't like she was giving up sex forever; she was just abstaining, taking a break, because she thought it would be good for her, the way some people who aren't even really Christians give things up for Lent. Her head was clearer and calmer than it was before the vow, when a space in the back of her head had always been devoted to the question of sex, of when and who and how and if, a churning little spot of energy that ran underneath and beside all her other mental activities. Now she'd freed up that energy and could just use it—well, what was she using it for?—to live.

What happened was this: on a Friday night—Friday nights at the Edgewater were an institution, and as usual the place was packed—Kelly looked around and counted nine men she'd slept or fooled around with. It wasn't the number that bothered her but that, looking at them, she couldn't stop picturing them all naked, and it was not an arousing picture. She was walking around trying to serve drinks and hear people's orders over the music and all the while seeing naked men, pale-skinned, dark-skinned, pot-bellied, muscled or flabby, hairy-chested or bare, hairy-backed or not, leaning against doors, sitting back in chairs, everywhere their freckled, spotted, rough or smooth skin. There was just too much skin. She took a deep breath and thought, *No more.*

That was last July, and she hadn't been with a man since. The chastity thing drove Manny crazy and he was always trying to set her up with somebody, most recently with his cousin from Kitchener who was coming to town for a visit. Manny's interest in her was by turns paternal, platonic, and sleazy. He often encouraged her to go back to school, patting her on the shoulder and telling her she was too smart for this dump, too young, too something; he'd also, every once in a while, look down her shirt or squeeze her butt. When he brought up his cousin, she was wiping down the bar while he flipped through catalogs of restaurant equipment. Manny dreamed about making the Edgewater more upscale, a thought that was wishful in the extreme. He wanted to put in stainless-steel chairs and sell microbrews. He also wanted to institute a no-jeans dress code, an idea that, when he floated it by a couple of regular customers, made them snort Miller Genuine Draft out their noses.

"He's a very interesting person, Kel," Manny said. "You guys would have interesting conversations, I bet."

"Okay, so I'll talk to him when he comes in. But that's it, talking."

"Well, okay, but really talk to him. Get to know him."

"Manny."

"What?"

"You know I'm off men."

"Off men? What does that even mean?" He looked around as if he had an audience for this question, but it was Tuesday night at seven-thirty and the place was almost deserted. "It's not normal, a girl your age. Hey, do you like these stools?"

She looked at the catalog. The stools were four feet high and upholstered in a black-and-white cow print. "Looks comfy."

"You know what else?"

"What else, Manny?"

"My cousin? He's only got one leg."

"Poor guy," Kelly said. "How'd he lose it?"

Manny looked at her over the catalog. "Motorcycle accident."

"Oh."

"It's not the whole leg that's gone, it's actually cut off at the knee. The left one."

"Poor guy."

"Well, it's not the whole leg."

When she came back from taking the order of the only occupied table, Manny still hadn't gone back to the catalog.

"So, that doesn't interest you at all?"

"What doesn't?"

"The leg."

"What do you mean, interest me?"

Manny shrugged and studied a page of light fixtures, chrome and colored plastic descending from some invisible ceiling. "He says girls love the leg, that's all."

"Great," said Kelly. "Then he doesn't need me to talk to, does he?"

Manny's cousin's name was Lone. At first she thought she'd misheard, and that his name was Lorne, like Lorne Green, but no, it was Lone. A nickname, Manny explained, that referred to his one intact leg. He came into the bar around nine-thirty, while Manny was in the back. By now there were a few more customers, including a guy who'd never been in before and who therefore thought the name Edgewater Bar & Grill implied that food was being served. Which it kind of did. But Manny had just added the "& Grill" to the sign a couple of years ago because he thought it sounded better.

"You can't even make me a sandwich?" the guy said. "Some fries?"

"I think we have some chips by the register," Kelly told him. "Do you want regular or barbecue?"

"If I wanted some goddamn chips I'd go to a goddamn store."

"Feel free," Kelly said.

"Hey, why don't you just leave her alone," said a voice behind her.

Turning around she saw a man walk up close, very close, to the guy's table and jab a finger at his face. He was thick-armed and barrel-chested, definitely a weight lifter, wearing a black Metallica T-shirt. Below, his body turned slim at the hips, and then there were his legs. He was wearing jeans, and the leg that wasn't whole was wearing jeans too, with only a hollowness below the knee, an airy, smooth sort of quality in the fabric, to signal what was missing.

"You must be Lone."

"And you must be Manny," he said, and smiled. "Just kidding."

"What's this, a reunion?" said the guy who wanted food.

"Shut up," Lone said.

"I'm handling this," Kelly told him.

"Not very well," the other guy said.

"That's enough," Lone said, turning to hit him, hard, in the face.

The guy howled, clutched his cheekbone, swore, promised to call the police, swore again, and left. Conversation at the other tables resumed.

"That really wasn't necessary," Kelly said, wiping down the table.

"He was a jerk."

"A jerk who hadn't paid yet."

"Lone, my man!" Manny shouted, coming out from the back, and they exchanged an elaborate handclasp. Kelly could see a family resemblance: both were stout and thick-chested, although Lone's chest had a lot more definition than Manny's, and both had bushy dark eyebrows and stubble-shadowed chins.

"Lone, Kelly, Kelly, Lone."

"We just met," Kelly said.

"Great," Manny said, clasping his hands together as if he couldn't stand that the handshaking was now over. "Let's sit down. Kelly, could you get Lone a beer?"

"Sure."

When she came back, they were sitting at her old table by the window, looking at the lights of the neighborhood reflected over the water, red from a traffic light punctuating the paler yellows.

"So, how's Aunt Linda?" said Manny. "Thanks, Kel. Come, sit down and join us."

"I don't know. She's okay, I guess."

"Yeah? How's Mark?"

"He's on drugs."

"Oh."

"Yeah, it's too bad," said Lone, scratching his neck and looking around the bar. "So, Kelly, tell me about yourself."

"Not much to tell, I don't think."

"Manny tells me you're, what, studying commerce?"

"I was. I'm not in school right now, though."

Lone shook his head and looked concerned. "Shouldn't quit school, Kelly. You miss a lot of opportunities. For example. I'm looking, maybe, for like a business partner? I'm thinking of opening a bar just like this one right here."

"Really," Kelly said.

"Yes, really," he said with exaggerated seriousness. His eyes were dark and small and bright. "I really am. And I'm going to need someone to, you know, keep my books."

"I bet you'd like her to keep your books," said Manny. "Since when are you opening up a bar?"

"It's an idea I have."

"I can't believe it. You never mentioned that till just now."

"I appreciate the suggestion," Kelly said, "but I don't think I want to move to Kitchener."

"Smart girl. See, Lone, I told you she had a good head on her shoulders."

"Is that what you told him?" Kelly said.

Marie-Claire said, "Cool."

She turned it over in her hands, the foot in one hand, the open, fluted top of the leg in the other. She'd come over as soon as she saw Luz sticking her own foot into the plastic leg, as if it were a boot. Luz had discovered it wasn't hollow all the way down when she looked up and saw Marie-Claire towering over her. That was the thing about Marie-Claire. She might be a stoner but she wasn't out of it. She grabbed the leg right away.

Luz put her shoe back on. "Is it from a store?"

"A store?"

"Like the models that wear the clothes in the windows."

"What? Oh, a mannequin? No way, Luz, this is, like, a pros-thetic." She ran her fingers down the leg's shin, gently, as if it were a real leg and might be tender. She touched the foot, which had no individual toes or anything, just one big curve, more shoe than foot. There was a strap at the top of the leg, with a little buckle.

"What's that?"

"It's for people that are missing a leg. They can strap this one on."

"And walk on it?"

"I guess so," Marie-Claire said. "Maybe." She stood up and rested one knee on top of the plastic leg, then tied the strap around the back of her knee and stretched her arms out, balancing. Her hands flashed in the sun. Marie-Claire wore a lot of rings.

"How do I look?" she said. Her hair was dyed black and stuck up above her head, and she was wearing three or four necklaces. She looked exotic and strange, like someone whose costume had tribal meanings, a picture on the front of *National Geographic.*

"It's backwards," Luz said. The foot on the plastic leg was sticking out behind Marie-Claire, in a ballerina's pose.

"Shit." She undid the leg and bent down to rearrange the strap, her face close to Luz's. She smelled like pot and sunblock. Marie-Claire was beautiful, a fact that seemed to horrify her, and she did everything she could to camouflage the situation. The rings around her eyes were thick and black, as if drawn with a Magic Marker, and her ears were pierced with safety pins. Her clothes were ragged and baggy and everything that wasn't black was olive green. She was regimented, like her own personal army. But whenever she got close Luz could see her smooth, light skin, the freckles on her small, upturned nose, the rosiness on her cheeks, her green eyes and her long eyelashes. All that was there, no matter what Marie-Claire put on top of it.

Marie-Claire stood up again. The foot was straight now, poking out next to her black running shoe like a faceless animal. She took a step with it and lost her balance right away, hopping around and coming back to face Luz, laughing.

"I want to try it," Luz said.

"It's going to be way too big," Marie-Claire said, but she took it off and buckled the strap around Luz's knee. Because she was too short to stand up straight with the leg on, she stuck it out in front of her, at an angle, like a tent pole. When that didn't work she picked up the leg and moved it to the back and started hopping along, dragging the leg behind her as if it were broken. Marie-Claire burst out laughing.

Luz tilted her head, raised her shoulders, and did a monster voice. "I am your servant, master," she croaked, dragging a little circle around Marie-Claire. "I will follow your orders."

"Oh my God, that's so funny," said Marie-Claire. She was wheezing. Luz was laughing, too, and they both had tears in their eyes. The mom with the stroller was looking over in their direction.

"I am your monster," Luz said. "I will live in your basement."

Marie-Claire shrugged. "Too bad, I already live in the basement."

"How come?" Luz asked in her regular voice. "Do your parents make you live there because you smoke pot?"

"Um, kind of. How do you know about pot?"

"From school," said Luz, moving away from the water's edge. If she didn't keep hopping she'd lose her balance. "And from my dad. And from you."

"God, your dad is such the aging hippie," Marie-Claire muttered.

"No he's not, he's a teacher."

"Right," said Marie-Claire, motioning her back. "Come here, you better take that thing off. It's like time to go." She bent down and undid the buckle.

"I want to take it home," Luz said to the top of Marie-Claire's head.

"And do what?"

"Keep it. I found it, it's mine."

"Okay, whatever. We'll see what your dad says. Let's go. Here, take my hand for when we cross the street."

"I'm not a *baby,* Marie-Claire," said Luz. She grasped the foot and held the leg out. "You can hold my leg, though."

They crossed Lakeshore together, a leg's length between them.

At eleven-thirty, Manny gave Kelly the rest of the night off.

"Gee, thanks," she said.

"Just don't say I never did anything for you."

"You never did anything for me, Manny."

"Oh, ouch. Okay, get out of here."

She was turning the key in the ignition when Lone came out of the bar, walked over to the car—with a slight but definite limp— and knocked on her window. "Hi," he said.

"Hi."

"I didn't think you were leaving so soon," he said, leaning down, his hands on the car.

"Manny let me go home early."

"Oh. Time off for good behavior." He smiled, then shyly looked down at his legs.

Kelly looked there, too. "Something like that," she said.

"I was wondering if you maybe wanted to go get a drink."

"Where? Here?"

"Oh, that's right. You do work at a bar." One hand came up and slapped Lone on the forehead, seemingly of its own volition. He shook his head, as if to clear it, and said, "Here. Someplace else. Whatever."

Kelly sighed and shifted the car into reverse. "You know, I'm really tired, but thanks anyway."

Lone put his hand on the side of the open window, inside the car, a gesture that aggravated her. If she backed away, at what point would he let go?

"Come on," he said.

"No."

"Why not?"

"Why should I? And why do you care? Because Manny told you about me?"

"If you mean he told me about your vow thing, well, yes," Lone said forthrightly. "I think it's interesting. I want to know why somebody would do something like that. Therefore I am interested in you. Therefore I am asking you to have a drink with me. Is that a good enough reason?"

"Maybe," she said.

He insisted on driving, so they left her car at the Edge. His van was outfitted with equipment that met his special needs. This was what he called it, special needs, in a tone that sounded partly confessional and partly bragging. When he started the van, Metallica flared briefly from the tapedeck, disappearing suddenly when he switched it off.

"Sorry about that," he said.

Kelly rolled down the window and felt the wind. She could smell the water, salty and close. It was nice, actually, not to be going home right away, to avoid the certainty of her apartment and her bed and a magazine to read until she fell asleep. If she missed anything about dating, she thought, it might be this: a moment of precarious silence in a stranger's car, nighttime air, hands in your lap, waiting for the night to settle into itself. This was the moment before things got defined, before you had to decide what would happen, who you'd be, what you'd do. She took a deep breath and watched the telephone poles flip by.

"This okay?" Lone said, pulling over.

They were out by the docks in Ste. Anne's, at a bar that was what Manny wanted the Edgewater to be. Upscale. Nicer decor, fancier people, waitresses in black skirts serving mixed drinks. A terrace was strung with colored lights, and voices rippled in waves of rhythm and laughter. Words stood out in small, quick bursts like names being called.

"Fine," she said.

As they approached the entrance, Lone jumped ahead of her, awkwardly, and opened the door.

"Thanks," she said.

He pulled out her chair for her, too. Once they'd settled their drinks, he said, "So why'd you quit school? You know that's no good."

"Did you finish school?"

"No," he said. "That's how I know."

"What do you do, anyway?"

He looked at her. His skin under the stubble was dotted with small craters. He was wearing an earring, she noticed, a thin, small gold band that looked like it was pinching the bottom of his ear.

"Not a lot," he said. "You didn't answer my question."

"I don't really know. I couldn't get into it, I guess."

"Uh-huh. Was it the same thing with men?"

"Not really."

"You don't talk much, do you?"

"I just met you," Kelly said.

"True enough," Lone said, then nodded and tipped his drink to his mouth. Ice rattled against his teeth. "That's a fact." He smiled and looked at her again, just at her face, and it made her blush.

She remembered this, now. The part of sex that wasn't about touching someone else but about *being touched,* feeling your own skin warm under a man's eyes and hands, alive to your own body, inside and out of it. She didn't know which was stranger, feeling somebody else's body for the first time or feeling how your own self could change.

"You look pretty," he said.

Kelly rolled her eyes a tiny bit.

Lone just smiled and shook his head. "Oh, you're a hard one," he said, and laughed as if this were a quality that he in particular was well positioned to appreciate. "You are."

When they got home, Marie-Claire let Luz watch cartoons with a book balanced on her lap so that when her father came home she could pretend to have been reading it. The TV room was dark and cool, and the bright sunlight that filtered occasionally through the curtains seemed incongruous and strange. Luz sat with her legs out in front of her on the couch: her own legs next to her new leg, all three of them pointing at the TV. During the commercial breaks she would look at the plastic one and sometimes put her hand on it, as if to keep it from walking off. Marie-Claire wandered around the house for a while—what was she doing, Luz wondered, was she going through the tin box?—and then came back downstairs and stood in the door of the TV room, pretending she was watching Luz, not the TV, but after a while they were just watching cartoons on the couch together. When Marie-Claire fell asleep, Luz got up on her knees and edged closer to look at her face. It was weird how you could see flecks of her makeup stuck to her skin. Mascara was glopped onto her eyelashes, and there were streaks underneath where it had rubbed off, little eyelash flutters that looked like the marks of a feather.

Marie-Claire opened her eyes. "What the fuck are you doing?" she said.

"Nothing," Luz said, and scooted back to her side of the couch.

When Luz's father came home from school he found them silent on the couch, Luz with Nancy Drew #114 and Marie-Claire with a copy of *Steal This Book* that she must've found upstairs. He put his backpack down in the hallway and came into the room. "Hello, young women," he said. "And how are we all today? Bright-eyed and bushy-tailed, I hope."

"Fine," said Marie-Claire. She put the book down on the coffee table. "The day was totally fine."

"Great, great," said Luz's father. "You taking care of my baby, Marie-Claire? Luz, is Marie-Claire taking good care of you?"

"Yeah," said Luz.

"Good," he said. Then his eyebrows came together sharply in the center of his forehead. "What is *that*?"

Luz cradled it protectively. "It's my leg," she said.

"Um. Marie-Claire?"

She shrugged. "We found it by the lake. Luz wanted to bring it home."

"It's filthy," Luz's father said.

"You liked it too," Luz pointed out to Marie-Claire.

"Yeah, I did like it," she admitted. "Actually, Mr. Howard, I'm thinking, you know, I might want to take it home with me."

"No!" said Luz.

Marie-Claire ignored her and turned to her father, sitting up straighter on the couch. She spoke fast and low, imitation enthusiasm bubbling out from under shyness. "I've been doing this sculpture? I'm trying to work on, like, people? This'll be perfect, because I'm very into humans, and, like, artificial parts, because it's like society, you know?" Her black-rimmed eyes opened wide, then aimed down at the ground before she looked back up at him through her long, mascara-thick eyelashes.

Luz thought, *please*. She knew this was all a lie. Marie-Claire didn't have any sculptures.

"I know exactly what you mean," Luz's father said. "Why don't you take it home."

"How come she gets to have it and not me?"

"Luz," her father and Marie-Claire said at the same time.

"Dad," Luz said, "it's my leg."

"Another way of looking at this, Luz, is that I really don't want you to have that thing in the house anyway. It's too, I don't know, it's not a toy. It's not meant to be played with."

"It's not fair," Luz said. Her shoulders shook and she started to cry.

"I know," Marie-Claire said, putting a hand on her shoulder while her father watched. "I know it's not."

Lone told her about the accident. He was twenty-one, at the height of his Evel Knievel years, and was coming down a hill in the Laurentians high on cocaine, shrieking his head off out of pure joy, when he took a curve too fast and smashed sideways into a truck coming in the opposite direction. He woke up in the hospital, and the doctors told him there hadn't been anything below the knee for them to try to save.

"What happened to the guy driving the truck?"

"Goddamn it," Lone said. "People always ask me that." He slammed his beer down on the table.

They were in his motel room, a Days Inn off the Trans-Canada. He wasn't staying with Manny because his apartment was a third-floor walkup.

"And I say hey, you know, I've been stuck with this prosthetic fucking leg ever since, what about that?" He grabbed his leg with both hands just where, it looked like, the real part ended, and shook it a little bit, for emphasis.

"So what happened to him?"

"He was fine," Lone said. "He walked away. Unlike some people I might mention."

"Oh, you mean you."

"Yes, I mean me. Very funny."

"Ha ha," Kelly said solemnly. She took a swig of her beer, swallowed and sighed. "Anyway."

"Anyway," said Lone. "So, do you want to see it?"

"Do I want to what?"

"Do you want to see my leg?"

Kelly shrugged. The truth was that she did want to see it, badly. "If you want to show me."

"Well, I only want to show you if you want to see it," he countered.

"Then show me."

Lone reached down, undid his left shoe and pulled it off, then his white athletic sock. Underneath was the pink plastic foot, toe-less, curved, as delicate as a woman's shoe. He started to roll up his jeans, then stopped. "You know what? This would be easier if . . ." he said.

"That's fine."

"Okay." He took off his other shoe and sock, then stood up and undid the buttons at his fly and balanced himself with one hand while he pulled his jeans down with the other. When he sat down again he pulled them off completely and sat there in his boxer shorts.

She found herself looking back and forth between his face and his legs, as if this were somehow the most polite approach to the situation. He leaned back and rested his arms on the sides of his chair. "That's the prosthesis," he said.

She nodded, and leaned closer. It was attached to the end of his leg with a brown strap. "Can I touch it?"

"Sure," he said.

She started at the ankle, which wasn't really an ankle at all, no bone, little contour, just a thinness above the foot. The plastic was scratched and peeling in places, having been through God knows what trouble. Her fingers went from the ridge of the plastic onto Lone's real skin, which felt weirdly, almost wrongly soft. She rubbed her fingers up and down the hair on the side of his leg, and Lone exhaled a little laugh. She lifted his leg a bit with her left hand and slid her right hand underneath. They were sitting close together now.

"That tickles," Lone said.

She unbuckled the strap that held the prosthesis to his leg and set it gently on the table next to the beer bottles. On the stub of his leg the skin was rippled and folded, as if the doctor had wrapped it like a present, and she slid her fingertips over the bumps. Some of the ridges were red, like welts. "Does it hurt?" she said.

"No." Lone put his hand on her shoulder.

While they kissed, she kept her hand on his leg.

Up in her room, Luz watched Marie-Claire walk away. She couldn't breathe without crying. Marie-Claire swung the leg back and forth as she walked, like a baseball player warming up with a bat. After she turned the corner, Luz climbed under her desk and pulled the chair in as close as she could and sat with her knees up to her chin. One of her knees had a scab from when she fell at the park a week ago. She scratched it off and watched blood well up through the skin. Hearing her father moving around downstairs, getting a drink out of the fridge, she knew he was going to sit down at the kitchen table and open the mail. Then he'd read the newspaper because he never had time in the morning. Then he'd call her downstairs and have her sit in the kitchen while he made dinner, asking her questions about what the day was like, and then she could watch TV for an hour before she had to go to bed.

She pushed the chair away, softly, and crept out from under

the desk. She could feel dry tears crinkling her cheek. She went into her father's bedroom and smelled the soapy smell that was always in there. When the floor creaked she stood still, but he didn't call upstairs or anything. Very slowly and quietly, she opened the bottom drawer of the nightstand, lifted the stack of *Macleans,* and pulled out the tin box. She put the joint in her pocket, closed the box and the drawer, then went into the bathroom and shut the door and looked at herself in the mirror. First she wanted to practice, to make sure it looked right when she said, *Marie Claire showed me how.*

Afterwards, they were lying in bed, drowsing in and out of talk and sleep, when Lone murmured softly, "God, you know it's so true." He shook his head.

"What's true?" said Kelly, looking at him. His eyes were closed.

He put his arm around her and stroked her hair. His skin was hot and sticky against hers. "Girls love the leg," he said.

She slept for an hour or two. When she woke up, Lone was breathing steady and slow, his hand on his chest. She got out of bed and dressed. Starting for the door, she stopped at the table and picked up the leg. She was afraid someone might ask her about it, but there was no one around. At the parking-lot pay phone she called a cab to take her back to her car at the Edgewater. There was a suggestion of light in the sky, nighttime opening up and letting go. She guessed it was around four.

Back in her car, she put the leg on the dashboard. Then she put it on the seat beside her, the foot dipping down over the side of the upholstery, but no matter how she placed it, the leg looked splayed out, violent, accidental. There was no point, she decided, in keeping it.

She got out of the car and walked behind the bar to the water, where waves splashed and foamed, swirling detritus around the rocks, and heaved the leg into the lake as hard as she could. It bobbed a few times before floating beyond her sight. This action felt deeply satisfying, as if it were a part of her own self she wanted to leave behind. Driving home on the highway she saw dawn lifting into the horizon, though it was still far off and had a long way to go.

Wonders Never Cease

The house was isolated and charming, and though they'd looked at other rentals, the first sight of this one was all it took. It was a red farmhouse at the very end of a country road, ten minutes from the small, picturesque college town, and behind it spread a hill covered, at the time they moved in, with lazy, late-summer wildflowers. The first floor had a fireplace, green wallpaper with a pattern of vines, and old-fashioned wall sconces with electric bulbs; the second floor was a warren of small bedrooms. Penny moved through the place gingerly, touching her fingertips to the wallpaper and wooden door frames, planning where things would go. Everything, for now, was still in boxes.

When Tom went off to school every day, she unpacked, starting with the kitchen. Then, upstairs, she made herself an office, for the freelance graphic design she'd arranged with her former employer, but had a difficult time focusing on it. In the back of her mind—or, more properly, in the back of her body, a warm liquid sensation, almost like sickness, a fever that threatened but never did descend—lurked other ambitions, shadowy yet insistent plans. This was the year they would start having children.

Sitting on an unpacked cardboard box, drinking a cup of coffee gone cold, she heard a car in the driveway. She was still used to city living, and it took her a second to realize that any vehicle this far down the road had to be coming to their house. Through the window she could see Irene, the landlady, getting out of her station wagon, holding something wrapped in foil. They were the first people she had shown the house to—it belonged to her daughter, who lived in Boston—and she'd taken an immediate shine to them. *Shine* was her word—"You're going to take a shine to this area," she'd said—and she was shiny, too, her small, plump face glossy with August sweat and dappled with marks left by the sun over the course of her seventy years. She came, she said, from farming people.

"I don't need to show it to anyone else," she told them that first day. "I know you're the right people for this place."

"We're definitely the right people," Tom said with his usual confidence, and Irene bestowed on him a beatific smile that revealed small, brown teeth.

Today was warm, and Irene was huffing visibly as she came up the driveway. She was a short woman, at most five feet, and the way she beamed up at the world made her look like a character in a kids' book, some smiling, helpful gnome. Penny opened the door before she could knock.

"I came to see how you're settling in," Irene said, once she'd caught her breath. In the morning sunlight, the spots and wrinkles on her face stood out in bright relief. "And to bring you a housewarming present. It's my special zucchini bread."

Penny offered her tea, which was accepted, then sliced the bread and laid it out on a plate. When she and Tom answered the ad in the paper, they'd received a tour from Irene and her husband, Henry, an equally shiny and tiny farmer wearing overalls and a panama hat.

"My husband's deaf!" was the first thing Irene said when Penny and Tom got out of her car. Beside her, sweat pouring down from beneath his hat, Henry nodded, as if he agreed completely.

"He can't hear a thing!" Irene went on, yelling in their direction with an enthusiasm that seemed entirely misplaced. Henry smiled. Through the rest of the tour he walked behind Irene as she showed them what she called the grounds: the house itself, the hillside next to it, and the shed at the bottom, which she said, with a rueful shake of her head, was full of her daughter's old things.

"How's Henry?" Penny said to her now.

"Deaf as a post," Irene said, and grinned. Penny felt obliged to offer, in return, a conspiratorial giggle, as if she, too, had a deaf husband somewhere around the house and fully understood just how vexing it could be.

"It makes some things hard," Irene said. "But it certainly makes some things a lot easier!"

Penny laughed again, out of obligation. The late-morning light was gathering force, turning toward noon, and she was conscious of time passing, of all the unpacked boxes. But Irene was settling in, rubbing against the straight-backed chair, as if that might make it more comfortable, stroking the arms with her spotted hands.

"It happened two years ago," she said.

From the fairy-tale rhythm of this sentence it was clear that her story would last a long time, and it did. But its gist was simple: Henry's hearing disappeared slowly, over a year, each day turning fainter and blurrier, like a repeated photocopy. She woke up in the middle of the night and found him sitting outside in the cold, looking at nothing, and when she spoke his name, he wouldn't answer. She thought he was distant, that maybe he didn't love her anymore.

"I considered therapy," she said. Penny imagined these two

sweaty, gnomish farmers sitting together on a therapist's couch, working through their issues. "I kept saying, 'Henry, it's like you can't even hear what I'm saying.' And it turned out to be true. Absolutely, literally, true."

"I'm glad you got that sorted out," Penny said.

For a moment, Irene just stared at her, as if she could tell Penny was trying not to laugh out loud, then she beamed again. "I am too, dear," she said.

She stayed at the table for two hours and half a loaf of zucchini bread, telling anecdotes about the early years of her marriage, explaining how to scrub the delicate porcelain of the upstairs bathtub, urging Penny to call as early as possible to order heating oil for the winter. She was offering, in her shiny, organized way, a complete manual for life.

That night, when Tom came home, Penny told him about Irene: the tea, the countless slices of bread, the endless advice. "Two hours disappeared," she said, "just like that."

"Don't worry about it," he said, leaning back in the same chair Irene had taken earlier in the day. Unlike Irene, he was gaunt and angular and very tall, and he could have reached across the table, without any strain at all, and touched her face with his long fingers, or her hair or her shoulder. "She's just making sure we're still the right people."

Feeling guilty for complaining about this harmless, doughy woman, she asked Tom about the students. This was his first real teaching job—if he did well, he hoped the appointment would be extended beyond a year—and he was beside himself with the satisfaction of being a real professor, finally, his own office in the history department building. Yesterday he'd taken out his wallet and shown her, with real pride, his faculty ID card.

The moment Tom paused, she stood up and reached for his

hand and led him upstairs to bed. She'd been doing this more and more lately, and was surprised by her own agenda. Things she'd never known she needed had recently crept up and shocked her with their force. She felt a sharp hunger for a certain kind of future. That is, she wanted Tom—as she always had—but she also wanted to own a home like this, with him, and for their kids to grow up in it, too. This need was mysterious and pure, like instinct or sex. It was as if someone had flicked on a light switch and suddenly she saw what was in the room with her, the room of her life, her heart.

In the morning she found herself alone again, unpacking, working through the many boxes of books upstairs, and it took her a bit longer to hear the car in the driveway. For someone living in the country, she was getting a lot of visitors. She came downstairs, expecting to see Irene again, but someone else stood at the door. He was around her age, thirty, and about her height, wearing a green T-shirt, jeans, and work boots. His short, curly hair was receding at the temples. She lingered behind the screen door.

"I'm the yard man," he said.

Beyond him, parked behind her car, was an old pickup, faded to the same color as his shirt. The morning was very clear, and in the distance she could hear the faint rush of the brook. His face was lined, and he had the smoky, too-sweet smell of someone who spends a lot of time in bars.

"I didn't know there was a yard man," she said.

"Well, there is." He gestured vaguely at the grass in back of him. He was wearing a bulky, too-big metal watch, and it slid up and down with the gesture. "The service comes with the house. Didn't Irene tell you? I just need to get the mower out of the shed and I'll take care of the place for you."

"Irene didn't tell me any of that."

"The mower," he said stubbornly, "is in the shed. Otherwise I'm going to have to break off each individual blade of grass by hand, and that's going to take a very long time."

As an argument, it was less than convincing. Penny stepped outside into the cool shade of the porch. She did in fact have the key to the shed, although Irene had made it clear she was not to use it. The shed was storage space, for the daughter in Boston. The man shifted his weight back and forth, from one boot to the other. He needed a shave. In their tour of the house Irene, with Henry silently sweating by her side, had gone over the minutiae of the rental contract, including the watering schedule of the plants, the idiosyncrasies of the washing machine, the tendency of the third stair to inflict slivers on unsuspecting feet. These codicils took hours. There was no way she would've neglected to mention a yard man.

"You're not the yard man," she said, and sat down on a plastic lawn chair on the porch.

The man shrugged, giving up without any struggle, and sat down on the other chair. He smiled resignedly. "You don't believe me," he said, as though it happened to him often.

They sat for a minute in almost companionable silence. He had thick, stubby hands he folded carefully in his lap. Penny should have been afraid—a quarter-mile at least to the nearest house, and his car parked behind hers—but she wasn't.

"What do you want?" she finally said.

"I used to do some work around the house," he said. "I'm guy."

She didn't understand. "Excuse me?"

"My name is Guy," he said, "although I'm also a guy. It's confusing, I know." He held out his hand to shake, which she did; the large watch slid down his arm, toward his elbow, like a bracelet on a woman. "My friends used to call me Some," he said. "As in, 'There goes some guy.' 'Who was there last night?' 'Some guy.' "

Penny laughed, politely. "That's funny."

"In a limited way," Guy said.

She still wasn't sure what he wanted. "So you worked for Irene's daughter? The one who's in Boston?"

Guy snorted, then looked down at his feet. "Christine's not in Boston," he said. "That old lady—Jesus. She's tough as nails, isn't she?"

"Where is she, then?" Penny said. "Christine."

"She passed on," Guy said, giving her a moment to register what this meant. "Car accident. A year ago now."

"I'm sorry," Penny said, conscious of the rote stupidity of the words.

Guy shrugged again, and stood up. The watch slid back down to his wrist. "You won't unlock the place," he said.

"No."

"All right, then," he said. "Thank you for your time." Once more he held out his hand.

She'd barely gotten back to the books when Irene came by again, this time bearing cranberry-walnut muffins and "a wedge," she said, "of fine local cheese." Penny sighed; the days were getting so crowded that she hardly had time to think. They sat in plastic chairs on the front porch, and the strips cut into the backs of Penny's thighs as Irene launched into an exhaustive anecdote about the amount of state taxes she and Henry had to pay that year. The story was complex, with figures and equations, and footnotes and appendices would not have been out of place.

"I see," Penny said, nodding. She was pinching the back of her knee, hard, trying to stay awake, but drifting back and forth between boredom and pain. She wished Tom were here; he was good at making excuses, polite yet direct, whereas Penny could go on nodding and smiling until she exploded into an obvious yawn. She wanted to ask Irene about her daughter, why she'd lied that Christine was in Boston, but couldn't see how to bring it up, especially given Irene's barrage of storytelling.

Two weeks passed. At intervals irregular enough that Penny could never plan to evade them, Irene continued to stop by, always bearing a gift: banana bread or blueberry muffins or a potted plant or brochures from the local chamber of commerce with pictures and maps of area attractions. Sometimes she brought Henry, at whom she would occasionally shout—"Henry thinks so, too, don't you, Henry?"—to include him in the conversation. He nodded and smiled and then fell asleep with a nonchalance Penny could only envy. Irene's sense of the boundaries between landlady and tenant was eccentric. She was always telling Penny what a joy it was to have her and Tom renting the house, making it impossible for Penny to ask her to leave. She was too sweet, too lonely, too short and smiling, too stubbornly pleasant. In the evenings, hearing herself complain to Tom, Penny felt like a small, bad person. Once she'd aired them, her complaints dissolved so entirely that she couldn't even understand why she'd even been annoyed, until the next time.

One hazy September day, Irene chatted through an entire afternoon. Penny had never met anyone whose conversation so clearly defined chatting. She tilted her gray head to one side, clucked her tongue, and chatted about how the doctor wanted to change Henry's blood pressure medication even though she couldn't see what the problem was with the current drugs. After she mused on this for a solid half hour she tilted her head to the other side and took up the subject of her own social security benefits—"It's all a mystery," she said, "to your average taxpayer like myself"—and various problems she'd encountered in her dealings with the government, the intransigence of bureaucrats, the crucial need for young people like Penny to begin planning immediately for the long-term future. There were always special circumstances, she said, that you hadn't planned for but happened anyway, whether you wanted them to or not, so it was important to be prepared.

Listening, Penny felt dread drizzling over her like rain. Was this what it meant to get old: your worldview blinkered, sexless, narrowed to administrative concerns? Taxes, medications, schedules and routines, a set of forms and formulae for the numbing worries that eased your transition to the final numbness of death? She thought about Tom, about the few gray hairs she'd noticed behind his ears, and she thought about the two of them in bed, her fingers moving through his hair in rhythm with their other movements. On the one hand was her vision of the two of them having children and growing old together; on the other hand, the idea that they might grow old like Irene and Henry made her want to scream. She found herself trapped between these competing feelings, each equally powerful and unexpected, with no sense of which one would win out in the end. It made her feel desperate and reckless. In her mind, overcome by the contest, she stood up and screamed the word "Motherfucker!" in Irene's face. She literally had to prevent herself physically—with more pinching—from screaming this in Irene's sweet, beaming, elderly face. Not because Irene was a motherfucker but because she so patently was not, because she was so permanently and rigorously removed from the world of motherfuckers. Penny trembled with the desire to do it. Then she really stood up.

"Thank you for the delicious bread, Irene," she said.

Irene—interrupted mid-tip: "You can use a vinegar solution for that"—rearranged her spotted face from shocked to compliant. "Of course, dear," she said. "Don't let me get in your way."

The books lined the upstairs shelves, and the wedding crystal glinted in the mahogany cabinet that was itself a wedding gift from Tom's aunt in California. She'd unpacked enough of the living room that she could take a break there and read a book without feeling distracted by the disarray. She was working on the bedrooms when she happened to glance outside and saw Guy standing in the yard, fiddling with his watch and checking the time as if he had somewhere more important to go. Which, it soon became clear, he didn't. He wasn't even tangentially involved in anything important. It was ten-thirty in the morning, and he was drunk, or had been drinking, anyway.

"There's some guy standing on my lawn," she said to him.

He smiled in broad appreciation of this remark. His face had been lightly touched by the sun. His T-shirt today was a sallow, mustardy yellow, and his gut made the fabric blouse above the hips. "I was going to break into the shed," he said, "but it's daytime."

"Why do you need to get in there so badly, anyway?"

"There are some items in there I need to collect," he said.

"I think maybe you should talk to Irene about that."

"That old bag?" He was weaving ever so slightly, like a tall building in a strong wind, and it fascinated her to hear him talk about Irene that way. "She hates me," he went on, "with a passion."

"Why?" she said, although it was not hard to imagine why someone like Irene would not be overly fond of someone like Guy. He was definitely a person who had at least a passing acquaintance with the world of motherfuckers. The treacly smell of hard liquor wafted from him like perfume.

"Christine," he said, "my love and life."

"You weren't the yard man for her, either, then."

"I don't know shit about yards."

Penny gestured to the plastic chairs on the front porch. "Would you like to sit down?" she said.

Guy and Christine first met in high school. She was sweet and shy, wholesome and blond. She wore glasses and wanted to be a veterinarian. Guy was a loser—a kid who hung around the parking lot and smoked a lot of cigarettes all day long. "She was a square peg, and I couldn't even find a peg." They both came home again after college. Christine didn't have the drive for veterinary school and settled for work as a kennel-tech instead. Guy got a job at a construction company and started saving money; he didn't know just what it was for, but liked the thought of it growing safely in his account. One winter afternoon, driving, he saw a tabby cat lying by the side of the road. Hit by a car, it was still alive, dragging itself, inch by painful inch, to the curb. He stopped the pickup and walked over. Its hind legs were red mush, but when he picked the cat up it clawed and bit him, then lay still. He put it in his lap and drove to the animal hospital, the cat's blood soaking his pants. Christine was on duty at the reception desk when he came in, and if the fluorescent hospital lights bleached her pale skin to white, then sight of the cat paled it even further.

She was almost intolerably shy—he remembered this from high school—as she took his name, mumbling, and led him into an examination room. He laid the cat down on the counter. It was panting shallowly in pain, blood oozing from its open mouth. Christine came back with a veterinarian, a bossy, red-haired woman who said the cat would have to be put down. She asked if it was his, he shook his head, and she told him to leave the room, then she and Christine together administered the shot that ended the cat's life.

He sat in the truck in the parking lot, waiting for her to get off work. When she saw him there, she turned around and went back inside. After a couple of minutes she came out again, her breath streaming in the cold, and got in on the passenger side. She had antibiotic lotion and bandages and cleaned his arm where he'd been scratched, and when she was done he drove her to the pub and they drank for an hour or so without hardly even speaking. Then he took her home.

After this evening he would stop several times a week to wait in the parking lot for her shift to end. They would go to the pub, or down to the river to watch the water, and in this quiet, unhurried way, over one long winter, they fell in love.

"Her hair," he said to Penny, "was so blond and straight it looked like thread against the pillow."

According to Guy, Irene never thought he was good enough for her daughter (Henry's opinions on the matter could not be discerned, as he was even then fading out of the hearing world). But Christine didn't care. She'd inherited the red farmhouse from her grandmother, and she asked him to move in with her. They planned a future: a garden in the back, a dog and cats, children to run through the house.

"This house," he said, looking at Penny. She nodded.

"Then, the accident. I was driving. I was *not* drunk—current appearances to the contrary. Irene blamed me. Maybe she was right to. I don't fucking know at this point, to be completely honest with you. All I know is that Christine got thrown from the car, and by the time I woke up she was gone."

Penny said nothing. There was nothing to say.

"While I was still in the hospital, Irene packed up the entire house. She moved my stuff into an apartment. Christine's things," he said, "she put in the shed." Exhausted by the effort of talking, he leaned back in the lawn chair, still looking at her. His eyes were bloodshot. In the distance, the shrill wheeze of a lawnmower cut the air.

Penny stood up. "Come on," she said. With the key to the shed in her pocket, she led him down the grassy slope to the door and unlocked it. Windowless, musty, and hot, the inside of the shed was as orderly as you would expect from someone like Irene. Cardboard boxes, all the same size, sat stacked evenly against the walls. A few pieces of furniture—a loveseat, a desk, a standing lamp—were shrouded in plastic, looking ghostly in the light. Guy moved around, touching each item with the tips of his stubby fingers. This close to him, the smell of alcohol was even stronger, and it was mixed with an acrid, unhealthy odor of sweat.

He pulled a Swiss Army knife out of his back pocket and began opening the boxes, setting each down on the floor before moving on, pulling some things out—a sweater, a doll, a book— and then racing on to the next, like a frenzied addict facing an unprecedented supply of his chosen drug. He heaved boxes aside and started in on new ones. At last he found one that attracted his full attention. First he pulled out a set of large books wrapped, like everything else, in plastic, then sat down in the midst of his mess and began turning the pages of one of them. It was a photo album. Penny came up behind him and looked over his shoulder, but for all he cared she may as well not have been there.

A blond girl graduating from high school in a light blue gown.

As he turned the pages she changed her hair and her glasses; had a vacation on a beach somewhere; went off to college and hugged a dog—her own or someone else's, Penny didn't know—and celebrated a birthday with three friends and a blazing cake.

Guy touched this last photo with his right hand. "Will wonders never cease," he said.

Penny wanted to ask what he meant. That a girl's mother would pack away her entire life and leave it to molder in a shed? That the girl looked the same as he remembered her, or completely different? That he still loved her, was that the wonder? She could not ask. There was a scuffling behind her, and she turned—expecting a mouse—and saw Irene in the doorway of the shed, sunlight flooding in around her, looking tiny and betrayed. As her gaze moved from Penny to Guy, it took on the unmistakable shimmer of hatred. It looked exactly as if she were thinking the word *motherfucker.* He glanced at her and turned back to the album without reaction. It was clear to Penny, as he touched the photograph, that his dishevelment, his smell of liquor and sweat, his too-big watch reminding him he had nowhere to go, all these things were the consequence of the girl's death and not, in any respect, the cause of it. And it was equally clear that Irene's primness, her financial and domestic concerns, even her shouting at her husband, were also consequences of this death, instruments she used to wall off the tragedy of her life— her loss, and her cruelty—and keep it hidden.

"Murderer," Irene said. "Murderer." She enunciated each syllable distinctly, evenly, and for the first time Penny saw her looking down instead of up.

"Guy," Penny said.

"She'll have to drag me out of here," he said matter-of-factly, "and I'd like to see her try."

———

After Irene turned on the heel of her orthopedic shoes and left, she disappeared from Penny's life for a long time, so completely as to seem almost imaginary. Penny sent the rent checks by mail and received no confirmation in return. She didn't see Guy, either. The shed was relocked, minus a few boxes, and she and Tom were busy. They were wrapped up in their life together, now finally and fully unpacked, and went to faculty dinners and took walks in the woods. On a quiet Wednesday morning Penny stood in the bathroom with the results of the pregnancy test in her hand, knowing that everything was about to change. When Tom came home that night she was sitting on the couch, where she'd sat, unmoving, for two hours.

He put his leather bag down immediately, sat down beside her, and took her hand. "What happened?" he said.

"It's now," she said. "We'll be parents now."

He leaned over and kissed her forehead solemnly, then leaned down and kissed her stomach, too. After that, his smile broke open and stayed for days, and it was the confident smile she'd counted on. At various times in the past she'd been annoyed by his self-assurance, his ability to picture himself a success. When he'd asked her to marry him, she'd seen in his eyes that he'd never doubted she would say yes. He'd also known that he could ask Penny to follow him to this town; that she would understand the importance of his job. She'd felt he could use a little more self-doubt, a little humility, but now she needed his strength. And he was as sure that they would succeed as parents as he was about everything else. In his certainty about the future she was able to locate a confidence of her own, and to forget the radically conflicting desires that had been tearing at her. All desire to scream the word "Motherfucker!" in somebody's face evaporated. She knew they would have the life she'd constructed in her mind, in this house or another one like it, a house with a family.

One day, returning to the farmhouse from a doctor's appointment with an ultrasound picture in her purse, she walked through the front door and felt two disparate emotions tumble strongly, suddenly, over her: happiness and guilt. The happiness was for her and Tom and the baby, the guilt was for Christine and Guy. She owned this life and they did not. She must be grateful, she knew, for the circumstances that had allowed her to imagine a future and watch it come true. Something had been given to her and Tom that had been taken from them, and there was no reason behind this gift. It was all mystery.

Leaves dropped from trees; cold winds blew. Dark came early, and she and Tom often fell asleep on the couch by the fireplace, his hand on her lap. Some days she was tired and sick, but more often, as time went on, they lay in bed in the morning and Tom would run his hands over her body, its new contours; at these times she felt a strong, greedy pleasure that obliterated all other thoughts from her mind.

But it was a small town. Once, on a freezing, hail-pelted January day, she ran into Guy. She was dropping off some dry cleaning, and the shop doubled as a laundromat. Guy was sitting on an orange vinyl chair, bent over a copy of *Ladies' Home Journal.* Above his head, laundry she assumed was his squirmed in a foamy circle. She laid her dry cleaning on the counter and watched him across the room; he didn't look up. At a certain point he put his finger on a page of the magazine—much as he'd touched the photos in the album that day—to examine a picture or help himself read, she wasn't sure which. His pickup truck was parked outside. For a moment she could picture him and Christine exactly: driving around town in that faded green truck, stopping for a drink at the pub, maybe heading down to the river to hang out and watch the river and kiss, pretending they were still teenagers. His hands on her neck, her shoulders, her waist; his lips on hers; her glasses fogging, her fine hair tangling as they moved.

Penny left before he knew she was there.

A few months afterwards she saw Irene, too, at the grocery store. Their carts almost collided in the cereal aisle. It was early spring but still cold, and Irene was wearing a long padded jacket and white boots; her eyes widened as she took in the sight of Penny's pregnant belly, bulging through her unbuttoned coat. When Penny said her name, the landlady looked up at her.

"When are you due, dear?" she said.

"At the end of May."

"Are you getting lots of rest? Rest is important, you know."

"I'm doing fine," Penny said. She put a hand on her stomach, a gesture that had grown quickly habitual with her, a means of instant comfort. Watching tension twist the muscles of Irene's face, she knew what must be going through her mind: all the advice, the recommendations and recipes, suggested names, tips on feeding and baby furniture, the knowledge of years. The older woman's face was almost pulsing with the longing to share it. Penny steeled herself to receive the onslaught, balancing her weight on both feet, knowing she might be standing there in the aisle for a while. But Irene just stood there, smiling thinly, fixed to the linoleum.

"How's Henry?" Penny finally asked.

"He's been fitted for a new aid," Irene said. "But he won't hardly wear it. He says he's gotten used to the silence. He says he likes the peace and quiet. Well, good luck, dear." And with a pivot of her grocery cart she turned around and walked away. Penny was left looking after her, then gazing up at the rows of cereals and granola bars. She'd forgotten what she came into this section to buy.

After this encounter, Irene did not call or visit. She must have thought about it, though. In fact she must've thought about it a great deal. Because in June, after the baby was born, she could not stay away. Penny was sitting by the window, enjoying the first warm breeze of summer while she nursed the baby, when a car pulled up in the driveway. She heard a door slam shut, and saw Irene coming up the driveway, carrying one of her baked goods, the sun reflecting brilliantly off the silver foil. Her shiny face was set in determination as she came to confront the unceasing wonders, the mysteries of sex and circumstance, that had brought her to the house again.

I Love to Dance at Weddings

Leda calls on a Saturday afternoon to announce she's getting married the following Thursday night. "Can you come?" she asks, her voice as innocent as milk.

Cordless in hand, Nathalie moves over to the garage, where Nick is thrashing away at a rocking chair with a piece of sandpaper. He refuses to use the electric sander because he says he can't really *feel* the wood. He's turning into the Michelangelo of home improvement. When he sees her come in, he raises his eyebrows and puts up his palm in the standard I'm-not-here gesture he uses whenever his mother's on the phone.

"We wouldn't miss it," Nathalie says.

"We are very, very pleased," Leda says, making this "we" sound royal. Nick, whacking at the chair, keeps almost missing the arm of it, threatening to take off a layer of his own skin instead. "Martin will be thrilled."

"How is Martin?"

"A prouder bridegroom you never saw," Leda says.

Nathalie smiles at this; she likes Martin. He's a retired medical instrument salesman who wears threadbare cardigans and tells old-fashioned, sexist jokes. The last one she heard involved three women together in a jail cell—a Navajo, an Arapaho and a "regular ho, from Dallas." It's the "from Dallas" that makes her like him. Martin will be Leda's fourth husband, and coincidentally he was also her second. They were married on a whim, by a captain on a cruise ship, and divorced six months later after an argument at a party.

"Can we, you know, do anything?" Nathalie says.

"You're a dear," Leda says, "but I'll go over this with my darling son. Could you put him on?" Nathalie holds the phone out to Nick, who shakes his head. They pantomine this back and forth—her holding, him shaking—until she hears Leda sigh pointedly on the other end. Then she drops the phone into Nick's dust-covered lap and goes back into the house.

Leda was married to Nick's father for twenty-seven years. Since he died, she's taken up marrying the way some women take up art classes or volunteer work. First it was Martin, then it was her ob-gyn—Rupert Thorne, whom everybody called by both names, including Leda, even after they were married—and now it's Martin again. For each of the weddings so far, Leda has gone whole hog, without regard for the fact that she is neither a first-time nor a youthful bride. (On the cruise ship she managed to rustle up a long white dress and a headdress made of orchids, which they apparently sold in the onboard boutique to people given to just such marital whims, and she'd browbeaten the ship's yoga instructor into serving as the maid of honor.) Each time, she says that when she was younger she didn't appreciate her wedding, and she might as well enjoy it now. This drives Nick insane. He says she's gone off the edge. Nathalie wonders, never out loud, if Nick's the best judge of the edge's location. He lost his consulting job a year ago and hasn't been able to find new work; for the past few months, instead of looking, he has been gutting their entire house and its contents. He's into stripping things down: walls, chairs, floors. He wants everything to be authentic and unadorned. Their house, he says, has a skeletal identity that has been wrongfully and deliberately obscured over the years of its inhabitation. At Home Depot, the clerks call him by name.

When he comes out of the garage his face is dark with annoyance. He sits down on the couch in their living room, which was once wallpapered and carpeted and now is fully exposed, down to a brick wall on one side and the bare pine boards beneath their feet. At least the upholstery's still on the furniture, though Nathalie doesn't count on it sticking around for long. She wouldn't be surprised to come home and find it all reduced to wire and string.

"You won't believe what she wants," he says. "A full-on church wedding, just like the last two. I don't even know where she found a place this fast."

"It's the off-season, I guess," Nathalie says.

"And you know what else? She wants me to *give her away.* I said, 'Mom, I think you're old enough by now to give yourself away.'"

"What did she say?"

"She said, 'I know, Nicholas' "—here he shifts into a disturbingly accurate falsetto imitation of Leda's sweetest tone of voice—" 'but it would mean a lot to me.' "

"So you're going to do it."

"Of course I am," he says. "She'd kill me if I didn't."

The next few days are an avalanche of last-minute activity, Leda calling Nathalie every twenty minutes at work, Nick calling every ten to complain about Leda. He and his mother bicker constantly, being so much alike, each of them obsessed with detail, having infinite attention spans for logistics. Whenever Leda comes over, Nick parades her through the house, talking about joists and finishes, and his mother not only nods but asks questions that make it clear she's *processing* the information. This is when Nathalie retreats to the kitchen—as yet untouched, thank God—and listens to Martin tell jokes about ho's.

When Nick and Nathalie got married, he and Leda took charge of everything: the flower arrangements, the invitations, the seating arrangements, the music. At first none of this bothered Nathalie; work was hectic, she wasn't a party organizer by nature, and she was relieved to have met a man so unconcerned with gender stereotypes that he could throw himself into wedding planning with abandon. The one thing she cared about was her dress, and she and her mother found the one whose simple straight lines and elegant drape suited her perfectly. She thought walking into the church in it—into the ceremony her husband had lovingly designed for her, for them—would feel like crossing a threshold into their life together, a border crossing to a new world. Instead, as she walked down the aisle, she felt separate and alone: the only self-contained element of the entire event.

Leda will have no such problems. She's arranging all the details and drawing everybody else in with her. She summons Nathalie on her lunch hour to help her choose a dress from the off-the-rack options at a store called Better Bridal Bargains. She sweeps out of the fitting room, all sixty years of her, in organza concoctions with full skirts, in beaded bodices and empire waistlines. She looks like a princess who's fallen victim to an evil aging spell.

"Honestly, I've always wanted to be married in a tiara," she says. "Haven't you?"

"I guess," Nathalie says, stealing a look at her watch. She has to be back at the office by one.

"You probably haven't," Leda says pityingly. "You're so practical, so lawyerly. I was almost expecting you to walk down the aisle in a navy blue power suit."

That is what Nathalie is wearing right now. She doesn't use clothes to draw attention to herself. Her outfit, like a doctor's coat or a mortician's black, enables a client to look past her, the individual woman, to the expertise she represents. Leda has never worked, having married Nick's father when she was still in college, so it would be unreasonable to expect her to understand. Nathalie looks Leda up and down. The bodice of the current dress is tight, clenching her torso into several horizontal rolls of fat.

"I'd have to vote against this one," she says. "It's not the most flattering."

"But it's the most *romantic*," Leda says. "It's like Martin's proposal. He said we should just do it, life is too short, we shouldn't wait. 'Let's get married this week,' he said, and you know what I said, dear?"

Nathalie waits.

"I said 'Martin Horst, when you're right, you're right.' This dress is like a fairy tale. I'm going to take it." She spreads the skirt out on either side, folds of fabric frothing like egg whites in her arms, and grins at herself in the mirror. Her short white hair matches the gown. She looks like she feels adored.

At home that night, Nathalie finds her husband sanding the chair again. It's a rocking chair that belonged to her grandparents, and over many years it has been painted successive layers of white, red, and green—most of which have been removed and now lie scattered in particles around the garage floor. It's less like he's sanding the chair than pulverizing it. In fact it looks noticeably smaller, the runners spindly and weak. She worries that by the time he gets through with it, there won't be any chair left.

"Hey, look," he says. "I'm finally down to the real color." He points to a spot, a nondescript light brown, on the arm.

"Okay," Nathalie says. She used to be more enthusiastic about these things before the house smelled permanently of paint stripper. "Have you taken care of the flowers?"

"Done."

"Called everybody on the list?"

"Done."

"Ordered the catering?"

"Done."

"Figured out what you're going to do for Martin's bachelor party?"

This makes him look up from the light brown spot. "You're joking, right?"

"Leda was hinting that he'd enjoy having one. She said maybe you and Michael Thomas could take him out."

Nick lowers his eyes to the light brown spot, squints at it, then bangs his head against it several times in succession. Michael Thomas is Rupert Thorne's son. He still insists on referring to himself as Leda's stepson, even though she divorced his father two years ago. (Rupert Thorne was having an affair with another patient, and apparently was always having affairs with patients.) A thin, jittery, forty-year computer programmer, Michael Thomas lives alone in an enormous house he bought early on in the tech boom. He adores Leda and took her side, one hundred percent, when his father told him about the divorce. Leda generously continues to invite him to family functions, which he always attends bearing tasteful but extravagant gifts: fine wines, tropical flower arrangements, fruit baskets. Like most very enthusiastic people, he seems a little unbalanced.

Without answering her question, Nick goes back to sanding. He's been doing this more and more the past few months: checking out of conversations and turning instead to the project at hand. What's disturbing to Nathalie is that she doesn't even necessarily mind. After all, she already knows where the conversation would go. In the first months after the layoff she kept trying to get Nick to talk, kept trying to boost his spirits, kept trying everything she could think of.

All it accomplished was to make him mad; he said he felt like a child, like her own project to fix. It reinforced his sense that she had her life together and he didn't. "The best thing you can do," he said, "is to leave me alone."

Nathalie is good at leaving things alone; she doesn't like to intervene. Her work involves labor disputes, and in conference rooms she often faces clients staring at her beseechingly, begging to be told what to do next with disgruntled former employees or tough-negotiating union representatives. She always lays out options and consequences rather than recommending any one course of action. She explains their liability, the strong and weak points of the case, and that is as far as she will go. The lighter the touch, she believes, the better. But at home these days she thinks maybe she isn't just leaving things alone; maybe she's on the way to leaving.

Martin and Leda are as giddy as kids. They show up at the rehearsal dinner, at Nathalie and Nick's house, holding hands and blushing. They keep turning around and smooching and pinching each other's sagging cheeks. There is a lot of eye-rolling going on in Nick's corner of the room. Michael Thomas, who arrived staggering beneath a present the size of an oven, keeps crossing and uncrossing his arms and saying loudly, "Aw." He says it every time they kiss, which means at least five times so far.

"She and my dad were never like this," he says to Nathalie in the kitchen. "He was a cold bastard with her like he was with everybody else. Once he got them into bed it was all over. Conquest was the name of his game. Frankly, I never understood what she saw in him."

Nathalie nods. After that divorce she and Nick had Leda over for dinner, and she got tipsy and confided that she'd married Rupert Thorne "for the sex."

Nick said, "I'd really rather not know this about you, Mom."

Leda shrugged, her cheeks a flourish of color. "It's not enough to base a relationship on," she said, "not one that will last forever."

"Thanks for the tip," Nick told her.

Now he's in a corner with Martin and Leda, listening to them talk. All week long he worked on wedding arrangements during the day and on his various projects in the garage at night. He looks exhausted, dark shadows beneath his dark eyes. Leda, on the other hand, looks radiant, wearing a pink suit with a corsage—what Nathalie thinks of as a mother-of-the-bride outfit—and a flower in her hair. She's staring at Martin with a wide-eyed, loving stare. Martin's elaborating a joke that involves an Englishman, a Frenchman, and a Belgian; Nathalie misses the setup, but the punch line is the single word *potatoes*.

Leda's laugh rises and flits across the room, a string of notes like pearls.

At dinner Martin rises and makes a toast. He is sixty-six; his ex-wife has moved to Florida, and his children live in Europe. His suit bags and pouches, and it looks like he's carrying rocks in his pockets. His eyes are watery; his nose hairs need clipping.

He raises a glass in Leda's direction. "To my darling bride," he says, "I let you go once before, and I will never be so foolish again."

Leda blows him a kiss.

Michael Thomas says, "Aw."

After dinner, while Nathalie and Leda clean up, Nick and Michael Thomas take the groom out for his bachelor party. Since Martin likes to go to bed early, this is at seven-thirty. Nathalie drives Leda home, and when she gets back, at nine, the light in the garage is on. Nick is standing over the chair, looking down to where it rests on its side at a weird angle. His eyes are bloodshot and he smells like booze.

"How was it?"

He grimaces. "Michael Thomas bought Martin a lap dance."

Nathalie pictures a nineteen-year-old stripper hovering over Martin's hairy nose, shaking her pasties in his face. She laughs. "Did he enjoy it?"

"He did until he tried to get up and give her some money, and he pinched his sciatic nerve or something and we had to take him home."

"Is he okay?"

"He says he will be. Let's go in, okay?"

Nick never wants to come in from the garage. His tools and handiwork are in here, all his gear and paraphernalia. She looks down at the chair and realizes it's not really lying at a weird angle. What it really is is broken. He has sanded it so hard that he snapped part of it off. He sees her see this and says, "I can fix it. You'll never even know."

"It's my grandparents' chair, Nick."

"It'll be even better once I fix it. It was structurally weak."

She sighs, heavily and on purpose. The garage is a blur of dark shadows, of Nick's head, of wood pieces scattered like detritus on the ground. "I don't know why you had to start messing with it," she says.

"This is what it's supposed to look like. Once I fix it, you'll see how much better it is."

"If you say so," she says. In the flick of his head she sees how annoyed he is that she won't get mad at him, won't lose her temper and yell. But what would be the point, anyway? She turns on her heel and goes to bed.

The wedding day is cool and blustery. It's November and all the leaves are golden and half gone from the trees. The small church smells overwhelmingly of potpourri, which Nathalie realizes comes from air freshener, the same spray Leda uses at home. Nick's aunts and uncles and cousins—all that could make it at the last minute—filter in, greeted by Martin, who's loitering by the door in a moth-eaten tuxedo that predates the Vietnam War. He shakes all the relatives' hands and cracks jokes.

"I guess you heard it's a shotgun wedding—but don't make any comments about Leda showing. She's kind of sensitive about it." Nathalie, who is handing out programs, smiles at this, and he winks. To the next aunt he says, "We had to have another wedding because the presents were so disappointing last time. I hope you acquitted yourself well." In a lull between guests he wanders over to her, his silver cummerbund rising halfway to his neck, and confides that he is nervous.

"You'll be great, Martin," she says. "It's going to be great."

"Where did your fine husband get off to?"

She shrugs. "Probably refinishing all the pews at the last second."

Martin looks at her, his rheumy eyes gleaming kindly behind his thick glasses. "Now, sweetheart. Be grateful his hobbies are harmless."

Harmless, Nathalie thinks later, as the organ plays the wedding march and Nick, his face a study in beleaguered patience, escorts his mother slowly down the aisle. She thinks, *It's not enough.* The minister, a solid twenty-five years younger than the two he is about to wed, greets the bride with a smile. She wonders if Leda knew, each time, that her marriage wouldn't endure— wonders when and how this knowledge dawned on her. And each time it happened, was she surprised? Behind her, one row back, Michael Thomas sighs with audible sentiment. Nathalie shoots him a look over her shoulder, and he leans forward and whispers in her ear, "Grouch."

Nick kisses his mother on the cheek and takes his seat beside Nathalie without looking at her. Leda's wearing the floor-length gown she chose in the store, its wide skirt buoyant around her, her exposed chest and shoulders wrinkled, age-spotted, as soft as cushions. She's also wearing elbow-length gloves, a veil, and— Nathalie can just make it out, its gems nestled and sparkling against Leda's white hair—a tiara. She smiles at Martin, her thin lips parted slightly. She looks like a travesty and a fantasy, both.

She and Martin promise to love each other, to honor and obey. Martin lifts up her veil and looks into Leda's eyes; she looks back, then they share a gentle, dignified kiss. One princess-gloved hand reaches up and squeezes Martin's arm in its ancient tuxedo. What she's seeing, Nathalie can tell, is love—the real thing, stripped down and authentic—and as they walk back up the aisle together, she looks down at her hands.

At the reception, which is held back at the house, Martin tells her a joke involving a mailman, a fireman, a policeman, and a farmer's daughter. Leda and Nick are dancing in the living room, swaying more than moving their feet, their shoes scuffling against the bare floor. Leda's gloves lie where they've been flung, in postures of abandonment and repose, over the back of the couch. Nick smiles down at his mother. They've made up, as they always do.

He sees Nathalie watching them and glances away, a gesture that is half anger, half apology, and wholly familiar. Michael Thomas comes over and asks her to dance. He's been leaning against a wall since the party began, tapping his feet to the music and looking longingly at the people on the floor. Passing by him earlier, handing out hors d'oeuvres, she even heard him humming along loudly to "The Way You Look Tonight." Now he stands before her, wide-eyed and eager. She shakes her head. Michael Thomas seems like the kind of person who's had dance lessons and isn't afraid to use them.

"Please?" he says. "Just one dance? I love to dance at weddings."

"I'm not really much of a dancer."

Beside her, Martin gives her a nudge—actually, less a nudge than a poke in the ribs, sharper and more forceful than she would've expected.

"Go ahead, dear," he says. "Who knows how long it'll be until Leda and I get married again?" He pushes her in the direction of Michael Thomas's skinny arms. She relents. Michael Thomas takes her hand and bows an exaggerated introduction. The two of them step and swirl, paired and clasped. She was right about him: he has *technique*. People head to the edges of the room, making room for them. He spins and dips her, and by the time the song finishes, she's breathless and grateful not to have been injured.

When Michael Thomas bows and retreats, Nick comes over and hands her a drink. "Impressive moves," he says.

"It was all Michael Thomas," she tells him.

Together they watch him scouring the room for other partners. Leda and Martin are dancing together now, cheek to cheek, eyes closed in rapture, swaying only the slightest bit. Nathalie sips her champagne and observes the happy couple. Next to her, Nick smells of cologne and sweat and shrimp canapés and wine; the rhythm of his breath as familiar as her own. She knows the two of them won't dance tonight. They'll stand side by side, as if on guard, waiting until the others are through.

Land of the Midnight Sun

Maxine was the good child; her little brother was the problem. When he kept getting in trouble at school, their parents conferred and took drastic steps. The doorbell rang one Saturday afternoon when Maxine was home alone, doing her trig homework. Her mother was working at the hospital and her brother was wherever he went when he left the house. Nobody knew what he did with his time. Maxine opened the door, and there was a boy standing on the porch; she'd never seen him before. On the street behind him, a horn honked and a car drove away.

"Can I help you?" she said.

"I am Yuri," said the boy, and just stood there. He was thin and dark-haired, pale-skinned, with high, prominent cheekbones. Despite the warm October weather he was wearing a wool sweater. Dark circles under his eyes made it hard to guess his age.

"Is your parents at home?"

"No."

Maxine noticed a black suitcase on the ground, bound by a leather strap. Yuri looked to the left and the right, as if checking the truth of her story. Finally he looked back at her. "I am exchange student," he said. "I live in your house one year."

"What?" she said.

"Then, if you like, you may come to Soviet Union and live in my house one year. But only if you like," he continued. "It is no obligation." His accent was halting and twisted, like nothing she had ever heard.

"I know nothing about this," Maxine said.

"It is glasnost program."

"It's like nobody tells me anything," she said.

"You have a brother," Yuri stated flatly, and fished a piece of paper out of his jeans. "His name is Brian. He is for me the exchange host."

"Nobody calls him Brian," Maxine told him. "We call him Bat."

Yuri gazed at her with his exhausted eyes. He reached into his jeans pocket again and pulled out a pack of cigarettes, then sat down on the porch and lit one, throwing his match onto the rock lawn.

"Because his room is like a cave," Maxine said.

Yuri nodded. "You are talking of the mouse with wings."

"Yes, exactly." She left the house and sat down next to him and waited until he was done smoking. Then she picked up his suitcase and led him to Bat's room. It was pitch black in there and smelled like an armpit. She usually avoided it.

"Well, here's your new home," she said. "You can watch TV if you want."

Maxine's mother made enchiladas that night and they all ate dinner together, in the dining room. This was such an unusual occurrence that Maxine and Bat stood in the kitchen beforehand, momentarily baffled, until their mother gestured to the chairs around the table. In their house people tended to be preoccupied by individual activities—work, school, juvenile delinquency, as the case may be. They rarely ate meals together, were rarely even home at the same time. Maxine enjoyed this setup as a rule, especially when it freed her own days from scrutiny, but she liked it less when Russians started showing up on the doorstep unannounced. She sat down across from Yuri, who had taken a nap that afternoon but still looked tired.

"Yuri, these are enchiladas," her mother said. "A local specialty. It's Mexican. We are very close to Mexico, I guess you know that."

"Ah, yes," he murmured, looking out the back window as if he might see Mexico right there. Maxine followed his gaze: there was nothing to look at, just some faded rosebushes blooming into the alley, then the square backs of other houses, all the same-looking houses in Carlsbad, New Mexico.

"I didn't make them too spicy, because I thought you might not be used to it. But if you do like hot food, you can put the salsa on it. Salsa comes from the chile pepper. Do you have chile peppers in Russia?"

"Chiles are a New World crop, Mom," Maxine put in.

"Oh, shut up, Max," Bat said, and Yuri looked at him. Bat was slumped in his chair, hair falling over his eyes. He also looked exhausted. Last year he'd been suspended for selling speed out of his locker; school administrators took it away from him, and since then he had had no energy. Their parents thought this could all be traced to their divorce.

Yuri lifted some enchilada with his fork. Strings of cheese stretched down to the plate. He chewed carefully, swallowed, and smiled. "This is delicious, Mrs. Watson."

Maxine's mother beamed at him. "Why, thank you, honey," she said.

————

On Sunday, as always, Maxine and Bat had dinner with their father at Furr's Cafeteria.

"Ah, the Russian's here. Welcome," he said to Yuri, extending his hand. "We're real happy to have you."

"Thank you," said Yuri.

They picked up the wet plastic trays and pushed them along the metal counter, past the salads and Jell-O. Yuri watched Bat carefully, Maxine saw, and said to each counter person, "The same as him, the same as him." He wound up with a plate full of starches, macaroni and cheese and fried potatoes, but seemed satisfied. At the table he gulped down two glasses of Coke, then went back with Bat for coconut cream pie.

"So, Yuri, what part of Russia are you from?" their father said.

"Like you know any part of Russia," Bat said.

"I live in the very far north," Yuri said. "I like the weather here."

"Okay, I seen this on the TV," their father said. "That's the land of the midnight sun. In the winter it stays dark, but in the summer, the sun shines all the time, right? Way into the night."

"Yes," said Yuri. He took a fork to his pie and tried it. When he smiled, the chocolate sprinkles caught between his teeth were as dark as dirt.

Yuri stuck next to Bat all the time. There was one other exchange student that year, a Swede who was living in Happy Valley and called Yuri on the telephone a few times, almost singing his name in his lilting accent, but Yuri discouraged his advances. He explained at the dinner table that he had come to America to meet Americans, not Swedes. At school Maxine sometimes saw Yuri and Bat drifting down the hallway together, or smoking cigarettes in the parking lot. Bat said he thought that Yuri was a spy, a Soviet agent brought over by their parents to watch his movements. "We're living in a police state," he whispered.

"You are like paranoid," Maxine said.

Yuri seemed to enjoy the desert. Bat had just gotten his license and bought an old Chevy Malibu—probably with his drug money, Maxine thought—and the two of them spent a lot of time driving around outside town, Yuri staring quietly at the juniper and yucca, the pink and pocked brown of the rolling canyons. They drove to the falls at night and swam in the turquoise water, or threw rocks at the ducks in the Pecos. All this Bat reported to Maxine, speaking in a hushed tone, when they met in the hallway at home.

"He's my shadow," Bat said. "But I have to say he's not a bad guy."

Maxine didn't see either of them very much. She was a junior and taking AP English and practicing for the SATs. More than anything she wanted to go away to school, someplace east, with leaves changing in the fall and tall brick buildings stacked with dusty books, anywhere away from the desert, from Furr's and JCPenney. Her history teacher, Mr. Vasquez, was coaching her on the SATs. He was a short man whose receding hairline revealed dark freckles on his head as it went. She wondered whether they'd been there his whole life, waiting under his hair, or had come into existence only as his scalp came into contact with the sun. In class he wheezed nervously and coughed a lot, but one-on-one, talking with Maxine about her education, he grew passionate and raised his voice. He felt strongly about her future. He talked about the Ivy League, which she always pictured as a huge dome, like a football stadium garlanded with vines, spanning all the New England states.

"The SATs are your passport out of here, Maxine," Mr. Vasquez said, and she very much wanted this to be true.

On Thanksgiving, Yuri took careful bites of the sweet potato and marshmallow casserole. "This is delicious, Mrs. Watson," he said. He said this about everything. Maxine suspected he'd been coached.

On Christmas Day he went into Bat's room and brought out small wrapped gifts: for Maxine and their mother, beaded necklaces; for Bat and their father, Communist Party watches. One had a hammer and sickle where the twelve should be, and the other had a tank. Bat got the tank version and loved it, showing it all around school. Some guy whose father was in the reserves called him a Communist, and after the fight Bat came home with a bruised cheek and a black eye. But he kept wearing the watch.

Yuri received letters from the USSR, odd, blocky handwriting on thin blue paper with many stamps, a single page folded over itself to make an envelope. One night after dinner he reached into the pocket of his jeans and unfolded one of these. Inside was a picture of his two little sisters, ten-year-old twins with black hair in braids.

"They're adorable," Maxine's mother said.

"Bat will meet them when he comes to Soviet Union to live with us."

"Well, we'll see about that," she said.

Maxine's mother came home from work and propped her aching feet in their nurse's shoes up on a chair. Maxine brought her a glass of iced tea. Her mother sipped it and asked her to spend more time with Yuri and Bat.

"I'm afraid they're becoming too attached," she said.

"I thought you wanted them to be attached. You wanted Bat to have a friend. You imported a friend for him from another country."

"Don't be so dramatic, honey."

"I have things to do."

Maxine's mother drained her tea and raised an eyebrow. "You're seventeen years old," she said. "Get out of the house."

So Maxine took the boys to the Living Desert, where they wandered listlessly down the nature trail and stared at the antelope. The antelope stared back just as blankly. Yuri stumbled and stuck his hand into a prickly pear, its spines puncturing his palm, but he said he was fine. They went up to the cages at feeding time and watched a snake choke down a bird. Then they walked around the nature center, looking at rocks split open to show the minerals inside.

"Okay, this is boring, Max," Bat said.

"Yeah, it is boring," Yuri echoed. His accent had picked up a Southwestern tinge, making him sound like a Russian cowboy. They went to the Dairy Queen and had blizzards. This was what there was to do in Carlsbad. Out of here, thought Maxine, looking at the white plastic chairs and the soft-serve machine. Soon.

She offered to take them to the Caverns, but Yuri refused, explaining that he was afraid of the dark. She didn't believe this for one second—he spent hours at a time with Bat in his murky room, listening to Pink Floyd—but she didn't protest. The boys went off together, arguing about something. Bat's face was less pale than it used to be, with all the time they spent out in the desert. Yuri, too, looked less pale, the circles under his eyes having faded to light purple. When she saw them now she remembered being with Bat on the Fourth of July, driving down to the beach with their parents to watch the fireworks over the Pecos, Bat as a little kid, with a summer tan and still Brian then, laughing his head off at the explosions.

Then Yuri knocked on her bedroom door, late.

"Bat's sick," he said. "He drank too much beer." He led her outside to Bat's car, where her brother was slumped heavily against the passenger window.

"Who drove home?" she said.

"I did."

"You know how to drive?"

"I have seen Bat do it."

They dragged Bat into the house and laid him on the bed. There was vomit matted in his hair. His lips hung slackly down to the blanket and he started to drool.

"We have to keep him on his side, so he won't choke on his vomit," Yuri said. "I learned this at your school."

"I'm glad American education's so useful," Maxine said.

They arranged Bat on his side, and he snorted a little.

She got a bucket from the hall closet and put it on the floor next to the bed. "Well," she said. "Good job, Yuri."

They went outside and sat on the curb in front of the house. It was three o'clock in the morning, in April, and the air felt humid and warm. Yuri smoked a cigarette. When he was done he lay down on his back on the thick grass and looked at the stars. Maxine wanted to ask him about the constellations, whether they looked the same from the USSR or different, but when she started talking she realized that he was asleep.

The next morning Bat couldn't leave his bed. He tried claiming he had the flu, but the stench of beer on his clothes gave him away.

Maxine's mother lectured him for a long time. Then she turned to Yuri. "I thought you were different," she said bitterly. He looked confused and said nothing. "I thought you would help him."

"Give him a break, Mom," Maxine said. "He's not from here, he doesn't know."

He stared at his shoes, as if they were discussing some other, absent person.

Maxine decided it would be good to get him out of the house, so she drove him out the winding road to the Caverns. "It's the only place you haven't been in Carlsbad," she said. "People come from all over the world to see this. You have to."

Yuri lit a cigarette and blew the smoke out the window. He shrugged. "If I have to."

She led him down the winding steps to the mouth of the Caverns. Families lingered in the sun outside, pressing the audio guides to their ears. Inside, it wasn't very crowded and they followed the spotlit path into the dark chambers. Maxine had been here a million times. The air was clammy and smelled acridly of bat guano.

"At sunset," she told Yuri, "the bats fly out into the sky, hundreds of them. The sky is all blue and orange and pink and full of bats. They spend the night looking for food and then come back in."

"Like your brother looking for beer."

"Yeah," she said, "something like that."

"Will they attack me, the bats?"

"I think they sleep during the day."

"Also like your brother!" Yuri grinned, and she smiled back at him.

She tugged at his sleeve, shyly, and walked to the start of the trail. Secretly, and even though it was always full of tourists, she liked the Caverns. She liked the twisted, gnarled formations, the marble colors in them, the improbable shapes. She liked the ones that stretched from floor to ceiling in tensed arcs, like rubber bands. They looked like they could move—and they were moving, in a way, if you thought about it; they were the movement of water made visible.

"The water drips all the time," she whispered to Yuri. "Can you hear it dripping? It leaves deposits behind. It takes years and years to make these things. Stalactites are from the top, stalagmites are from the bottom."

Yuri grabbed her hand, and his palm was sweaty. "I do not like caves," he said.

"It's okay," she told him, "Come on. It's a little slippery, so walk slow." She pulled his reluctant hand and led him farther down. The path circled lower and lower until it brought them to the darkest part of the cavern. The formations were barely visible, pale and pink, like shy ghosts. Above them people stood higher on the trail, their voices echoing through the chamber. The lights up there looked as clustered and distant as a faraway town, as Carlsbad did when you were driving in from Artesia. Yuri stood behind her. He put his hands on her hips.

"Do you feel okay?" she asked him.

He nodded and his hair brushed against her cheek. He clasped his hands over her stomach. She thought of his two sisters, their braids flying as they ran across the snowy steppes, their pale faces turned to the sky. She thought of the beaded necklace he'd given her, curled up in her jewelry box for safekeeping.

"You are very pretty," he said in her ear.

She loved his accent. He put his hands on her chest, one palm cupping each breast, his fingertips making tiny, almost unbearable movements over the fabric of her shirt, like water flowing in slow, insistent drops. She stood still.

Six months later, Maxine received a letter from Yuri. It was written on thin blue paper in blocky handwriting, just like the ones he used to get from his family. On the stamps were pictures of the crown jewels of Russia.

Dear Maxine,

How are you? I am fine. It is quite cold where I am right now. There is already snow but I do not mind it because the sun shines on the white snow and makes it very bright. I am often wearing my American sunglasses which makes other boys in my school very jealous. I hope that your mother will let you visit me in Soviet Union one day. I am still practicing my English for when I may go back to the States but I am getting worse because no one here speaks as good English as I do. I am the best. Oh well.

Love, Yuri

P.S. Tell Bat that the Russian beer is not very good, but the vodka is excellent. Ha ha ha.

In Moscow, she walked alone to the Kremlin, drifting past its spiky towers and tiers of gold domes. Among the crowds she could hear the drone of tour guides reciting historical facts in English and French. This was ten years later. Her husband, Ross, worked for a pharmaceutical company in Chicago and was allowed to bring Maxine on this business trip. The Russians were in dire need of pharmaceuticals, he said, they needed new drugs for the new Russia, and he was busy with them from morning to night. Maxine had wanted badly to come along—never having traveled much—but now that she was here, on her own, she felt listless and cold and had to fight the urge to stay in the hotel room with her work. She was in graduate school, and school was the only place she seemed to feel at home. To get herself out of the hotel she began to treat the trip as a type of class and pored over the guidebook, learning to decipher a few of the signs, memorizing random architectural details. Each day she assigned herself sights to see: museums and palaces and armories, grand old buildings with vaulted ceilings and gilded paintings and firearms.

She bought a set of nesting dolls for her mother—the outermost shell a stocky, dark-haired peasant girl, the innermost a baby so small that she could squeeze it in her palm—then walked out into Red Square. Russians strode quickly past her, their faces set, carrying plastic shopping bags. Back home, in Chicago, she had read about food lines, poverty, and political chaos, but there were few signs of this, at least in the places within walking range of the hotel. She had an uneasy feeling that things were being concealed, were beyond her reach, whether because of the country or her own failing, she wasn't sure.

She shivered in her light coat and crossed her arms over her chest. With a slightly guilty feeling she retreated to the hotel room and ordered soup and coffee from room service. She opened her guidebook to the map of Moscow, then flipped to the map of Russia. She tried to remember the name of Yuri's town, far in the north, but had forgotten it. Only Bat would remember the name. He lived in Oregon now, where he operated his own business, a company that sold hemp products through the mail. Despite their parents' fears, Bat seemed to have turned out all right; he was kind of a hippie, maybe, but he supported himself and had a small house in the woods.

Maxine stood in the chilly hotel room and looked out the window. Traffic blared below her. She and her brother hardly ever spoke, and he rarely went home to visit. She thought of his face when she and Yuri came home from the Caverns that day. He was sitting in front of the TV, drinking a Coke, and they sat down next to him, close together on the couch. Bat started to say something, but then, looking at them, stopped. At the time she wasn't thinking about Bat at all. She was too wrapped up in remembering the minutes she'd just spent, how she and Yuri had walked up the hill out of the darkness of the Caverns, his fingers brushing against hers, furtive, barely there, yet electric. They emerged into the sudden, blinding desert sun and it shocked her, as if she'd been expecting midnight.

Meeting Uncle Bob

Spike proposed to me at the bus station. It was November and we stood outside shivering and smoking cigarettes, our breath merging with the exhaust from departing buses. Spike stuck one hand in the pocket of his jeans, blew smoke, and said thoughtfully, almost to himself, "We should get married."

"What did you say?" I said.

"On second thought, never mind," he said. He dropped his cigarette to the ground and picked up my bag, then his.

"What do you mean, never mind?" We had never discussed marriage before. Spike smiled and put his arm around me, guiding me toward our bus. He kissed the skin below my ear.

"Maybe we should talk about it later," he said. "After you've met Uncle Bob."

On the bus he pulled out a book, slouched down, and began to read. I looked out the window as we wound out of the city and hit the highway. The day was dense and overcast, the sky crouched down close to the earth. We passed small towns with churches and bars strung along the road, wooden steeples, neon signs. In places the road was cleft through rock, leafless trees high on either side. The bus was cold and I leaned closer to Spike, who put his arm around me but didn't talk.

His real name was Leslie. When he was ten he wanted a tougher name, so he picked Spike, and it stuck. He'd spent every summer of his life in Vermont with his uncle and cousin, and this was our first trip there together. I was nervous. I was twenty-two, about to graduate without any real plans, and Spike was the only thing in my life I knew for sure I wanted.

We stepped off the bus into a deserted parking lot. It was dark and snowing dizzily, flakes that turned red in the taillights of the bus before dissolving on the pavement.

"It looks like Uncle Bob's late," Spike said. "He's usually late. Are you cold?"

"Very." He stood behind me and wrapped his arms around me, his cheek against mine. This led to kissing. When Uncle Bob pulled up he honked the horn and we jumped. Spike's teeth hit my chin.

"That's Uncle Bob," Spike whispered.

He was a pale, round-faced man with a dollop of chin, like a piece of dough stuck under his mouth. He jumped out of the truck and shook Spike's hand, then mine, and helped me into the cab.

"Heat's broken, so you two snuggle," he said. Everybody's breath blew whitely toward the dashboard. Spike pulled me closer, and I leaned my head against his shoulder while he talked to his uncle.

"Your mother says you're thinking of dropping out of graduate school," Uncle Bob said.

"I am," said Spike.

"I'm supposed to talk some sense into you."

"Okay," said Spike. He leaned forward and looked at Uncle Bob, and both of them laughed.

Ten minutes later we pulled onto a dirt road and the headlights played uncertainly over rocks and trees and snow. The road turned out to be the driveway leading to a small wooden house. Smoke rose from the chimney and lights glowed in the windows.

"Is someone here?" Spike said.

"Miriam is."

"Who's Miriam?"

"She's my lady friend. You get to bring a lady friend, I get to bring a lady friend." He smiled at me and parked the car.

"I never thought of myself as a lady friend before," I said.

"Well, you are now." He patted my shoulder. "Congratulations."

Spike took the bags and Uncle Bob went around to the passenger side of the truck, holding out his hand to help me climb out.

The house had been in their family for generations and was beautiful inside, small and old with hardwood floors and a stove with a pipe running up to the ceiling. I smelled garlic and tomatoes.

"This is nice," I said to Spike. As we took off our coats, Miriam came out of the kitchen and introduced herself. She was wearing a black turtleneck and dark red lipstick and she looked about my age. Uncle Bob kissed her on the cheek, then disappeared to make drinks. I lit a cigarette and stood next to the stove; three hours of continuing cold had left an ache in my legs and arms. When Uncle Bob returned from the kitchen and handed me a glass of red wine, I took a big, grateful sip, and felt warmer and, right after that, sleepy.

"So," said Uncle Bob. He rubbed his hands together and laughed. There was something impish about him, gleeful and young. It was hard for me to imagine him in his professional life, being competent and busy and medical. He was supposed to be an obstetrician.

We ate spaghetti and drank red wine.

"So how's Michael?" Spike said.

"Who the hell knows," Uncle Bob answered glumly. He turned to me. "My son's a graduate student in East Asian languages. He's learning how to forget English. He only speaks Mandarin now."

"I know," I said. Michael had come to see Spike once. We took him to a Chinese restaurant, where he drank plum wine and refused to eat the food.

"I call him on the phone and he quacks like a duck," Uncle Bob went on. "I'm supposed to learn goddamn Chinese to speak to my own son?" He kept looking at me. "I'm not an unreasonable man."

Miriam leaned across the table and whispered loudly, "Michael has issues. Since his mother left."

"He's sensitive," Spike said.

"I'm sensitive, too," said Uncle Bob. "I'm so sensitive I can hardly stand myself. As a matter of fact, everybody in this family is sensitive."

"That's true," Spike said.

Uncle Bob smiled broadly. "Take my wife," he said, "please." He laughed and I laughed, too, just to be polite. Miriam didn't. "She was so sensitive she had to move to California." He spoke the word California in a mincing, high-pitched tone, and he put his hands up in the air, as if he were doing a little dance in celebration of the state. Miriam put her hand on his shoulder and he took it and touched it to his cheek, a sweet gesture, I thought. "Sunny California," he said. "Going to California in my mind."

"That's Carolina," Spike said gently. Uncle Bob went into the kitchen and brought a large jug of wine to the table. Miriam—I assumed it was her—had made a little centerpiece of pine branches and there wasn't space for both, so Uncle Bob threw the centerpiece into the fireplace, where the needles melted and snapped, and set the jug down instead.

"Jesus Christ, Bob," she said.

"Oh, lighten up," he said. He poured us all more wine. "It's a wise man who buys in bulk," he pronounced. "Ancient Chinese proverb."

"Ancient Irish drinking," said Miriam.

"Shut up, Miriam," he said.

"So anyway, Miriam," Spike said, dropping his cigarette ash into the remains of sauce on his plate, "how did you two meet?"

Miriam shrugged. "It's a small town. Everybody meets everybody else. And you? How did you and Lucy meet?"

Spike and I looked at each other. At the beginning our relationship had been a secret, and we had discovered that's how we like it, the world it made for the two of us. He had been my TA in "The Bible as Literature" the spring before. In class he said the Bible contained the greatest and most basic stories of our culture, then asked us to put our notes aside and retell stories from our reading to the class. Tell whatever you remember, he said. He walked around the room, pacing and talking, and I thought he was sweet and fierce and slightly terrifying, like a raccoon trapped in your basement. My friend Stephanie and I used to mock him outside of class. Spike? What the hell kind of name is Spike? We imagined some foolish woman having sex with him and moaning, Oh, Spike, give it to me, Spike. Then, all of a sudden, that woman was me.

"It's a small school," I said to Miriam. "Everybody meets everybody else."

Halfway through the semester I came upon Spike in the quad. It was early spring and the campus bloomed sedately with the first flowers. He sat under a tree with a bottle of wine in a paper bag, smoking a cigarette.

"Ruth, right?" he said when he saw me.

"Lucy," I told him. "My name's Lucy."

"I know." I realized he was referring to the story I'd chosen to tell in class, Ruth and Naomi. Ruth said to Naomi, Wherever you go, I will go; wherever you live, I will live. I liked that story, the devotion in it, Ruth making that permanent promise.

"Are you allowed to do that—at school?" I said, looking down at the bottle.

"School," Spike said. "Do you want a sip?"

"Okay," I said. "But aren't you, you know, religious?"

Spike laughed. He passed the paper bag over to me, and I sat down next to him.

"It's just a divinity degree," he said. "Not the seminary or anything."

I took a swig from the bag and swished it around like mouthwash and winced. It was pretty bad wine. Spike laughed and told me I was funny. We spent all that summer together. Every night we sat on Spike's porch, drinking beer and talking in the dark. I never talked so much in my life: three o'clock in the morning, sometimes four o'clock. We'd fall asleep holding hands. More than once, after we had sex I cried, from the closeness of it.

"Must have been fate," Uncle Bob said now, "because you are such a beautiful couple." He refilled the wineglasses and toasted us silently.

"I don't believe in fate," said Spike. "Or God. That's why I'm leaving school."

"Shit, Spike," said his uncle. "Nobody believes in God anymore. That doesn't mean it's not interesting."

"Some people do," said Miriam. Her red lipstick had worn off, except at the outlines of her mouth, and the real color of her lips was pale. "I do."

"Sure," Spike said, putting his elbows on the table in an irritated jerk. He ran his hands through his hair. "And fanatics and terrorists and people who wage wars."

"That's not true," Miriam said.

"People who prevent women from having abortions. Isn't that right, Uncle Bob?"

"Not everyone here is Catholic, you know," Miriam said. "Not everyone here has to rebel against the pope."

"What are you, Lucy?" Uncle Bob said, turning to me. I was smoking a cigarette and trying to stay out of it.

"I wasn't raised any particular way," I said. "I'm not anything."

"Everybody's something," he said, kindly.

"I for one am Jewish," Miriam went on.

"Well, congratulations," Spike said.

Spike and I climbed the stairs to the guest room. As I went, I steadied myself against the walls with the palms of my hands. I was drunk, a lazy, liquid kind of drunk, not a loud and talking kind. I was learning to like this about drinking, that there were so many moods to it; in this it was like sex, one physical situation that could go in a million possible directions. Spike pulled his clothes off and dropped them in a pile on the floor. I lay down on the bed and watched him.

"Are you okay?" he said. I said I was. He stood looking out the window, in only his long underwear.

"How old do you think Miriam is?" he said. "I mean, she's got to be younger than I am."

"So?"

"So I'm worried about Uncle Bob. Ever since Aunt Mary left, he's been meeting these crazy women. He's always got these crazy women up here."

"She didn't seem that crazy to me."

"The last one was a Jehovah's Witness," Spike said. "She left Uncle Bob because he wanted to celebrate Christmas, for crying out loud."

"I don't think Miriam celebrates Christmas, either," I said, and closed my eyes.

Spike climbed on top of me and stroked my hair and kissed my forehead. I kissed him back but then stopped. I liked to drink with Spike in general and I liked to have sex drunk, too—it made everything velvet, blurred edges, smoothed time. But I was spinning.

"Sorry," I said. "Can't."

"Let's get married," he said. I looked for his eyes in the darkness, hoping they would stop the spinning, but they didn't. He touched my nose, which was very cold, and then traced my lips with his fingertip.

"I don't know," I said.

"You love me. But?"

"I love you but I wasn't thinking about getting married. I mean, not right now."

"I love you but," Spike said. He put the palm of his hand on my neck, moved it to my breast. I arched my back to press against it. He stuck his fingers into my armpit, and I laughed and clamped down my arm.

"But what?"

"But nothing," he said, his fingertips walking along on my collarbone and down my chest. "But nothing at all, not ever."

The bed was the worst I'd ever slept on in my entire life. Lumps in the mattress competed with broken springs to torture my back. I woke an hour later in agony, and Spike was groaning in his sleep, tossing back and forth, like a fish dying on land. My head hurt and my mouth was dry. The moon shone over Spike's face. With his eyes closed, his cheek against the pillow, he looked like a child.

From the other bedroom I could hear a bed squeaking and Miriam's voice saying, "Yes, yes, yes, yes, yes."

Without waking, Spike reached up and pulled me close to him, warm together against the cold air of the room.

In the morning, the house smelled of syrup and bacon. We sat up in bed and spent a while kissing. There was a holiday sort of feel to things. Downstairs, Miriam was mixing pancake batter and Uncle Bob was building a fire in the stove. He winked at us.

"You two sleep all right?" he said.

"Well, okay," I said.

Spike collapsed on the couch. I walked through the kitchen and stepped out onto the back porch, squinting as the sun glinted against the snow. The air smelled clear and fresh, and there were no other houses in sight. The land sloped down to a rocky valley and up to a clearing on the other side. The wind rattled pine needles over the snow, and maple trees stretched their naked branches to the sky. I was only a little hungover. After a minute I went back inside and offered to help Miriam with breakfast, but she said she was all right. She hummed to herself as she stirred the batter. I poured coffee for me and Spike and went back into the living room. Uncle Bob was lighting the stove.

"So, Lucy, you didn't sleep all right?"

"I slept okay. It's just, well, to be honest, the mattress isn't very comfortable."

"It's not? Why isn't it?"

"It's lumpy, Uncle Bob," Spike said from the couch. I sat down next to him, and he rubbed my back.

"Well, God, Spike, you should have said something. God, you kids, I'm so sorry. I'm really sorry." He stretched out his hands, looking dismayed.

"It's not a big deal," I said. "We'll survive."

"Absolutely not," said Uncle Bob. "I mean, if a person comes to my home, I'd like that person to do more than survive. I'd like that person to have a good night's sleep. That's the very least I can do, isn't it? As a host? Well, you know what I'm going to do? I'm going to buy a new bed."

"You don't have to do that," I said.

"Yes, I certainly do. I can't have you kids coming to my home and not sleeping. You should be able to relax in your Uncle Bob's house. I just can't have it any other way. I'm buying a new bed."

He wouldn't talk about anything else over breakfast. As soon as we were done eating, he and Miriam drove to a furniture store in Rutland. Spike and I did the breakfast dishes. Then we went back to the old, uncomfortable bed and had sex.

They got back at around two in the afternoon. We were reading next to the stove, Spike engrossed in a paperback thriller he'd found in the guest room, and me battling *Middlemarch.* I had to write a paper on it, but kept falling asleep in the middle of chapters.

"Spike!" cried Uncle Bob as he came into the room. Cold air blew in behind him. "Come help me with this goddamn bed."

Miriam sat down next to me. She looked tired.

"Good book?" she said, and I made a face.

With great difficulty, Uncle Bob and Spike dragged the old mattress down the stairs and across the living room. It was a feathertick mattress, lumpy and huge and mottled white. It looked like a dead animal, say a polar bear—something they'd hunted and killed but that continued, even after its death, to overwhelm them. I stood in the kitchen as they dragged it in there.

Uncle Bob let his end drop. "I need a break," he panted. His face was red. He looked at me and Spike. "I bought this bed with my ex-wife. Let that be a lesson to you," he said, and shook his head.

Finally they managed to get the mattress outside and they left it in the snow behind the house. Then they carried the new one up the stairs. The whole thing took hours. Miriam stood at the base of the stairs, saying, "To your left, Spike," and "No, you have to lift and angle it," until Spike lost his temper and told her to leave them alone. She went away muttering. I stayed in the living room.

Finally, Uncle Bob came downstairs and sat down next to me. "Lucy," he said. "I think Uncle Bob needs a drink."

"Thanks for the bed," I told him. "You really didn't have to do that."

"But I did, didn't I?" He smiled widely, that impish look again. "You know, you're the first girl Spike's ever brought here."

He and Spike started drinking whiskey to celebrate the new bed. It was already dark when Uncle Bob got the idea to burn the old one instead of taking it to the landfill. He got some kerosene out of the garage and told Spike to help him drag the mattress down to the valley. Spike seemed to like the idea. Miriam came out of the house, scowling.

"What are you doing, Bob?"

"Burning this old mattress."

"Where? Under all that tree cover? Are you crazy?"

Uncle Bob looked at Spike and me and shook his head, as if appealing to our common sense. "You know," he said, "when a middle-aged man takes up with a younger woman, it's supposed to be so he can have fun. It's not supposed to be that the younger woman just looks like a younger woman but is really a middle-aged woman inside."

Miriam turned sharply around and went into the house. I looked at Spike but he didn't say anything. It didn't seem right for nobody to follow her, so I did. I didn't know what to do. I went to our room and sat down on the bed. I could hear her sobbing. After a while she used the bathroom and then walked back to her bedroom. I went out to the hallway and knocked on the open door.

"Are you okay?" I said.

She just looked at me. "Bob," she said, and shook her head. "Fucking Bob." She pulled out a compact and put on her red lipstick, pressing hard against her lips, and seemed to get calmer and angrier. "Fucking Bob, he drives me crazy," she said, and smacked her lips together. She stared at the floor as if Bob, or a picture of him, were sitting there. "I have to stay with him, though. I owe him my life."

"What do you mean? You can't stay with him if you aren't happy together," I said, and I believed this to be simple and true.

She looked at me with pity. "When I met him I had no life. I was pregnant, I had no money. He helped me. So you see?"

I didn't. "I still think you have a choice."

"If I ever left Bob I'd be in trouble again in a second. I just know it. In a second. He knows it, too. That's the thing about me and Bob, he's crazier than I am. It keeps me steady, you know what I mean?"

I looked out the window. Snow was falling thickly, but a fire burned tall and strong in the valley, and I could see two shadowy figures around it—a weird scene, magical and sinister, like a page from a fairy tale.

"I guess I'll fix dinner," Miriam said. She didn't seem upset anymore.

I walked downstairs and went out the back. Snow piled on my

hair and my shoulders. I found Spike and Uncle Bob each with a bottle in hand. On top of the mattress they'd piled boxes, broken chairs, some twisted pieces of metal I couldn't identify. Wind whipped the flames around loudly.

"Housecleaning!" yelled Uncle Bob when he saw me. "I decided to get rid of some things. I know the traditional time for this is spring, but you know what Spike says."

"What does Spike say?" I said, looking at Spike.

"Spike says Uncle Bob is not a traditional man," said Uncle Bob.

"Want some whiskey?" Spike asked me. "Is everything okay? Are you okay?"

I nodded. It was blazing hot next to the fire and freezing a couple of steps away. The two of them seemed not to notice, standing so close to it, their faces flushed. Outside the rim of fire the world danced into darkness. Miriam emerged from that darkness, her red lips even redder in the firelight. When Bob saw her he dropped to his knees. She laughed.

"Forgive me, forgive me," he said. He stood up and put his arms around her, and they kissed. He looked at Spike and me, triumphantly, and said, "The love of a good woman. That's all I need."

Spike gestured for me to come close to him. I shook my head and he gave me a questioning look. He walked toward me and stumbled as he took a step. When he reached for my arm I moved away and walked past the fire, picking my steps over rocks, going as quickly as I could. The hill was steep and tangled with roots I could feel even under the snow, until I reached the clearing.

It was peaceful there. The smell of the fire carried, though neither the sound nor the shadows of the flames. An early star had come out and the sky was a dark, smoky blue. I kept walking fast through the snow. I could hear Spike following me, his steps crashing messily. *Hurry to me.* I wanted him to have to run, possibly trip, fall, bruise himself somewhere: anything to get to me. He was closer, was almost upon me, and then he stopped. I heard him retching. I turned around and saw him bent over, vomiting into the snow.

"Jesus, Spike."

"I'm sorry."

When he finished he took my elbow and steered me away from the steaming snow. He walked me over to a pine tree at the far edge of the clearing. With his back to me he washed his mouth out with snow. I leaned against the trunk of the tree and looked back down the hillside, toward the fire, my heart beating fast in my chest.

"Marry me," he said.

His cheeks were shiny with melted snow and his eyes were bright. I felt like no one would ever see straight through to the heart of me like he did. Years passed, we divorced, I got myself sober, strong, everything a normal person is supposed to be, yet some nights I still feel this. I remember—the world was cold and white all around me and, like a bride, I lifted my face to his.

Babylon

Robert fell in love for the first time when he was twenty-nine, and he was vastly relieved. He'd started to think that he wasn't capable of it, that in his soul—or heart, or brain chemistry, or wherever the center of a person was located—something essential was lacking. Over the years he'd dated enough women to know he was straight, and he'd cared for some of them a lot; in college, he and his girlfriend Marisa had even tossed around names for potential children. But when Marisa suddenly got sulky their senior year, stopped laughing at his jokes, and eventually announced she'd been nursing "a thing" for his roommate for almost a year and had recently found out he had "a thing" for her, too, that she was therefore breaking up with him and would love to still be friends although she'd understand if he couldn't handle it, he wasn't shattered. Pained and irritated—especially when forced to listen to them having loud, panting sex at all hours of the day and night on the other side of his dorm-room wall—but not shattered. This, he thought, was where he failed. He never felt himself split open like a melon, offering all his vulnerable fruit to the world.

Then he met Astrid at a wedding in Babylon, Long Island. He'd worked with the groom, a financial analyst, for years—the bride was an analyst, too, as were many of the guests, and the reception was full of tedious jokes about the marriage being *productive* and *cost-beneficial*—but they rarely saw each other outside the office, so he sat at a table in the corner, dateless, making small talk about global markets with a woman from Morgan Stanley while she picked at her Chilean sea bass. The main thought on his mind was that once dinner was over he could go home. In the back of the room he saw a thin blond woman lingering uncertainly, as if she, too, were anxious to leave. She had the bad posture common to many taller women, and kept scanning the room vaguely, as if she'd lost whomever she came with. But after watching her for a few minutes, nodding and grunting through the conversation at his table, he decided she wasn't looking for anybody at all; she was just looking. Lying about needing to visit the men's room, he excused himself and walked over. Up close she had wide, clear blue eyes and delicate wrinkles that sprayed out from them. Even her nose had three little wrinkles on either side.

"Are you tired of all the market jokes, too?" he said.

She jumped as if he'd touched her, and when she glanced over her shoulder, he realized that she'd felt invisible. For a second he considered going back to his table but then saw the Morgan Stanley woman glowering in his direction, having figured out that he'd lied to her in order to go talk to a blonde. *Men,* he could practically see her thinking.

And then she smiled. "You're not into . . . markets?" she said.

"Well, I'm a computer guy, so I shouldn't complain. Our weddings are much, much worse," he said. "When we have them, anyway." He told himself to stop talking. Her blue eyes were fixed on him. Her skin was very pale, almost translucent, blue veins visible at her temple. Her smile broadened even further, and he understood that he was staring. He felt very warm.

"I'm Astrid," she said. "I have to leave now, but would you like to have dinner sometime?"

"God, yes," he said.

The band began to play. She wrote down her phone number, a Manhattan exchange, and walked out of the room as the happy couple began their first married dance together. All my life, he thought, I'll remember this day.

He waited two days to call, not wanting to appear too eager, also not wanting her to forget who he was. As he was dialing he realized she didn't know his name, and almost hung up, but she answered just as he was about to put down the receiver, catching him off-guard. "Hello?" she said, her voice cool and placid.

"This is Robert?" he said squeakily. "We met at Marcy and Brian's wedding last week in Babylon. The really boring one with all the financial humor, if that's not an oxymoron. Financial humor, that is." To all this she said nothing, and he wasn't even sure she was still there. He closed his eyes. "I was wondering if you still wanted to have dinner."

"Oh, of course," she said. "Why don't you come over here?"

The immediacy of this response violated every precept of dating in New York. He pictured her blue eyes, her white skin. She wasn't beautiful but there was something about her, some dim, pale radiance, that made her looks extraordinary.

"That sounds great. I don't want to put you to any trouble, though."

"I like to cook," she said. "Can you come tomorrow?"

"Oh, of course," he said. On the other side of the phone he could hear her exhale in a smile that echoed his. After she told him where she lived, they got off the phone. The easiness of it made him all the more nervous; made him want her all the more.

———

At the appointed time he showed up at the apartment with flowers, wine, and chocolate. This was overkill, he knew, but she didn't seem the type who'd read too much into it, although he hardly knew what type she was at all. She opened the door wearing a white button-down shirt and jeans, an outfit that on another woman might have looked studiedly casual, yet on her looked simple and relaxed. Her blond hair, which had been swept up at the wedding, fell loose and straight to her shoulders. He kissed her on the cheek, and she blushed, pink seeping into her white skin like a watercolor.

"Come in," she said.

Entering, he smelled food cooking and another smell beneath it, maybe of flowers. Her apartment was feminine without being fussy: a blue couch, a matching armchair and a brown jute rug, a bookcase with a stereo, framed black-and-white nature photographs on the walls. The living room was, if anything, a bit abstract, like a picture in a catalog. Then again, she'd probably cleaned up before he got there.

There was an awkward flurry of gift-giving and putting the flowers in a vase and drink offering, and then they were sitting next to each other on the couch, wineglasses in hand.

"What are you making that smells so good?" he said.

"Chicken Mirabella," she said. "My mother always used to make it for guests. Do you mind having chicken? I know it's not very exciting."

"Of course I don't mind. Do you want any help?"

"There isn't room for more than one person in the kitchen, but thanks anyway."

"Thank you," he said, blushing, "for cooking."

"It relaxes me," she said.

And she did look relaxed, sitting there on the blue couch in her white shirt, her long fingers cupping the base of her glass. She made him feel as though ordinary rules didn't apply. So he leaned over and kissed her, once, on the lips. When he sat back he was trembling a little.

"Thank you," she said. "I'd better go check on the food now."

While she was in the kitchen he walked around the room. Her apartment faced a courtyard where a small tree grew wizened and stunted in the permanent shade. He could see a man on the other side watering the plants in his window. He wandered over to her stereo, thinking to put on some music, but she seemed to have only classical, and he decided against it. Then, on a bookshelf below the stereo, he saw a sculpture of a woman's breast—just the breast, and so lifelike that for a second he was afraid to touch it. It had pale brown flesh and a darker brown nipple, which was erect. Picking it up, he discovered it was floppy and cool to the touch. He stood there frowning, holding it carefully in both hands, wondering why on earth such a thing was in this blue, abstract apartment.

"It's from my work," Astrid said beside him, and he turned guiltily, not having heard her come back into the room.

She held out her left hand, palm up, and he placed the breast on it like a child surrendering chewing gum to a teacher. But she took his right hand in hers and guided his index and middle fingers to the surface of the breast. "I'm a physician's assistant in a women's clinic," she said. "This is to teach women how to look for lumps." Her hand was warm, and the breast was cool. She moved his fingers around the breast in a circle from the outside to the center, pressing inch by inch, stopping to make sure he could feel the lumps, little pits as hard as seeds. Rather than looking at him, she was gazing down at the breast, concentrating. When they got to the nipple she said, "You have to pull on it to see if there's any discharge." Then she dropped his hand and put the breast back on the shelf, and it dawned on him that he'd been holding his breath. He exhaled. "Let's eat," she said.

They ate in the living room, and over dinner she told him more about her work. Originally she'd thought she might want to be a doctor, but had decided against giving up that much of her life to medical school and residency. In her current job she felt like she was helping people and could still get home in time for dinner every day. She asked about his work, and he made self-deprecating jokes about how boring it was, and she laughed at them. The food was excellent, he told her, and she blushed. After dessert, a homemade apple pie, he stood up, his head swimming a little from the wine, and insisted on doing the dishes. When she wanted to help, he said, "There's only room for one in the kitchen, right? Go sit down and relax."

She smiled, and from the kitchen he could hear her moving through the small apartment to the bathroom. He washed all the dishes and placed them in the drying rack. Like everything else, the kitchen was small but well organized. He was whistling. Scraping the last few scraps of chicken out of the pan, he saw the garbage can was full, so he tied the bag and pulled it out, then looked in the pantry for a replacement. Instead he found a stack of empty containers from Dean & DeLuca, all the courses of their dinner matched by the labels: the chicken Mirabella, the mesclun salad, the apple pie. She must have transferred the food into pots and pans to look as if she'd cooked it. He stood there staring at the containers, amazed that she'd lie about cooking; but then, suddenly, it made her more human to him, more endearing. Didn't he want to seem perfect to her, too?

———

He started seeing her every weekend, then every few days, and before long he was sleeping over at her apartment almost every night. Most of the time they ate out, or he cooked; she never did, and he never mentioned the containers from Dean & DeLuca. Every night she fell asleep at ten o'clock, exactly; even if they were at a movie, out with friends, or in a restaurant, he would see her eyelids drooping like a child's, and she'd lean her head on his shoulder. In sleep her body grew even more attractive to him. She slept on her back, one arm flung over her head, her breasts flattened against her chest like the model he'd handled that first night. Her breathing was regular and deep. Often he willed himself to stay awake and watch her, feeling how deeply in love he was.

When they had sex she wrapped one leg around him, one arm around his back, so he was half-captured and half-free. Her skin grew hot to his touch, her hips rocking violently against his. They had sex in her apartment, in his, in a restaurant bathroom, in Central Park under a blanket. When she came she said his name over and over, in a low, throaty murmur he found unbelievably sexy.

During the day they never spoke. She said the clinic was a women-only space ("Even the phone?" he said, and she nodded), and that she was usually too busy to talk on the phone anyway ("Even at lunch?" he said, and she nodded). If he had something urgent to tell her, he left a message on her cell phone, which she'd check while eating lunch at her desk or before leaving. At first this annoyed him, but after a while he came to like it: at dinner they each had a full day's worth of anecdotes and gripes to share. She complained about the arrogance of some of the doctors and said women were harder to work for than men, since they were threatened by things she said or by patients who liked her. Sometimes, as with the breast, she brought items home from work: a medical smock, a pamphlet about ovarian cancer. Once, in a Chinese restaurant, when he asked if she had change for a tip, she fished around in her purse and emptied the contents onto the table—keys, lipstick, tissues, her wallet, a long thin silver object he picked up and examined. "What's this?" he said.

Astrid opened her wallet and took out some ones. "It's a speculum," she said calmly.

"A what?"

"They use it to take tissue samples."

He stared at her for a second, the instrument cold in his hand. "Why do you have it?" he said. "Are you planning on doing something once I fall asleep?"

She shrugged and started loading things back into her purse. "I don't know. There's something about it that fascinates me, I guess. Not so much the equipment but what they do with it. How far they go into your body, how much they know."

"Maybe you should go to medical school."

"No way," she said, sliding the speculum into her purse. "I couldn't handle it."

This was the one thing about Astrid that frustrated him: she put herself down all the time. No matter how much he tried to talk her out of it, she always said she could never be anything other than an assistant in an office. She, on the other hand, encouraged his vague plan to quit his computer job and go to graduate school in public administration. He had an idea about working in a hospital, streamlining care, and in his most elaborate fantasies Astrid worked in the same hospital and they commuted to work together and ate lunch together in the cafeteria, and he always knew where she was, every second of the day.

She loved him too. He could feel it glowing out from her, in the warmth of her skin, in the way her voice changed when she spoke to him. It was like the first time he did coke, in college. He closed one nostril, inhaled, and, within seconds, thought, *So this is what everybody's talking about.*

A year after they met, he proposed to her in Central Park, and she said yes.

"I guess it's about time you met my family," Robert said that night in bed. "Let's fly to Chicago. For the weekend. And we can go to San Francisco whenever you want. Thanksgiving, maybe?" She'd grown up in Oakland, an only child, in a two-bedroom house he'd seen pictures of.

"We won't have to," she said calmly. She was in her sleeping pose, eyes closed, arm flung up, about to drift off. It was a quarter to ten. "They're here now."

"What do you mean, they're here?"

"In Babylon."

"Your parents live on Long Island? How come you never told me?"

"We aren't close."

"Astrid, this is very weird."

"Look," she said, an uncharacteristic edge in her voice. "Not everybody comes from a perfect family. I'm not even sure I'll want them at the wedding."

He put his arm around her. "Okay," he said. "Okay."

The next weekend, at his insistence, they went to Babylon to meet her father, Dr. Henglund, a podiatrist, and her mother, Barbara. Driving out, he tried to get her to talk about them, but she just shrugged and looked out the window. Looking back, he could hardly remember her mentioning them at all.

Dr. Henglund was very tall and very thin. He wore a white button-down shirt and light brown slacks and exuded an air of distant, medically enhanced menace, like Laurence Olivier in *The Marathon Man.* His white hair was cropped very close to his balding head. Barbara was a slightly wrinkled version of Astrid, with the same placid blue eyes, the same very pale skin. Her hair was also cut short and fitted her head like a sleek, gray-blond hat. Unlike Astrid she had no stoop, and she greeted Robert with formal politeness, shaking his hand. They all sat down in the living room, on separate chairs, and Barbara served white-wine spritzers without offering any other choices.

"This is a beautiful house," Robert said, although in fact it was plain, sturdy, and underfurnished, with very little on the walls. "Astrid and I met out here in Babylon. At a wedding. I'm sure she told you."

"Indeed," Dr. Henglund said.

Astrid said nothing. Since stepping into the house she'd adopted the posture of a young girl: sitting straight in her seat, knees together, hands clasped in her lap. She looked around ten years old. Whenever her father spoke, she fixed her gaze on the floor.

Everybody was quiet. He couldn't smell anything cooking. When Astrid told him they were expected at five o'clock, he'd assumed there would be dinner, but now he wasn't sure. He felt a sharp pang for Astrid, for having to grow up with these people, and he felt a great heat too, knowing that his family would enfold and enclose her, that together they would have a life completely unlike this one, whatever the hell it was.

"Do you miss California?" he asked Barbara.

She looked at him and frowned, seemingly almost puzzled. "Well, no," she said.

"Astrid tells me you're in computers," Dr. Henglund said.

"Yes, though maybe not for long," Robert said. When he was nervous he talked too much and too fast. "I might go back to school. Astrid's really supportive, and I'm trying to convince her to go back to school, too. She's too smart to be just a physician's assistant, but she just tells me not to be so pushy."

Again Barbara gave him a puzzled look. It was like he was speaking a different language. He turned to Astrid for help, but she was gazing out the window at the yard, where a row of rhododendrons burst with loose, open flowers.

There was no dinner. After another ten minutes of minimal conversation, Astrid stood up and said they'd better be going. They drove through suburban streets back toward the highway, and she asked him to stop by a park.

"Now you know why I don't see them very much," she said. "They're cold. They're the coldest people on earth, I think."

In the warm interior of the car he turned and held her, and she lifted her pale face and kissed him hard, smashing her mouth against his, her hand groping his pants. She climbed on top of him awkwardly, pulling his shirt loose, her nails scraping against his chest. Things got out of hand and they had sex in the car, and then he drove home with Astrid leaning back in the passenger seat, her eyes closed.

The visit to Chicago went much better. His parents and sisters, as relieved as he was that he'd finally found someone, loved Astrid. His sisters teased him that she was out of his league, and the family took up this joke and kept insisting that he'd better schedule the wedding as soon as possible, before she wised up and changed her mind. Once they got back to New York his mother was calling twice a week—not to speak to him but to Astrid, conferring over every detail of the wedding. If Astrid regretted not having these conversations with her own mother, she never said so. A hall was reserved; invitations were engraved and addressed. He took one in to work to give to Brian, wanting to tell him personally. They hadn't socialized any more regularly since Brian's wedding than they had before, so Brian hugged him and said, "I didn't even know you were with someone, man! Congratulations!"

"Thanks," Robert said. "I owe it all to you, in a way."

"How's that?"

"Astrid. I met her at your wedding."

"You did? Astrid who?"

"Henglund."

Brian frowned. "Must be a friend of Marcy's," he said.

At home that night, when he asked Astrid about it, she said that she'd been there as someone's date, a guy she didn't know well and never saw again. "As soon as I saw you," she said, "I knew."

A week later his secretary told him a woman was there to see him, and for a moment his heart lifted. (This was another fantasy he had, about Astrid surprising him at work, wearing a trenchcoat with nothing underneath it.) But it was Barbara Henglund, who stood for a minute examining his office—the picture of him and Astrid on the desk, the black-and-white photograph of Central Park she'd given him on the wall—and then sat down with her purse in her lap. "I got the invitation," she said.

"Oh," he said, smiling at her, but she didn't smile back. "I hope you'll be at the wedding," he tried.

"Astrid hasn't had a lot of boyfriends," she said.

He didn't know what to say to this. "And?"

"I don't think you know her very well," she went on.

Robert sighed. He didn't know what was wrong with these people and didn't much care, except that he was glad Astrid had gotten away from them. "I know everything I need to know," he said. "Astrid works in a clinic, she's from California, we've been together almost every day for a year, and we'll be together for the rest of our lives. I'm sorry if you find it hard to accept, but that's how it is."

Barbara Henglund nodded several times, quickly, as if in agreement. "Astrid is troubled," she said slowly. "She's been alone a great deal."

"She isn't alone now."

"She also isn't from California. She's from Babylon. She grew up in that house. We've lived here for thirty years. And she doesn't work in a clinic. She's a paralegal. Her office is only ten blocks from here."

He stared at her for a long moment, and finally shook his head. "That makes no sense," he said.

For the first time, Mrs. Henglund's expression seemed to soften. "She used to only lie about small things. Whether or not she'd cleaned her room. Where she was going with her friends. Then she went off to Barnard. We liked the idea that she was close by. Her transcript came after the first semester. All Fs. We found out she'd been going to NYU, lying about being enrolled there. In all those classes she had straight As."

"That's the most ridiculous thing I've ever heard," he said.

"She was in therapy for years," Mrs. Henglund said. "I thought it was over."

When she stopped talking the world was soundless. He looked over her shoulder at the clear glass wall of his office. In the corridor people were strolling past, papers in hand, chatting. None of it was possible.

"I thought you should know," Barbara Henglund said, then stood up and turned to go.

"I don't believe you," he said.

She looked at him, pity distending her lips into an expression that was almost, but not quite, a smile. "Dustin, Rawlings & Livermore," she said. "Forty-seventh Street."

At five o'clock that afternoon he was waiting outside the building. It really was only ten blocks away. He told himself this was crazy, that he'd go home and never tell her about the vicious lies told by her crazy mother, that they'd sever all contact with her family and never go to Babylon again. Crowds of office workers streamed past toward the subway. The day was rainy and gray.

Then he saw her unmistakable blond hair. As if in a dream he reached out and grabbed her arm. In movies, he thought, a guy searches for the girl he loves in a crowd, runs after her, and when she turns around it's never really her.

But Astrid turned around. "What are you doing here?" she said.

He looked at her. "What is this? What are *you* doing here? What are you?"

Her expression didn't change. "How funny to run into you," she said. "I was just doing an errand."

He dragged her to a nearby bench, people on the sidewalk frowning at them, wondering if they ought to intervene. "Love," he said, "your mother came to see me. She says you work here as a paralegal, that you're from Babylon, not California. Just tell me she's crazy, okay? Tell me who the guy was that you went with to Brian and Marcy's wedding."

Astrid was wearing gray trousers, and when she crossed her

legs on the bench she looked, for a moment, as composed as ever. Then her eyes met his, and he saw the tears and knew his life was over. "I used to like to go to weddings," she said. "I was . . . lonely. There are weddings every Saturday at that hall."

He put his head in his hands, felt her arm wrap around his shoulder, then stood up and shook off her touch, feeling like he was choking. Her hair was in the corner of his sight as he walked away, not knowing where he was going.

It turned out everything was a lie. Her job, her background, even her name—which was Sophia, though she preferred to call herself Astrid after a favorite aunt. That evening in her apartment, relentlessly questioning her, he stripped away lie after lie, and Astrid, sitting on the couch where she'd first lied to him about the dinner she hadn't cooked, admitted to all of them, tears always trembling in her eyes without ever seeming to fall: yes, she'd lied about her job; no, she couldn't explain why. There were lies upon lies, lies without sense, lies without end. There was no reason why being a physician's assistant was better, worth lying about, than being a paralegal. There was no reason why California was preferable to Babylon. He kept asking her *what the point was,* and she kept shrugging. He grabbed the model of the breast from her bookcase and shook it at her, its rubbery flesh cold in his hand. "What about this?"

"I can't explain it," she said.

For the first time in months he slept in his own apartment. In the morning—from work, where he was calmer—he called his parents. His mother made arrangements to fly in immediately from Chicago, and when she arrived she set about canceling all the plans that had been made for the wedding. He didn't call Astrid and didn't hear from her. He thought she must be too ashamed, and that she deserved it, for the magnitude of her betrayal.

It was over.

A week went by. His mother called everybody who'd been invited and explained that the wedding was off. He worked all day, and at night his mother gave him some Valium, which he took obediently, just as he'd taken antibiotics from her as a child, and he'd be asleep before eight.

Then one evening he came home and his mother told him she thought he needed help. She'd made an appointment with a therapist for the next morning, without asking, and he was too tired, or sedated, or will-less, to protest. In the office he explained what had happened mechanically, as if it were somebody else's story. The therapist, a scholarly looking man in a green cardigan, listened to him and nodded slowly. "Recovering from this shock will take you some time," he said.

"Thanks for the tip," Robert said sharply. The therapist nodded again, and Robert sighed and rubbed his forehead, where there seemed to be a permanent pain. "What gets me is why. Why would she make these things up? They were such useless lies."

"Often this kind of behavior is related to a childhood trauma or abuse," the therapist said. "Although of course I can't say for sure, not without seeing her myself."

Abuse. Into Robert's mind came the vision of Dr. Henglund, the podiatrist, the coldest man in the world. He'd sensed evil in him as soon as they had met. He thought of Astrid fingering the rubber breast, pocketing the speculum that probed the female body. *How far they go into the body, how much they know,* she'd said. It was the invasion she found fascinating, Robert thought, a vulnerability of the body that must have spoken to her of her own.

He thanked the therapist and, that afternoon, drove out to Long Island, to Henglund's office.

On the wall in the waiting room was a poster showing crippled and deformed feet, hammer-toed, misshapen, archless. On the opposite wall, another poster displayed happy feet, unconfined and lacking bunions, romping in a field as if they'd never once needed shoes. He ignored the nurse and walked right into the examining room, where Henglund was crouched before a woman's foot, holding it like a prince with a slipper. Seeing Robert, he straightened up and excused himself to the patient, a middle-aged woman with red lipstick and enormous hair, then led him into an office and sat down behind the desk.

"Astrid is home with us now," he said solemnly, leaning forward with his hands clasped, his flesh sallow against his white coat. "We are taking care of her." His air of menace was even stronger now.

"I can't prove it," Robert said, "but I believe this is all your fault."

"Indeed," Dr. Henglund said. "Your response is understandable, I suppose. One always looks for others to blame when confronted with a difficult situation."

"Fuck you," Robert said. "What did you do to her?"

Henglund raised one white eyebrow behind his glasses. His eyes were blue and eerily pale. "This is no longer your concern," he said.

"If she stays with you, it's the end of her," Robert said. "You made her what she is."

Henglund touched the tips of his long fingers together. "It's been my experience," he said, "that we make ourselves."

Robert left the office in disgust and drove to the Henglunds' house, parked on the street, and walked up the driveway.

Through the front window he could see Astrid sitting on the living-room couch reading *The New York Times*. Her expression was calm. When she lifted her head, he thought she'd heard his approach; but then she said something in the direction of the kitchen, and he knew she must be talking to her mother. As he watched her he felt himself disintegrating, dissolving. He understood then why people with broken hearts killed themselves. It wasn't the pain so much as the nothingness, the formlessness of the days and months and years to come, that was unbearable.

Without her there was nothing. Yet he had no idea who she was.

As he stood there watching her through the window she turned and saw him, fixing him with eyes that were, he now realized, the same as her father's. Her hair hung limply to her shoulders, unwashed for days. He saw how tired she looked, how miserable, how bereft. Then she smiled sadly, tightly—a smile that said she knew she'd betrayed him, that in so doing she'd betrayed herself.

Without thinking, he beckoned to her, and she put down the newspaper and came outside. He didn't even know what to call her.

"Will you take me home?" she said.

He nodded. In the car, driving back, she put her hand on his knee, and he let her. After a while she moved her hand up to his thigh, and he let her do that too. He walked with her upstairs to her apartment, and in the living room she thanked him for taking her away from Babylon. Without thinking, the same as the first time, he kissed her, and she kissed him back, pushing her tongue into his mouth, running her hands up his back. He grabbed her and took off her shirt. A button popped and landed on the floor. She pulled him down on the couch, and he pulled down her pants and then his own and thrust inside her, one foot braced on the floor. "Robert," she said.

Afterwards they took off the rest of their clothes and moved to the bedroom, where they slept for a little while, his arms around her. The room was dark when he woke up, alone in bed. He could hear her moving softly around in the kitchen, opening the fridge door, it sounded like, pouring a glass of water. The sheets smelled like her. He lay there in the dark, waiting for his love to come back.

Ghostwriting

When Marcus left home for college, he took his books, his clothes, his porn magazines (she checked), and the decrepit couch in the back room. He tried to take the dog, too, claiming the resident advisor had approved it, but Karin wouldn't let him. He said she'd never even walked the dog—which was true— and she said she'd have to start, and when he voiced some skepticism she was affronted, and they were hardly speaking by the time his father showed up to drive him to school the next morning. Fighting helped both of them get through the moment. Karin was able to hold off until it got dark that night, when she found herself sobbing in his bedroom. She felt bankrupt. She'd been cleaned out.

The dog crept hesitantly into the room. Karin lay down on Marcus's bed and tried to get her to climb up, to join her in her sorrow. Cynical about her motives, the dog refused. Instead she whined and stamped her paw until Karin let her out the back. In the kitchen she dried her tears and watched the dog standing in the yard, yellow light from the back porch glinting obliquely in her eyes.

The next morning she started a journal, having read in magazines about the cathartic powers of self-expression. *Who am I?*

she wrote on a piece of lined paper. *An ex-wife, a part-time copy editor, a mother in an empty nest. A new stage of my life is about to begin.* After staring at these lines for a few minutes, she added, *If I write any more of this crap I will kill myself.* Then she took the dog for a walk.

Nonetheless, change was in order. She'd spent a long time taking care of Marcus, feeding and clothing and *watching* him through the divorce, puberty, his college application essays, and now that he wasn't around she had an unbearable amount of free time. Not time, exactly, but focus. What to look at, what to think about? She walked around carrying her grief inside her, private, growing, fed by her own energy, just as she'd once carried him. In the end she turned to work. When she was young she'd lived in New York and edited full-time, mostly cookbooks and travel guides; then she got married, moved to the suburbs, and went freelance, following the money into corporate and medical newsletters. Now she began inching her way back, wanting something more interesting than investor portfolios and trends in drug research. What she got was work for a local magazine, feature articles about neighborhood chefs and do-gooders and hometown stars with small parts in Broadway plays and TV shows. One day the managing editor told her about a local author he knew who was looking for editing help on a mystery.

Karin had never worked on fiction before, and the idea attracted her. The managing editor gave her the writer's phone number and address, and she set up an interview for the following day. On the phone the author, whose name was Donald St. John, was professional and cool, seeming to reserve judgment. Karin had never heard of him, but spent the evening before the interview at the bookstore. His books were historical mysteries, small paperbacks with lurid covers—busty maids in tight corsets discovering bodies with knives in their backs. She opened the first page of the most recent one. *Annalise Gilbert had long suspected that the master of the house had a secret.* As it turned out—she flipped to the back—the master of the house had a woman chained in the basement for sexual purposes, and had murdered the maid who'd discovered this secret. The master of the house had issues with women, Karin thought, and decided to wear pants to the interview.

Donald St. John lived in the strangest house she'd ever seen. Though the first floor was a standard Dutch colonial with brick walls and black shutters, the second floor had been renovated with floor-to-ceiling windows all around, and must have cost a fortune to heat. Parked in her car outside, her samples and résumé in a briefcase in the passenger seat, Karin checked her hair and makeup, which was so understated as to be invisible. Since her hair had gone gray it had gotten even curlier and she had trouble containing it in an elastic band or a barrette, so she just let it hang around her head in an ugly, effusive triangle. She'd hated the way she looked for so long that the glance in the rearview mirror confirming it felt like reassurance. She walked to the front door feeling like she was being observed through those enormous windows, though she couldn't see anyone. The door was opened by a woman around her own age, petite and Hispanic, wearing a fuchsia turtleneck and a white apron over black pants. She smiled at Karin passively.

"I'm here to see Mr. St. John."

The woman nodded and silently led Karin into the living room, where she sat down on a sofa. Arranged on the coffee table were copies of upscale travel magazines. The maid, if that's who she was, smiled again and disappeared. For a few minutes Karin heard not a single sound, then Donald St. John strode into the room. He was tall and lean, with brilliant blue eyes and long white hair, wearing a plaid flannel shirt and blue jeans.

"Thank you for coming," he said in a rich baritone. His wrinkles were handsome.

It was as if men got an entirely different kind of aging, Karin thought, as if they were ordering from a different catalog. Quickly she ran through the compensating factors—prostate trouble, erectile dysfunction, undignified chasing after young girls and sports cars—but they didn't seem like enough. "It's nice to meet you," she said.

"Please, this way."

She followed him upstairs to his office, where his floor-to-ceiling view was of trees, a creek, and, beyond that, a broad swatch of cookie-cutter homes in a new subdivision that ruined his horizon. Motioning her to a chair, St. John sat down behind his desk and wheeled from spot to spot looking for something in his stacks of papers. As he did so he said he'd heard wonderful things about her from Sid, the managing editor, and was prepared to hire her on the spot. Karin sat there with her briefcase still on the floor beside her, wondering exactly what she'd gotten herself into.

Finally he said, "Aha! Here we are," pulled out a manila folder, and handed it to her.

She opened it and read, _The Hospital Is Haunted: Chapter One. People in the quaint mountain town of St. Lucent had known the hospital was haunted for many years._

When she looked up, Donald St. John finished writing out a check, and passed it over to her. It was for fifteen hundred dollars. "I'll just give you that now, and you can tell me when I need to give you more," he said. "How soon can you start?"

"I can start now," she said.

"Good." He scooted closer on his wheeled chair. "Now, listen. I've gotten up to chapter five, and I'd like you to take a gander at chapter six. There's an outline at the back with the basic story. When you've got a draft, call me up and we'll take a look."

She looked into his blue eyes, wondering if he was entirely sober. "I'm a copy editor, mainly," she said.

"You work with language, though, yes? And you have wonderful references. Just try it," he said heartily. "If it doesn't work out, it doesn't work out. No harm done. You've read mysteries, right?"

She nodded.

"Then you know that to those of us behind the scenes, they aren't mysterious at all."

She nodded again.

"Stay to lunch," he said.

Unable to stop the momentum, she kept nodding.

"Excellent. Corazón is a wonderful cook."

All three of them sat around a yellow Formica table in the kitchen. Corazón remained silent while Donald St. John spoke at great length about a trip he'd recently taken to the south of France, photographing the landscape and eating local stews. Their own lunch was a Mexican soup so spicy that Karin ruined her cloth napkin by having to wipe her nose so often. Corazón evidently spoke no English. As soon as she politely could, Karin refused coffee and left, carrying the mystery in her briefcase.

At home that evening, a glass of wine in hand, she read the first five chapters in one sitting. Ages ago, in college, she'd written poetry, but she had long since stopped thinking of herself as a creative person. She had become a competent person instead. In the first fifty pages of the book, a male doctor was killed and a female doctor was raped by a ghost, the latter act described with loving, brutal specificity. The female doctor's best friend, Rose, a sexy but hard-nosed hospital administrator, was determined to put a stop to these crimes and didn't believe in ghosts. Rather, she suspected the hospital's new doctor, a testy, handsome, brilliantly accomplished brain surgeon named Rusty McGovern. In the outline, the evidence piled up against Rusty, as did Rose's attraction to him, until he turned up at just the right moment to save her from the raping ghost.

The writing varied from mechanical and simplistic to outright awful. Rose had *shiny auburn hair that cascaded down her back like a brown waterfall,* Rusty was *part Irish, part Cherokee, and all man.* Karin's first thought was that of course she could write this stuff—much better, in fact. St. John was right, it wasn't that mysterious at all, and she went to sleep that night looking forward to the next day's work just as, when a child, she'd looked forward to a new year at school.

Chapter Six, she typed in the morning. In this chapter Rusty stepped outside of the hospital one gloomy, rainy night—all the nights in the quaint mountain town of St. Lucent seemed to be gloomy and rainy—and discovered a dead dog lying by the entrance to the emergency room in a pool of blood. He was bent over the canine corpse when Rose happened to exit the hospital, and of course she believed he'd killed the dog. Rusty arrogantly refused to try to persuade her that it was only a coincidence, and they argued until Rose, convinced of his guilt, drove away into the night (though, according to the outline, she would later discover that Rusty had thoughtfully arranged for the dog's burial in St. Lucent's quaint pet cemetery). While Marcus's dog snored beside her, her legs twitching in dreams, Karin felt she was able to describe the corpse with some exactitude. If not creative, she was certainly *accurate,* and there was satisfaction in that.

That weekend, when Marcus called, she told him about her new job.

"Who is this guy, anyway?" he said. "You just went over to his house without knowing anything about him?" For years now they'd played these roles—him protecting her, both of them acting as if she were the vulnerable one.

"He's a successful writer, and Sid knows him," she told him. "Don't worry about me."

"There's a lot of creeps out there, Mom. You can't be too careful."

"I'll be fine. You worry too much."

He sighed and asked after the dog.

"She misses you. She sleeps by your bed sometimes."

"It's weird not having a dog," her son said. "I wake up in the night thinking I forgot to feed her. It's like I have a phantom limb, but instead it's a phantom pet."

"I know," she said.

The next week she wrote another chapter, following the outline—the raping ghost continued to maraud, with increasing frequency and violence, throughout the hospital—but adding her own touches. She grew more confident as the writing went on. Deciding the plot was too simple, she introduced some other potential suspects: a cranky, balding internist who had wanted to be promoted to Rose's job; a lesbian nurse who'd once made advances that were spurned. Other characters she simply fleshed out. To the mentally disturbed custodian, for example, she gave every annoying mannerism she remembered from her ex-husband, Mitchell—the constant, vaguely sexualized jiggling of change in his pockets, the refusal to clip his nose hairs, the tendency to eat or drink something and then say, "Oh, this tastes terrible, try it"—while keeping the physical description of him very different, as she was mindful of the legal dangers. Writing became more fun every day. The characters were garish and crude, but this was the whole style of the book. She didn't think St. John would mind the liberties she was taking. He seemed to her like a man at the end of his rope, a burnt-out case. Why else hire a ghost writer?

Indeed, as she wrote, the question of St. John began to occupy space at the back of her mind. How did a person become a mystery writer in the first place, she wondered. And now that she was writing his book, what did he do all day? Karin had other work to do, other deadlines, but this was somehow always the file that remained open on her monitor. She was even enjoying the almost mathematical progression of the book's formulaic plot. Each chapter set up clues that would come to fruition later in a tidy, satisfying sequence; even the dead dog turned out to have a role, as it had been killed just when it was about to bark at the ghost.

Before she knew it, almost, she'd written four chapters. Not wanting St. John to know how much time she was devoting to the book, she waited a few days before e-mailing him the work she'd done. She expected him to write back immediately—at least to acknowledge receipt—but after three days she'd still heard nothing. Not knowing what else to do, she began writing chapter eight, in which the custodian and the lesbian nurse were now in cahoots, though she wasn't quite sure about what. No word yet from St. John. She was too distracted to concentrate on her other work, the medical journals and newsletters. All she thought about was *The Hospital Was Haunted*. At night she even dreamed of its creepy linoleum floors and Gothic shadows, waking not afraid but feverish, itching to get back to writing.

Finally an e-mail arrived: *Come for lunch tomorrow.*

This time she dressed up, in a dark purple dress, a black blazer, and boots. She put on lipstick and corralled her hair into a bun—not a librarian's but a sexy one, at least she hoped, with a few fetching loose strands. She wasn't out to seduce Donald St. John; she just wanted to dress like someone who had taken command of the situation. As she sat in the car checking her makeup, she glanced up at the second floor, mentally preparing herself for the conversation to come, and was stunned by what she saw. St. John was walking around the room without a stitch of clothing on. Clearing a stack of files from his desk, tapping a book's spine into place on a shelf, he roamed around his office and then stood at the window surveying his spoiled view. His body was pale, vaguely muscled, bulging at the hips above legs that were thin, delicate, practically feminine. At his crotch was an enormous spray of dark hair, thickly streaked with gray. Karin looked down at her lap, blushing, finding it impossible to fathom. Was this show being put on for her? Or was it his daily habit to inspect his kingdom like this? Was she imagining the whole thing?

People in glass houses, she thought, shouldn't walk around naked.

When she pulled her briefcase out of the car, her hand was shaking. Corazón met her at the door in her usual smiling silence, then led her upstairs. By the time she entered the office, St. John was dressed in a white button-down shirt and khaki pants.

He smiled a perfunctory, vacant smile. On his desk was a single file folder, and he motioned her to a chair beside it. "So, Karin," he said in his stagey baritone, "lovely to see you. Tell me, how *is* everything going with you? How is your family?"

"My son is a freshman at Penn," Karin said, sitting down. The folder was open, and she could see that the manuscript inside started with chapter six, her first chapter. She knew the opening by heart. *Rumors flew wildly among the nurses about the custodian, Jack. Some said he was an orphan who had grown up on the grounds of the hospital. Others said he'd been to jail for killing a man in a barroom brawl. Still others thought that he was brain-damaged as a result of a drug overdose. One thing they could all agree on: Jack couldn't be trusted.*

"Penn, really?" St. John said. His heartiness couldn't have been more forced. "Excellent school. I'm a Yale man myself."

She was unable to stop picturing him naked, which made conversation difficult. "Are you married?" she said.

"God, no," he said. "I'm a lone wolf. Marriage would be hell for me."

"It's hell for a lot of people," Karin said, "but they do it anyway."

"Indeed," he said, nodding sagely, "you're quite right." Then he cleared his throat and wheeled his chair over to the manuscript. "Well, about your work."

Her stomach seized. She crossed her legs and waited.

"Let's take a look, shall we?" He read the first paragraph out loud, paused, then sighed, rubbed his eyes with the palm of his hand, and looked up at the ceiling as he spoke. "The problem, you see, is that it's not well written at all. It's awkward and blocky. It is simply not publishable."

"I see," she said. The blood rushing in her ears made it hard to hear what he said next.

"I'm not saying you can't get there," he said. "It's just that you have a ways to go. It's like—how can I explain this? Do you like baseball? It's like the difference between the major leagues and the minors. What you've done with my book is not *wrong,* but it's minor-league. I suppose it's not surprising for a novice. I knew I was taking a chance. On Sid's word, of course. He's a big fan of yours. I understand you and your husband have been friends with Sid for many years, children going to school together, that sort of thing. These sorts of connections are epidemic in our little area, I've found."

Finally he stopped talking. Karin knew she could never speak the thought in her mind: that she'd had to make the writing awkward and blocky so it would match his own. That he was a terrible writer. That, if anything, the problem with her contribution was that it wasn't bad *enough*. St. John was looking down at the manuscript, his brow furrowed pensively, and she realized he wanted her to beg for a second chance. She stood up. "I'm sorry you were disappointed. I'll send your check back."

"Wait a minute," he said. "Life is disappointment. If nothing else, the two of us have learned that much by our age, haven't we? Why don't you try again? Just pitch it a little higher this time." Now he stood as well. "Corazón will see you out."

Driving back, Karin cursed St. John and all his terrible, terrible books. It couldn't be true that she had done such a bad job. She refused to believe it. At home she took the dog out, jerking her along by the leash at a breakneck pace until she dug her paws into the ground and refused to go farther, begging her with soulful eyes to be reasonable.

For days, instead of looking at what she'd written, she plotted revenge and vowed to expose him as a hack. She could write her own best-selling mystery series, whose very first villain would be an aging writer living in a glass house; she would accept accolades at the launch party, and when St. John approached her with his pitiful congratulations she would pretend not to remember his name.

Over time, she let this idea go. The problem was that the hospital and the town of St. Lucent and Rusty and Rose and even the custodian had somehow lodged themselves in her brain, and she wasn't prepared or able to let them ago. She didn't want to write another series; she wanted to write this one. The book, she felt, had become hers.

She couldn't concentrate on anything else. When Marcus called, she was evasive about her work and asked him so many questions about school, his grades so far, that he got angry and said, "God, Mom, get your own life and stop bugging me about mine." That night she couldn't even sleep. All she could think about was *The Hospital Was Haunted.*

Finally she stopped resisting and started writing again where she'd left off. From here on out, she would write without lowering herself to St. John's level. Refusing to think of it in baseball terms, she'd finish the book and polish it until it shone.

She reached the end in three weeks, writing fast and easily, not even looking back as she went. She worked in two extra murders and a romantic but steamy sex scene between Rose and Rusty, who, with those skilled hands, was as brilliantly accomplished in bed as he was in the operating room. But while they were in bed, someone else died, and Rose, tormented by guilt, vowed not to have anything to do with Rusty until the murders were solved. The streets of St. Lucent ran with blood. But at least this murder exonerated him, freeing the two of them to pursue the raping ghost together. This unity went against St. John's original outline—which kept the reader convinced of Rusty's guilt until the very end—but Karin no longer cared. In her version, all fingers pointed to the custodian until the penultimate chapter, when—surprise, surprise, and she hoped Mitchell understood how magnanimous she was being—he was cleared of suspicion. The actual murderer was the lesbian nurse. Karin felt a little bit bad about this, not wanting to marginalize the gay character, but she endeavored to make clear that there was no connection between lesbianism and homicide. The nurse was a frustrated lover, that was all; the knowledge that she couldn't have Rose had driven her insane. It was the perfect ending, because you wouldn't suspect a lesbian nurse of being a raping ghost.

In the final pages, Rusty and Rose vowed to leave St. Lucent together and establish a clinic in Tucson, Arizona, where the sun always shone. Every last plot strand was sewn up.

For a week or so after finishing, she was on a high. Food tasted better, and she slept long, satisfied hours. She baked cookies and sent them off in a care package to Marcus. She finally completed some of the other work that had been piling up and sent that off. She even cooked for herself, dishes with gourmet ingredients accompanied by a glass of wine.

When she was ready, she e-mailed the entire thing to Donald St. John. Then she moved on with her life, not waiting to hear back.

It took him three weeks to reply. One day she came home from the grocery store and found an envelope from him in the mail. *Dear Karin, I'm terribly sorry to say that I don't think that it's going to work out. Enclosed is an additional payment in recognition of all your efforts. Best wishes, Donald St. John.* A check fluttered to the ground.

Without even pausing, she got back in the car and drove to his half-glass house. She almost expected him to be standing naked on the second floor, waiting for her, but he wasn't. When she rang the doorbell, Corazón took a long time coming to the door, and her hair was disheveled, her cheeks flushed.

Karin looked at her. "Is the master of the house home?" she said.

Corazón nodded and let her in. Standing in the living room, Karin heard her go upstairs and then come back down, evidently alone. Minutes passed. He couldn't just ignore her by hiding upstairs. She looked at the art on the walls, bad oils of strangely colored fruit in misshapen bowls, the kind of thing you saw in suburban coffee shops. Glancing at her watch, she saw that fifteen minutes had gone by. It was ridiculous.

"St. John, I'm coming upstairs," she called. "I'm coming to your office and I don't care what you're wearing." There was no answer. She started up the stairs. The door to the office was closed. There was no sign of Corazón. She pushed through the door without knocking, and St. John was sitting at his desk, wearing a gray V-neck sweater over a white shirt, with his hands poised over the keyboard, like a photograph on a book jacket.

"Karin," he said, "I'm sorry. I just wanted to finish this one section before we spoke. Forgive me—you know how it is when you get in the groove and don't want to lose it."

She sat down across from him at the desk.

"I'll just be a moment, I promise," he said. His white hair was standing up all over.

Her own hair, she realized, was a mess, too—she'd left the house in sweatpants, without giving her appearance any thought at all—but she didn't care. She only wanted to know what he was writing, if he was redoing *The Hospital Was Haunted* to suit his own horrendous taste. She darted around behind him, and before he swiveled in his chair and stood up to block her view of the monitor, she read: *Dear Mother, I hope you are recovering well from the operation on your hip.*

"What on earth are you doing?" St. John said. His voice had risen, in perplexity or anger, and practically squeaked at the end of the question.

"Where's the manuscript?" Karin said, and started searching

the office, opening and closing folders and filing cabinets. She thought surely he would have printed it out, as he had the last time, but she didn't see it anywhere. Perhaps it was already gone, already sent off, under his own name, to his agent or editor or whoever he sent these things to. He had taken it away from her. He'd seduced her with the project and then robbed her of its satisfactions.

"Corazón?" he called. "Can you come up here, please?"

Corazón ran up the stairs and stood there watching the two of them, unsure of what to do.

The master of the house, Karin thought, with a woman at his beck and call. What a life he had, this Donald St. John. "You," she said, "are a raping ghost."

"And you are a very disturbed woman," St. John said. "I think you'd better leave my house before I call the police."

"I want my book," she said.

"Karin, my dear, it was never your book. It was my book and always will be. I realize that you became very invested in it. But surely you've understood all along that this is my work. You can't simply step in and take over, my dear."

"Stop calling me *my dear*," she said, shaking her head. She saw the movement reflected in the glass behind her, her crazy halo of graying hair, her desperate and ghostly eyes. Donald. St. John made a beckoning gesture with his hand and Corazón came and stood beside him, frowning, for the first time, at Karin. She saw that he was genuinely afraid of her. He thought she was going to attack him, and Corazón, this silent little woman, was the only protection he had. "Did you even read it?" she asked him.

"I began to," he said slowly. "I'm afraid I didn't quite finish."

You couldn't afford to, could you? she thought. *You knew it would be better than anything you've ever done.* She took a deep breath and something slowed inside her, a quiet tectonic settle marking the ebb of her rage. She felt a great wave of pity for him, for the gigantic emptiness of his life. "I'm going to leave now," she said. "I'm going to leave you to think about what you've done."

In the car she was tempted to turn back—to go to his computer, find the copy of her book on his computer, delete it, wrest it from him—but she fought the urge. Whatever he did with it, she thought, whether he published what she'd written or did it over himself, she would be there in its pages. Some shade of her would remain.

The dog greeted her happily when she got home, licking her hand, and she stroked her head and led her into Marcus's room. She lay down on his bed and the dog curled up on the rug beside her, no sound but their breathing, measured, rhythmic, ever calmer. On the wall was a poster of a rock band whose music she'd yelled at him not to play so loud. On a shelf stood his cross-country running trophies and a collection of marbles in a glass jar. She closed her eyes and thought of Rose and Rusty, their work at the clinic in Tucson, the adobe house they lived in behind it. *They were happy together in the desert sun. Still, Rose sometimes woke in the night, listening to the sounds of the darkness. Of course, after everything that had happened in St. Lucent, she knew that ghosts didn't exist. But another part of her understood that every house was haunted.*

Local News

The cold is killing in Cranston tonight—a homeless man, thirties, Caucasian, found huddled and frozen inside a Dumpster behind a convenience store. I drive over with Mario to film the EMTs carting him away. He's already in the ambulance by the time we get there, so the footage is just a shot of the Dumpster, rimmed by yellow police tape, and an interview with the clerk who found him.

"Threw in the trash and there he was," the clerk, a twenty-year-old with a lip piercing, says. "His lips were all blue and stuff."

The night air slashes my face. I want to ask him if his tongue ever sticks to the piercing when it's freezing cold, but I don't. Two years on the job have taught me to keep to the subject at hand. So instead I thank him, walk over to the cops, and ask the usual questions.

"Any ID?" I say.

When Jeff sees it's me, he turns his back and lets his partner Aurora handle it.

"Nothing so far," she says. "We're going to ask around at the shelter. I'm thinking he was drunk and fell asleep in there. You keeping warm, Joanne?"

"Not at the moment," I say.

"You too skinny, that's why." Aurora, who's forty-five and has grown children, thinks of me maternally. She also thinks that if I just agreed to marry Jeff and started having babies, all our problems would be solved. He's already back at the patrol car, ignoring me.

"Go home and warm up," she says.

"You take care too, Aurora."

In front of the camera, I take off my hat, and my ears burn. No matter how cold it is, I still have to take off the hat. Behind the lens, Mario's wearing a sheepskin hat with earflaps, and earmuffs on top of that.

"Police are investigating the death of a homeless man due to bitter cold in Cranston tonight," I say into the microphone. I wonder why cold is always *bitter,* never *melancholy,* never *peeved* or *furious.* The cold tonight feels whiny and pissed off—something about dampness in the air, about a lack of sparkle in the frozen brown slush. The cold is upset in the manner of someone who's been unhappily married for twenty years and just can't take it anymore. I talk into the mike about the weather forecast (still cold, getting colder), the crowded conditions at all the shelters, and the need for everybody to drive safely. Cold's a story we've covered a million times before, and I can tell Mario isn't even listening. I put my hat back on and we take the van back to the station. The heat of the vehicle makes me yawn. Then the scanner crackles. I hear the code for a fire, and tell Mario to turn the van around.

"Come on, man, really? It's ten-thirty."

"News never sleeps," I tell him, and he rolls his eyes and lights a cigarette, to get back at me, because he knows I hate smoke.

———

When we get there the fire's climbing up into the night, several stories of flame rising above the building itself. For a state surrounded by water, Rhode Island's terrible with fires. This one's in a dilapidated strip mall in Woonsocket, and it started late at night, which probably means no one was around. Although if no one was around, how did it start in the first place? I step out of the van and prepare to be investigative. The scene that greets me is painted in neon: the orange sizzle of the rising flames, the pulsating lights of the fire trucks, the bright jets of water arcing from the hoses. People from nearby neighborhoods are standing around, watching. A car pulls up, screeching to a stop, and a fat middle-aged man climbs out and runs up to the closest cop.

"What the hell happened?" I can hear him saying.

To my surprise I spot Jeff talking to another officer, their cars parked nose to nose. I go over and stand in front of him, where he can't act like he doesn't see me. "What are you doing here?" I say.

"Happened to be in the neighborhood. Aurora likes the soup at a place around the corner."

"So what's the deal?"

"Portuguese kale, for two-ninety-five," he says. And then he adds, because he's never sure I notice when he makes a joke, "That's the soup."

"Yeah, I got it," I say. "So what happened, exactly?"

"We're still trying to find out." He looks at me critically. "Your nose is really red, you know. Watch out you don't get frostbite."

"I'll work on it," I say. His nose is red, too, but I don't point this out. I feel it isn't my place anymore. Two weeks ago he said that if we didn't start talking about marriage, he'd walk away; this week he's barely said anything to me at all. "You're wasting my time," was the last thing he said to me on the subject. I didn't know how to tell him that time is exactly what I *don't* want to waste. I have plans that go beyond the local news, beyond the here and now. I never pictured myself as a policeman's wife, waiting up for him at three in the morning; in fact I never expected, when we first spent the night together, that it would go any further than that. When I think about my future, it takes place on a stage that's shiny and huge, in New York or L.A., with me on TV at six o'clock bantering with the middle-aged male anchor in the blue power suit. My future isn't in cruising around the Ocean State in the News Ten van all hours of the night. I have to admit, though, that I'll have a hard time forgetting Jeff's warm chest and the little scar above his right eye and the fact that he genuinely seems to like bringing me coffee in bed in the morning. When your real life collides with the one you've been dreaming of, it's hard to know which should win out.

The smell of the fire is dense and vicious—bitter, like the cold—and it singes my nostrils. The air is layered with toxic, plastic-scented fumes. Mario's filming and yawning at the same time. I scan the crowd, scouting for interviews. The fat guy who got out of the car earlier is trying to get into the store, apparently trying to get *into* the fire, and he's being held back, practically bear-hugged, by a cop I don't know. The fat guy squirms and wriggles like a child in his embrace. I wave at Mario and we go over.

"Sir, is this your store?"

The light of the camera calms him down, and the cop nods at me and lets go. Nobody goes anywhere while they're on film. He mutters in the guy's ear, "Everybody here needs to go stand on the other side of the parking lot, behind the fire trucks, understand?"

Another hose goes on, and the noise of the water and the fire together drowns out our voices. I motion to the guy to follow me back to the other side of the lot, then glance over my shoulder to make sure Mario's not spacing out, which he sometimes does when he feels I've kept him out too long.

"Is this your store?" I say again, pointing the microphone in his face. "What's your name?"

In the glare of the lights his eyes are tiny and black, set back in his face like raisins in a cinnamon roll. He looks bewildered and angry. I'm not sure he speaks English.

"What's your name?" I say again.

"Everything . . . everything's burning," he finally says.

"In your store? Do you own the store, sir?"

"I never thought it could burn. All the inventory—how could a store like that burn?"

"What kind of store is it, sir?"

He looks at the fire, then back at me. Some unidentifiable specks of ash float over us, sparks showering around them. "Water beds," he says. "How could they burn?"

I didn't know people still slept on waterbeds. The fire's burning ferociously, and distant shouts among the firemen sound frantic. Popping and exploding noises are flying along with bits of debris, and I realize these are from waterbeds bursting in the air like pricked balloons. The water from the hoses steams in the frigid air and all the snow around the lot is melting. I tell Mario to film some more of the fire and get back to me in five minutes, then I focus on the water-bed guy, putting a hand on his arm. When I offer my condolences, he opens up.

His name is Luther Hodges. He's been in the water-bed business since the sixties, and has seen his fortunes rise and fall, but he's convinced they're about to rise again. The water bed is making a comeback, he tells me, his little black eyes flashing. His store is called Sleeping With the Fishes, or was.

"Who would do this?" he asks after I've elicited this much information.

"I was about to ask you the same question," I say. "Do you have any enemies? Any really dissatisfied customers?"

This offends him. "People love their beds," he says. "I sell a quality product under warranty."

The cop who was embracing him earlier comes over and says he's ready to ask Luther some questions now.

"Officer, do you have any theories as to how the fire started?" I ask.

"No comment at this time, Joanne."

"Police authorities," I say into the microphone, "have no comment at this time on the cause of the fire."

I crawl into bed after midnight, my clothes reeking of smoke in the hamper, and barely wake up in time to answer the phone at four in the morning. I'm still in the mindset of assuming it's going to be Jeff. But it's Luther Hodges.

"You've got to help me," he says.

"I'm in bed," I say, wondering, not for the first time, about the wisdom of a person who works in television having a listed number.

"They think I did it," he says. "They're gathering evidence, they said. I need someone on my side."

"Did you do it?"

"Are you crazy? It's my own friggin' store."

I yawn and sit up. "What kind of insurance policy do you have, Mr. Hodges?"

There's a pause after this in which I almost fall asleep again. "That's what the cops wanted to know, too," he says. "You know, just because a person has an insurance policy that covers fire doesn't mean he *wants* his entire life to go up in smoke."

"I'm hanging up, Mr. Hodges," I tell him. "I'm a television reporter, and I need my beauty sleep."

"Just hold on a minute," he says, but I don't.

I sleep late, wake up, read three papers, watch CNN. My free time's mostly in the morning, and until recently I'd spend it with Jeff. He liked to cook, preferably old-school breakfasts with eggs and sausage and hash browns. After eating we'd go right back to bed. Half an hour later I'd get restless and want to leave the house, but he'd hold me down, his big hands on my shoulders, telling me not to be in such a rush all the time. It was a friendly argument, but an argument nonetheless. With him gone, I find there's all this space in my life, phantom and new, like when you put on your clothes after successfully dieting off five pounds. Except with the pounds you know you're more than likely to fill up the space again.

The phone rings every hour on the hour, and the caller ID says it's Luther Hodges. He leaves these messages that sound offputtingly breathy and excited—less distressed than porno-graphic. He wants to meet me for a drink and protest his innocence.

"This case will be tried in the court of public opinion," he says when I finally pick up the phone. "You have a responsibility to garner all the facts."

"Like what facts?"

"I'm being set up," he says.

"By whom?"

"I can't tell you over the phone."

I roll my eyes and agree to meet for a drink that afternoon, let-ting him pick the place; you can tell a lot about a person from the kind of bar they deem a suitable rendezvous point. He chooses a chain restaurant on 195, a neon-lit catastrophe with a sports-bar theme. When I get there I find him hunkered down in a booth with two hands around a pint of beer. In front of him is an order of fries served in a plastic football helmet.

I sit down opposite him and pull out my notepad. "So, Mr. Hodges. Who do you think set the fire?"

He leans forward over the table, then looks to his left and his right. It's three in the afternoon and the only person around is our waitress, a bored nineteen-year-old in a Patriots jersey. I wonder who he thinks could be listening. Luther Hodges, I decide, watches a lot of thrillers on late-night TV.

"My ex-wife," he says, "has some very shady acquaintances."

"I see. And what's your ex-wife's name?"

"Shannon Hodges. She lives in Pawtucket. All her friends are no-good characters."

I write on the pad, so that he can see, *Shannon Hodges. No-good characters.* I underline the *no-good.* People like to feel that their words are being taken seriously. When I was in school, before I had much practice interviewing people, I used to worry about how to get them talking to me. Now that I've been working for a while, I know the real problem is how to shut them up.

"And what would she stand to gain by burning down your store?" I ask. "Is she a beneficiary on the insurance policy?"

"Ha!" Luther Hodges says, his little black eyes sparkling with malice. "The fire's incidental. She doesn't care about the store one way or the other. She never did. All she wants is to set me up. To see me suffering gives her great happiness, and it always has."

I hear this kind of thing from married couples all the time, and it's another reason I don't like to put all my eggs into a basket labeled *Life with Jeff.*

"She's very, very clever." Luther taps on my notepad with his index finger, for emphasis. "You'll have a hard time catching her. She's great at covering her tracks. This case could make your career."

"There's no need for you to worry about my career, Mr. Hodges."

"Call me Luther," he says, "and I'm not worried. I seen you on the news. Lipstick on. Hair blowing. You look like a million bucks even when it's twenty below. I know you're going places."

"I'll be in touch," I tell him, and leave enough money to cover my drink.

I check in at the station—nothing pressing there, just another story about plummeting temperatures and rising oil costs—to pick up Mario and then drive out to Pawtucket. The sun's shining and the roads are dry. Shannon Hodges lives in a rundown duplex behind a chain video store. When she comes to the door, though, she doesn't look shady at all. She's wearing office clothes and looks tired but respectable. I can smell something cooking, and the news is on in the background, which always reassures me. She recognizes me right away.

"You're on TV," she says. "Boy, you're young."

"Can we come in?"

"Shorter than I thought, too."

"Can we please come in?"

"Is this about Luther?"

"It's about the fire at his store."

"I saw it on TV," she says, and opens the door.

Mario goes into the living room and starts setting up. I ask her if she'll sit on the couch and answer a few questions. The place is dumpy but clean: flowered couch, wicker tables, doilies on everything.

She sits at the corner of the couch and smoothes her skirt. "I only have a few minutes," she says. "I'm expecting company for dinner."

"Someone special?" I say.

She narrows her eyes. "Luther and me are divorced."

"Where were you last night?"

"At work. I'm a manager at a clothes store at the mall. We stay open till ten, it takes till ten-thirty for everybody to cash out, I'm home by eleven. You can check the time cards if you doubt it. Did Luther tell you I set the fire in his stupid store? That son of a bitch."

I look at her.

"Please don't put me swearing on TV," she adds.

"Does your ex-husband have a lot of enemies? Who would benefit from this?"

"He doesn't have any enemies I know about," she says. "But on the other hand, he doesn't have a lot of friends, either."

"How's his business doing, do you think?"

She raises her eyebrows. "Do you know anybody who sleeps on a water bed?"

"Not personally."

"My point exactly. For years I told him, Luther, you gotta go high end, and get into ergonomics, those fancy mattresses from Sweden you see advertised in the back of magazines. Did he listen to me? Never."

After we're done, she walks me and Mario to the door. "I'll definitely be on tonight, right?" she says. "I wanna tell my mom to watch."

As we leave, a man gets out of a car across the street and starts for Shannon Hodges's door. He's younger than Luther, and taller, so I can figure why Luther would try to pin the fire on his ex-wife. There are simple explanations for most things.

————

Heading back to the station, I consider calling Jeff to see how he's doing, just to hear his voice. But when I get there, Luther Hodges is waiting for me.

"Mr. Hodges."

"I told you to call me Luther."

"What do you want, Mr. Hodges?"

"I got something to show you."

I check my messages. I thought there might be one from Jeff, but there isn't. Instead there's one from a contact of mine, confirming that Luther Hodges does indeed carry massive amounts of fire insurance. I'm not following any other major story at the moment, and don't have to tape anything for tonight, so I agree to go with him. I'm curious about what he might want to show me. We take my car—I feel trapped if someone else is driving—and he directs me back to the scene of the crime. The water used to fight the fire has frozen into massive, sturdy, ghost-white icicles. Folds of ice droop thickly over the building, and beneath them you can just make out the bones of the charred wreck itself, the contours dark and shadowed. The whole thing is kind of gorgeous, as fragile and decorative and pale as an enormous wedding cake. It could all break apart at any second, is what I'm thinking, looking at it. There's police tape everywhere, but we ignore it. Luther leads me around back, to a cracked window that isn't fully iced over. We peek inside, and I can see the husks of the water beds laid out in the dark like crypts. The icicles creak in the wind, an anxious, spooky sound.

"See that?" Luther says, but I have no idea what he's pointing at. "That's the Queen Elizabeth," he says, "the cruise ship of water beds. The ultimate deluxe model. I bought two for display purposes. They cost thousands of dollars. If I sold just one I'd be back on track. It was an investment, don't you see? So why would I burn it down?"

Suddenly he's sobbing, this fat little man. Not tearing up, but serious sobs that steal his breath. I take his arm and lead him back to the car. Sitting in the passenger seat, slumped and soft-fleshed, his doughy cheeks aflame with cold, he makes me feel a little teary myself. I pat him awkwardly on the shoulder. Without saying anything, I pull out of the parking lot and drive to the nearest bar I can find. Luther follows me inside, as obedient as a child. We drink one shot and then another. It's a neighborhood place, and the locals eye us in an unfriendly manner. We do our best to ignore them. I can't tell whether I'm being recognized and I don't care. Several drinks later I announce to Luther that I'm driving him home. He starts to cry again, and I sigh.

"You do believe I'm innocent, don't you? It's important to me."

"Of course I do," I tell him, although I don't. I think he's sobbing out of regret for his own dumb behavior, not over being wrongfully accused. I think it's only a matter of time before he gets arrested. Which makes me wonder what the hell I'm doing here, exactly, in this bar, with this man, investigating this half-interesting story. What if this is going to be my life from now on? What if, because I haven't chosen marriage and kids with Jeff, this is what I get? It doesn't seem fair.

Just because a person has an insurance policy that covers fire, it doesn't mean she wants her entire life to go up in smoke.

I drive Luther to an apartment building that hasn't seen better days and probably never will. When I pull up in front, he asks if I want to come in. With three or four drinks in me, I decide it might not be a bad idea to wait a while before driving home. But once we get inside he offers me another drink, and I say yes. He pours me a Scotch, neat, in a small glass.

His apartment looks like a motel room, with a bed and a TV in the living room and not much else. There are some dog-eared *Reader's Digest* books stacked in the corner, which look like church-basement giveaways. In the kitchenette is a small counter with two stools in front of it, and I sit down on one and sip. The Scotch is gone almost before I know it. Luther keeps puttering around the apartment, picking socks up off the floor, putting dishes in the sink, pulling lint off the sleeve of his sweater. And talking the whole time about how the fire's ruined him, how his wife left him once the water bed business started to go downhill, how he kept telling her that water beds would come back in style but how she didn't believe him, how she had no faith and wouldn't take the leap, how she wanted security, for everything to be *pinned down.*

"Let me ask you a question," he says while pouring me more Scotch. "Do you think we're living in a classical or a romantic age? I think it's classical. I think there's no big emotions left, no passion. Everyone's concerned with self-preservation. It's about money, it's about safety. You know what I mean?"

I look at the *Reader's Digest* books. "Where do you get this stuff?"

"I read things," he says.

"Is that a water bed you've got there?"

He shoots me a look.

"I've never actually been on one," I say.

He holds out his arm in a gesture of welcome, the bottle of Scotch still in his hand. I lie down on my back, expecting it to swish and sway. Instead it feels basically solid, like any other mattress. Unfortunately I'm encountering other problems: the spins, for example. The water bed and I seem to lift up off the ground together, hurtling through space on a mission to some faraway planet. My palms feel very cold. I keep losing my grip on my glass. Luther Hodges is lying next to me, talking about back muscles and the even distribution of weight. The bed spins and flies, part water, part solid. I'm leaving earth and I'm all alone—no Jeff, no Mario, no camera—and it almost makes me cry, the agony and confusion of it, and I grab Luther by his grimy collar and pull him down closer to me, so that on this mission at least I'll have a warm body along for the ride.

I wake up regretful.

A few hours later I wake again and find I'm still in the apartment. In my dream I'd showered, dressed, and left Luther behind—but apparently never got around to doing it for real. A middle-aged man is lying next to me, smelling of middle-aged sweat. I think I've just violated a bunch of journalistic ethics. I remember what one of my journalism professors used to say: "When you find you're starting to break all the rules I've taught you, you'll know you're finally working in news."

I get dressed slowly, my stomach several steps behind me. Luther's snoring is soft and buzzing and regular, like a small appliance. He doesn't budge as I leave the place, stepping out into the cold morning. The temperature's the same as it has been, but today the cold doesn't feel bitter. It just feels numb, inevitable. I'm not even surprised when Jeff and Aurora pull up to the curb. Why wouldn't they be here? It's their case.

I walk toward them, all of our three breaths pluming in the air. I can see that Aurora knows right away what has happened, and that Jeff doesn't, because his brain won't admit to it, won't let him see it, even though there are simple explanations for most things. I know that this, as much as my future in news, explains why I couldn't ever marry him. He isn't unobservant; he just can't imagine that someone he loves could be so different from himself.

"He must be asleep," I tell them. "I couldn't get him to come to the door."

"Probably passed out," Jeff says.

"Probably," I agree.

He looks at me closely, and for a second I think he registers my hangover, my bleary eyes, my skin that Luther Hodges has touched with his doughy little hands. "You're up early," he says.

"News never sleeps," I say.

I head home and shower and check messages. There's only one and it's from Jeff, from last night. He's calling to tell me that the homeless man in Cranston has been identified by workers at a downtown shelter. So far as they know, the guy didn't have any family. He gets to the end of the message and then stops talking for a couple of seconds, as if he expects me, impossibly, to say something back. It's the moment of hope that gets me, that pause on the line before he hangs up.

The Swanger Blood

The kid was screaming, and Gayle's sister seemed helpless to stop him. He stood on the steps of the swimming pool in the backyard, its serene turquoise water shimmering in the afternoon sun, oblivious to his complaints. Gayle, watching, was tempted to cover her ears. It had been two years since she'd seen the kid, and in that time something had gone seriously wrong. To begin with, his head had grown way out of proportion to his body, although she couldn't quite tell if this was part of the problem or only some sorry accompaniment to it. More disturbingly, from the second she'd arrived at the house he'd been screaming his head off, almost literally: his wide, chubby face swollen and red, his enormous head flung back, wobbling above the tiny stem of his neck as if threatening to detach. All this because he wanted to eat macaroni and cheese and Gayle's sister, Erica, didn't have any in the house.

"Be soft, Max," Erica kept saying. "Be soft."

The kid did not want to be soft. Softness was last on his list of priorities.

"It's not fair!" he screamed, his face getting, impossibly, even redder. Twin streams of mucus ran out of his nose and down his chin. His little hands kept twisting the hem of his striped T-shirt in an anguished, strangely adult, Lady Macbeth–like gesture.

Erica knelt beside him, her face level with his, wheedling. "Why don't we go inside and have some bagel pizzas?"

"I hate bagel pizzas," was the kid's response. "You said I could have mac and cheese, and I want mac and cheese! It's. Not. Fair!"

"I could run out to the store and get some, if you want," Gayle said. At this her sister turned and stared as if she'd suggested capital punishment, or jail time, or selling the kid into slavery. It was not, apparently, the appropriate solution.

"What are you thinking?" Erica said. She always asked rhetorical questions when she was mad. "He needs to learn you can't always get what you want. Isn't that right, Max? Isn't that what you need to learn?"

"No, it's not. It's *not* what I need to learn *at all*!" He curled his hands into fists and beat them against Erica's chest. Gayle flinched. He was hitting hard.

"Okay, that's enough," Erica said. "You're taking a time-out." She scooped him up by the waist and carried him inside, his legs thrashing behind her like he was swimming. Gayle wondered what she'd do when he got too big for her to pick him up. The head alone would soon be too big, at the rate it was growing.

While her sister and the kid were waging the mac-and-cheese war inside—she could hear, through the sliding glass doors, the muted arias of his continuing screams—Gayle sat down in a lounger by the pool. A mountain laurel hung over a corner of the shallow end, its blue flowers bent down, as if drawn to the blue water. It was a brilliantly sunny day in early April, eighty-five degrees, the perfect season to be back in Texas. She always tried to line up sales conferences in sunny places this time of year: Florida, Arizona, southern California. There were conferences going on in every state, every weekend, at every hotel, and Gayle sometimes thought it wasn't sales that kept the economy going, wasn't in fact any particular industry or service, but the conferences themselves. She'd chosen this one so she could see her sister and family, a decision she knew she'd regret almost immediately but had made anyway, because her parents would have wanted her to.

The glass doors slid open, then closed, smooth on their runners. Erica's husband came outside, carrying two glasses, and handed her one.

"Henry Higginbottom," Gayle said, and took it. "Hank." In the eight years he and Erica had been married, Gayle had never gotten tired of saying his name. They hugged. Henry was wearing khaki shorts and a button-down shirt and he sat down in the lounger next to her. His legs were pasty white. He had a job teaching biology at the university. All the Higginbottoms were nerds: teachers, lab technicians, civil servants. They all wore glasses, too, and in the wedding photos—taken on a day as bright as today—their eyes were often hidden behind the lenses, which caught and reflected the Texas sun.

"So, how's the conference?" he said.

"Oh, you know." Gayle sipped her drink, which was gin, and enjoyably strong. "Power Point slides, vendors, cocktails. The usual. It's nice to take the afternoon off."

"Always be closing," Hank said. "That's the extent of what I know."

"That's pretty much the gist of it."

"So have you been? Closing?"

"Sure."

"I'd suck at it. Schmoozing and handshaking."

Gayle shrugged. "It's easy if you don't take it personally. It's just your job, you know? It's just the things you sell. It's not *you*."

"So basically you're saying you have no soul."

"I leased it to the company," she said, "in exchange for a thing called money."

Hank laughed, and she smiled at him. The two of them had always gotten along.

In the distance, the kid kept on screaming. Then, in an instant, he stopped, and behind his glasses Hank raised his blond eyebrows.

"She used the secret weapon," he said.

Moments later, Erica and Max came outside holding hands. Max had a pacifier in his mouth, and the redness of his face was paling to a moderate rose.

"I thought we were trying not to do the pacifier thing anymore," Hank said.

"Were you in there just now?" Erica said.

"Okay," he said.

"I'm going swimming," the kid removed his pacifier to say. He ran to the other end of the pool, where the steps were, and sat down on the top one. He was still wearing his regular clothes, a T-shirt and shorts. He had Higginbottom coloring, light blond hair and alabaster skin. Without looking at them he started splashing quietly around the top step, humming to himself, seeming perfectly happy. It was as if Erica had given him a quickie lobotomy inside the house.

"Drink, honey?"

"No, thank you," Erica said tightly. She pulled up a lawn chair and sat down next to her husband. She'd gained a solid fifteen pounds since the last time Gayle had seen her, and her dye job had grown out so her hair was now half blond, half dark brown: half Higginbottom, Gayle thought, and half Swanger. She wasn't working these days, and Gayle had hoped maybe she'd be more relaxed than usual, but this was not the case. She was staring gloomily at Max, who was making a boat capsize in the water, over and over again, and imitating, in his high, delicate voice, the siren wails of imaginary people being thrown overboard. He'd taken out the pacifier and set it on the cement amid a scattered rainbow of toys. Gayle waited for Erica to say something about this, but she didn't. The three of them just sat there watching the kid play, as Gayle had noticed parents often did: too exhausted to maintain their own conversations, they gazed at their children as if they were television.

"He's sure gotten a lot bigger," she eventually said.

"Shockingly," Erica said.

Gayle and Hank exchanged looks.

"Max has been having some trouble at school," he said. "It's been a little rough around here lately. We keep getting these calls."

"I keep getting these calls," Erica said. "Hank doesn't get the calls."

"Young rebel," Gayle said. "What's going on, exactly?"

Hank glanced at Erica before answering, but she was still staring at Max in the pool. "There's been some aggressive behavior, I guess? I'm sure it's not a big deal. Happens to lots of kids, I think."

"Aggressive behavior," Gayle said. "What kind?"

"Well, one thing, most recently, is that he pulled a teacher's pants down. She was telling him that he had to pull his pants down to go to the bathroom, and he insisted that she do the same thing."

"Only fair," Gayle said.

"That's what he said. But she refused, and I guess he just

grabbed her waist pretty hard and pulled her pants down, and her underwear came down too, so she was exposed in front of like twenty kids. She wasn't very happy about it."

Gayle snorted. "I bet not." She looked up at the blue Texas sky. She was wearing a skirt—she'd come straight from a lunch meeting—and the sunlight hit her shins with a pleasant weight. "The little monster. Must be the Swanger in him."

"What's that supposed to mean?"

"Oh, come on, Erica."

"Come on where?" Erica said, opening her eyes wide. The skin beneath them was puffy and dark.

"Well, we had our own issues, I guess, is all I'm saying."

"We did not."

"We did too."

"What kind of issues?" Hank said.

"I guess in today's parlance you'd call it aggressive behavior," Gayle said. "Kicking, hitting, biting."

"Biting?"

"That was you," Erica said, "not me."

"Well, the biting was."

"You bit people?" Hank said.

"Just Erica," Gayle said. "Sank my teeth right into her flesh." She hesitated for a second, knowing that telling this story would make Erica mad. Although virtually everything Gayle did made Erica mad. All their lives it had been this way, and even more so since their parents had died, leaving the two of them abandoned, undiluted. They'd died within months of each other—both of cancer, as united in illness as they'd been in marriage—shortly after Max was born, and Gayle and Erica had just barely made it through the funerals without arguing. Yet Gayle still called her sister, still wrote and visited, the same as when they were kids and she wouldn't stop going into Erica's room, even when her parents told her to leave well enough alone.

"Why'd you bite her?"

"She had my doll. My Cabbage Patch doll."

"I remember Cabbage Patch dolls," Hank said. "Vaguely."

"She took the doll, and the birth certificate, and everything."

"You weren't taking care of her," Erica said. "There was *mold* growing on her back."

"That was because of the air-conditioning unit," Gayle said. "Not my fault."

"A responsible parent would've noticed."

"I was like eight," Gayle said. "So anyway, I went into Erica's room and took the doll back. And okay, I took some of her stuff, too. Her My Little Ponies and Strawberry Shortcakes."

"She took all my toys," Erica said.

"It's okay, honey," Hank said, and put his pale hand on her arm. Gayle wondered what was with all these *honeys*. Judging by Erica's reaction, or lack of one, it was a completely useless endearment.

"And I arranged them in a, uh, tableau, would you call it, Rica?" she said.

"I wouldn't call it anything." She turned her entire body toward her husband. "It was the most sadistic thing you ever saw in your life. Those poor dolls. Some of them were hanging in little nooses from the bookshelf. And the other ones, Strawberry Shortcake and Raspberry Tart—they were being, you know, molested by the ponies and stuff."

"Raspberry *was* a tart," Gayle said, "and Strawberry wasn't as innocent as she looked, either."

"You are sick," Hank said.

"She always has been," Erica said. "I bet Dino finally figured that out. What happened to Dino, anyway, Gayle? I thought you two were engaged."

Gayle gazed at her levelly, choosing not to blink, just as she would at accounts who tried to string her along, get free drinks and lunches without ever committing to the deal. "He ordered a child bride from the Philippines instead," she said, and Hank laughed. "Anyway, so Erica took back all the toys, plus the Cabbage Patch doll *and* Aerobics Barbie, and set them on fire in the backyard."

"You did not," Hank said.

"I was very upset," Erica said. "You should've seen that tableau."

"The smell of burning plastic was all down the street. It was intense," Gayle said. "We had this babysitter who always took naps, and when she woke up the stuff was already melting. She never worked in that neighborhood again, I'll guarantee you. We both got into a lot of trouble, and our parents locked us in our rooms while they tried to figure out what to do with us. I was so mad at Erica for burning my toys. I've never been so mad in my whole life. To this day I don't think I've ever been that mad. Our parents unlocked the doors when we went to sleep that night, and I crept out of bed in my nightie and went into Erica's room and put my teeth on her arm, and I didn't stop until I tasted the blood in my mouth. She screamed like you wouldn't believe."

"Jesus," Hank said.

Erica sat rigid in her chair.

The wind blew coolly against Gayle's cheeks, and she realized she was flushed. In her memory she could taste the blood, its unmistakable metallic warmth, this liquid iron at the back of her throat. Over the years she'd tasted her own blood plenty of times—chapped lips, hangnails, paper cuts—but never anyone else's, except Erica's.

"Aerobics Barbie?" Hank said after a while.

"She came with a little radio," Gayle said.

"You never told me any of this," he said to Erica.

She reached out her forearm and showed him the scar: a jagged half moon sunk forever into the skin.

"I always thought that was from a shot or something," he said.

"Nope," Gayle said. "From me. So anyway, maybe that's where Max gets it from, his Swanger blood."

The kid had gotten out of the pool and had his pacifier back in his mouth. He had a different toy in his hand now, something in flesh-colored plastic, and he was spinning by the edge of the water to make it fly around his body in circles.

"Will you stop saying that?" Erica said.

"She's only kidding, honey," Hank said. "Don't take it so seriously, okay?"

"Don't tell me what not to take seriously, *honey*," Erica said, standing up. "I've had about enough of you telling me not to take things so seriously."

Hank put his drink down on the concrete patio. "I only meant—"

"It's not like the Higginbottoms are God's gift to the world, you know," Erica snapped. "Every single one of them would rather have a drink than an actual conversation with an actual human being. It's not like they're so perfect."

"I didn't say they were," he said. He stood up with his glass in his hand. "I'm going to get another drink. Gayle, do you want another drink?"

"No thanks," Gayle said, although no one was listening to her.

"Don't walk away from me," Erica ordered. He did. "Max, stay out here with your Aunt Gayle."

If the kid heard this, he didn't show it. The glass doors slid open and closed, twice.

Gayle kicked off her sandals and sat down by the side of the pool, sticking her legs in the water. Max was on the other side, sitting on the steps of the pool again, making noises that sounded like gunfire and bombs. He'd taken his shirt off, and his skinny little chest was as white as office paper.

"Hey, Max," she called, "what are you playing?"

He ignored her, focusing instead on his symphony of explosions. It was a war zone over in the shallow end. His fair hair was plastered to his big head. Gayle's thoughts moved, listless with gin and sunshine, to Dino. The child-bride thing wasn't actually that far from the truth. Although the girl was not technically a child; she was twenty. Old enough to be legal, young enough that she wouldn't give Dino a hard time about marriage and children.

"The perfect woman," Gayle had said, and Dino had only nodded; he was always honest, which was supposed to be one of his good qualities. "I don't know why you were with me in the first place," she'd told him, "if *that's* what you want."

"No, you're great, Gayle. But—you push too hard. You can't let things, I don't know, unfold."

"I put my cards on the table. What's wrong with that?"

"Nothing, I guess," he'd said thoughtfully. "You just sometimes have the wrong cards."

"Oh, I could kill him," she said now, to herself but out loud.

This made the kid look up. "Kill the beast!" he said. He was holding up the flesh-colored toy: a figurine of a man with muscular arms, wearing a red shirt. One of the arms was partially extended, the other bent, but whatever he was about to shoot someone with had gone missing. "I'll lock you and your father in the cellar, unless you marry me!" the kid said.

"No offense, Max," Gayle said, "but I don't really know you that well. Plus we're related and everything."

The kid's eyes were glazed and unfocused and he kept shaking the figurine at her, its one arm extended; she understood it was the figurine who was supposed to be speaking. "Kill the beast, chase you with wolves, lock you up!"

"The beast?" she said. "Like Beauty and the Beast?" The figurine nodded its whole body wildly in agreement. Leave it to this kid, she thought, to concentrate on all the most violent parts of the fairy tale. In his hands, it wasn't a story about love; it was an action movie, a mob scene, a hostage-taking. "Do you really want to kill the Beast? Isn't he a good character in the end?"

"Not to me!" the figurine said loudly.

"Well," she said, thinking of Dino, "I guess I know how you feel."

The kid made a strangled, wordless noise and threw the figurine in the water, where it floated on its back, its muscular arms extended toward the bottom of the pool. Then he threw a plastic ship at it, and the two toys rippled slowly forward, spinning as they floated toward Gayle. For a moment he stared at her, a look of shock and desperation on his face; he hadn't intended this to happen. Then he stepped farther into the pool and started splashing the water in an ineffectual attempt to turn the toys back in his direction. Actually he wasn't splashing the water so much as slapping it, hard, all the while making animal sounds of frustration. Just as he had slipped into a happy mood earlier, he seemed now to have lost, in an instant, all ability to form words.

"Max," Gayle said, but he ignored her. The toys he'd flung away were suddenly the only ones he wanted, and all the others lay abandoned behind him. His face was getting redder and redder, and a pink flush was spreading down his white chest, too. The sun was hot and strong and he was going to get a burn, she thought; so was she. She dipped her hands in the pool and splashed her face. When she opened her eyes, the kid was all the way in the water, paddling frantically toward his toys, having difficulty holding his huge head above the water, and terrible gasping noises were coming out of his nose and mouth. He'd moved about three feet into the center of the pool, out of the shallow end, but the wake of his awkward swimming had only pushed the toys further away from him.

"Max," Gayle said, "can you swim?"

The kid's eyes—pale blue, unfocused, Higginbottom eyes—moved toward her, his lips moving soundlessly, and his arms flailing around in a circular movement that didn't look even close to the crawl. Gayle saw the enormous blond head sink lower and lower until it was beneath the surface of the water, and his pale, small feet were kicking in a sideways frenzy that wasn't going to do him any good at all.

She jumped into the pool and swam over to him. The kid was spazzing out in the water, his limbs going in all directions, and when she reached him he kicked her in the stomach, hard. She kept trying to grab his body, but his skin was slippery and each time he wriggled out of her grasp. Her skirt twisted itself around her waist. Something scraped her leg—a toenail? a toy?—and she couldn't see clearly, the water so frothy from all the commotion. Finally she got hold of his midsection and heaved herself up. The kid was scraping his hands up and down her arms, and she broke the surface saying, "Ow, damn it, Max," and he was screaming with what she thought was panic but then realized, as his arms kept extending behind her, was rage: he was still reaching for his toys and couldn't get them. In his anger he kneed her in the chest and she choked and sank down, the two of them wrestling. She couldn't believe how strong he was, how capable he was of pulling her down. *He'll kill me,* she thought for one crazy second. Then, with a last push, she got him into the shallow end and carried him out. There was a piercing sound in her ears, which, she now became aware, had been going on for some time. It was her sister, who tore Max out of her grasp and wrapped him in a towel and her own arms, shrieking all the while.

Gayle stood up, dizzy, heart going madly, dripping in her clothes. She pulled her skirt down over her thighs. Behind Erica and Max, Hank stood by the glass doors with another drink in his hand, watching.

"Are you okay? Are you okay?" Erica was saying to her son, and Gayle couldn't hear what, if anything, he was answering. Erica looked at her over his head. "What the hell were you thinking? I can't leave you alone with him for five minutes? Were you trying to kill him? What the hell is your problem?" She burst into tears and hugged Max again, her two-colored hair mingling and dampening with his wet blond strands.

Gayle rubbed her arms. Her legs were shaking. There were streaks on her biceps where the kid's fingernails had broken her skin. "I was trying to help," she said, and looked at Hank, but he said nothing.

"I don't know why you even had to come," Erica said, sobs thickening her voice. "What do you even want?"

If this were a sales deal, Gayle thought, she would have the perfect answer to that question; she would be able to calm Erica down; she would know exactly what to say to close. But it wasn't, and she didn't. She stood there wet and shivering and silent. The kid was turned away from her, his body hidden by the towel that fell to his feet. She only knew that, though she had been misunderstood, she was bound to come back. It was just the way things were, and it was never going to leave her, this craving she had for blood.

In Trouble with the Dutchman

I'm more of a cat person, really—I prefer a warm purr on the lap to the bouncing, slap-happy kisses of dogs. But when my husband, Phil, brought Blister home from the park, I have to admit that I fell in love with him just as deeply, as swooningly and childishly, as he did. Phil'd been out jogging, which he did every weekend (although I knew, from having accidentally driven past him once, that he jogged five blocks to the park, walked to a bench, and sat down for a while before jogging back), when Blister came up, prancing, and licked his ankle. Blister was a small dog, knee-high, with short black hair that shone like an oil slick in the Saturday afternoon sun. He was wearing a red collar with a round tag that bore his name. After petting him a little, Phil looked around for the owner, who was nowhere to be found, and after a further while he brought him home to me, when the previously mentioned falling in love happened and there was a lot of petting and fetching and wagging and speculating about his name, which seemed to suit him perfectly in some strange way, and there was also, I'll be honest, some baby-talking to the dog, and after looking for posters and ads in the paper we took him to the pound, and since no one claimed him in fourteen days, Blister was ours.

We don't have kids. Phil doesn't want them, and I kind of do but not badly enough to push; but with Blister we made a family. Phil works days, as an actuary, and I work the night shift in the clean room of a computer-chip manufacturer, so we cross paths at home like the proverbial ships in the proverbial night. Before Blister, we were often so tired that we'd just sit on the couch, not talking, watching an hour of shared television before heading off in our separate directions. After Blister, we'd venture out into the neighborhood, to the park or along the weedy industrial lots behind the shopping center, where Blister could run off leash, investigating trash, spills, and the accidental wildlife that thrives along the unkempt edges of suburbia. We'd talk, Phil and I, not about anything major—just our days, people who were annoying us at work, that kind of thing—and although I hadn't realized that our marriage was in any danger, I could feel cracks being mended, a kind of basement-level fortification, and I knew that the dog was saving us.

Even in the freezing winters we walked Blister, or he walked us, even in ice storms when his paws slipped comically over the glittering carapaces of lawns, even in black afternoons after the end of daylight savings. The dog walk was our together time. And then, in March, Phil got his promotion and started working longer hours. The money was welcome but the hours were difficult; for one thing, I had to walk Blister alone, by myself, in the afternoon. When Phil finally got home, Blister would greet him in a frenzy, curling up beside him on the couch, his black chin on Phil's thigh; but I only heard about these things, because by then I was already gone.

At work I wear a bunny suit, helmet to booties, the entire thing, and have to move slowly, so as not to disturb the complex air-filtration system, and I don't talk much, either. I use a scanner to examine chips for defects. People say it must be hard working nights, the same tasks each shift, in silence. This, however, is not the case. It is an atmosphere of almost one-hundred-percent calm. I move through the shift in a trance, my mind in total focus, my body swathed and clean. The chips are made out of a square wafer and then cut out into circles, and the chemicals on them produce gorgeous and geometric patterns of pink and blue. When a chip comes under the scanner and I look at it—carefully, carefully—it reminds me of a jewel sparkling in a store window. It shows me that human beings can make something perfect and beautiful. I love what I do, and don't want to give it up, not even to be at home in the evenings on the couch with Blister and Phil.

So I started walking Blister by myself. I took him to the park, where he fell briefly in love with a Jack Russell named Zelda, and became fast friends with a lumbering Rottweiler named Chekhov. I teased him that he had a weakness for the literary types. Without Phil, the industrial avenues behind the shopping center seemed ominous and lonely, so I avoided those and paraded him around the neighborhood instead. In the dark late afternoons, with a prancing, curious black dog by your side, you can see straight into people's houses and lives: families arguing around dinner tables, children staring gape-mouthed at television sets, couples getting drunk by candlelight. During those walks the world seemed to me pitiful and exposed, lacking in some critical defenses. I tried explaining this to Phil a few times, at breakfast, but he was tired and hurried, gulping down cereal while trying not to spill milk on his tie, and I never felt he understood exactly what I was talking about, although I'm sure, I really am, that he tried.

———

March goes in like a lamb and out like a lion, or the other way around, but this particular March was roaring and hostile from start to finish. We'd been hit by the worst kind of weather: hours of snow one day, and then it would warm up and turn sleety, with ice storms that caused power outages and car accidents. Being outside made my skin feel raw and itchy, the air like a thousand pricking needles. My walks with Blister got shorter, and he'd stare at me reproachfully as we turned toward home. I found a new route, a short loop through an apartment complex whose height cut the wind a little, and I'd let him poke around its small yard while I huddled beneath a fire escape. This is where we were when it happened. I've gone over it a million times in my head since then, thinking of how I might have prevented it, but my memory never varies: the rush of wind; the muffled sounds of traffic through my wool hat; the appearance, as if from nowhere, of another dog.

I'm no expert on breeds, but I know what a pit-bull mix looks like. I hate those big, strong snouts of theirs, which remind me of a dinosaur's jaws, made for chomping other forms of life. This dog and Blister stood nose to nose, immobile, tails straight to the sky. I had Blister on the long, retractable leash, but was afraid to tug because I didn't know what the other dog would do if he moved. Everything was terribly quiet.

Then, from the shadows at the edge of the apartment complex, a man materialized in a red Gore-Tex jacket, his face hidden by the hood. "Sweetpea," he called in a singsong voice. "Come here, Sweetpea."

If I could have searched in my mind for the most unlikely name on earth for this dog, Sweetpea would probably have been the one I chose. This dog was staring at Blister as if contemplating which limb he was going to tear off first, but Blister was holding his ground. I was standing there paralyzed, which I will regret for the rest of my life.

When Sweetpea lunged, the leash lurched and took me with it, like a fisherman at the mercy of a monstrous fish. I heard snarling and a howl like a baby's, ghostly and keening, and then a sick crunch of teeth meeting flesh, and I saw the red of the Gore-Tex jacket, and both names, Blister and Sweetpea, were being yelled repeatedly, then something tripped me and I landed on the ground, the breath was knocked out of me, like it hadn't been since I was a little kid, all the air pushed from my lungs, the atmosphere of the world collapsing. The dogs were fighting, snapping at each other's throats.

"Sweetpea! Sweetpea!"

He finally got control of his dog and put it, still snarling, on a leash. Blister was lying on the ground. I breathed in, painfully, and crawled over to him. When I put my hand on his fur, it came away wet with blood. I said his name over and over, like a prayer, and his tail flapped lazily like it did when he was half-asleep. I turned to the guy in the red Gore-Tex and screamed, "Help me!" at the top of my lungs.

"I'll get my car," he said. He took off running with the dog and I stayed there with Blister, watching him breathe, willing him to keep breathing. It seemed like hours later when a car pulled up and Sweetpea's owner got out. He carried Blister to the backseat of the car and said, "Tell me where you want to go."

At the animal hospital they took Blister away and made me stay in the waiting room. I was crying—hysterically, I'll admit—and couldn't stop. I was also trembling and shaking. I didn't care who saw. Self-control was not a thing to be considered. The guy in the red Gore-Tex took off his coat and folded it carefully on the plastic seat beside him, and I hated him for that, for taking so much care with a goddamn coat after his dog tore mine to pieces.

"You should've had your dog on a leash," I finally said between sobs, and had to repeat it several times to make myself understood. We were surrounded by photos on the walls and photos on magazine covers: all images of healthy, glossy dogs and cats, and they hit me like reproach.

"She got out," is all he said. His singsong voice was actually an accent—Haitian, I guessed. He was in his forties, and neatly dressed in a blue shirt and chinos; he had high cheekbones and a trace of a beard and a compact, athletic build. "She belongs to my niece. I am sorry."

"You'd better be fucking sorry," is what I had to say to that.

He nodded. Then he leaned forward, his hands clasped over the knees of his neatly creased chinos. "You are bleeding," he said.

"It's from the dog. It's from Blister."

"No, I think it's from you."

There was a dark splotch on my pants, below my knee. He knelt down in front of me, without asking, and quickly unlaced my boot and rolled up my corduroys and there it was: a rip in the fabric of my calf, jagged and bloody. My white sock was red. He touched his fingers to my leg and I swatted him away.

"Your dog bit me! Your fucking dog bit me, too!"

"She belongs to my niece," he said, still kneeling in front of me.

I started to wail. "I'm going to be late for work," I said.

His name was Jean-Michel and he came from Port-au-Prince. He worked in a hotel downtown, nights, like me. He'd come here five years earlier and lived with his brother, who was a doctor, and his brother's wife and their daughter, who was nine years old. The niece, Mireille, was beautiful and intelligent, but she was growing up wild. Her parents both worked and were very busy, and they did nothing to discipline her, and instead they bought her too many gifts, including new clothes all the time, earrings, CDs, and the dog. Jean-Michel told me all this in the waiting room at the animal hospital while my bloody calf throbbed and dripped onto the floor. His voice was low and melodic, and he seemed to think that he could soothe me with it, and he was right. I sat there listening to him while they worked on Blister, and I said nothing. Every once in a while I blew my nose into the cuff of my sweatshirt.

I interrupted him once, to ask him to call Phil and my supervisor at work. He took a notepad out of his pocket, wrote down the numbers, nodded, then did it. When he came back I said, "Thanks," and he shook his head and said, "No. Nothing to thank."

A veterinary assistant, looking all of nineteen, her hair in two long braids, came out and examined my leg. "Ooh, that's gotta smart," she said, bending down. Her braids flapped around my ankles.

"Blister," I said, "how is he?"

"You should get that looked at as soon as possible."

I was in no mood for advice.

"If you aren't here to talk to me about Blister," I told her, "get your fucking braids away from my leg." I rolled down my pant leg over the bite.

Jean-Michel smiled weakly at her. "She's very upset," he said.

Fifteen minutes later Phil came in, his nose red, his eyes wild, and said, "What in the hell happened?" and when Jean-Michel started to explain, Phil looked at him as if he couldn't understand a word he was saying, as if he were speaking a language that was eerily similar to English yet not English, and Jean-Michel trailed off into silence.

"Phil," I said, "go find out about Blister."

He barged past the reception desk into the hospital room and was gone for a long ten minutes. During this time Jean-Michel wrote down his name, address, and phone number, tucked the piece of paper into the pocket of my coat, and left me alone with the glossy photographs of healthy cats and dogs. When Phil came back he was crying, so I thought the worst, but he took my head in his hands and told me that Blister was torn up, that Blister was bloody and weak, but that Blister was going to be fine.

At home Blister recovered quickly. He had to wear that lampshade on his head for a few days, kept knocking into things without understanding why, and Phil and I had some good laughs about that, but he didn't seem to mind. I recovered, too. They couldn't give me stitches because dogs' mouths are septic, so I had a hole in my calf that reminded me of a tin can ripped open using an improper tool; it hurt like hell before it got better. Phil contacted the animal-control officer, who went to Jean-Michel's house next to the apartment complex and examined Sweetpea. When a dog breaks out of a fenced area and attacks a person, the officer told us, it's designated a dangerous dog. The owner must put up collateral against the possibility of the dog ever attacking anybody else, and if it does, the dog will die. This information was relayed with a certain amount of relish. The owner, he added, must also take out quite a lot of expensive insurance. And at his behest Jean-Michel's brother, the doctor, sent us a check to cover my medical expenses and Blister's.

March turned to April, though the weather didn't get any

better. One day I was home alone with Blister—the walking wounded, as Phil called us—when the doorbell rang and Jean-Michel stood there on the front porch in that stupid red Gore-Tex jacket. I let him in, he took off his boots, and then we sat down in the living room.

"So," he said, his voice still low and melodic. "You are all right. I was concerned."

"I'm okay."

"Ellen," he said. "Is it all right if I call you Ellen?"

"Call me whatever you want," I said. "I don't care."

"I've come here today, Ellen, to tell you that we are going to contest the dangerous-dog designation. My family, we cannot afford it. The collateral, the insurance. It is too much."

Blister came into the room and lay down at his feet. Jean-Michel reached down, stroking the dog's head while looking at his healing wounds, his buffed nails long and elegant. The palms of his hands were a much lighter color than the backs, and I found myself staring at the two colors as he gestured.

"What am I supposed to say?" I asked him.

"You will be called to trial," he said. "To testify about what happened. I wanted to ask you something, because I have a feeling about you. I can tell that in your heart you are a kind woman, Ellen. I wanted to ask you to be kind. At the trial, be kind."

"Be kind?" I said. Nobody had ever asked me such a thing before. I had never thought of myself as being kind, or unkind, either. The issue had never crossed my mind.

Jean-Michel's eyes were dark, dark brown. As I looked at him a strange thing happened. I fell a bit in love with him then, in that one look; it was simple and immediate, like walking through a doorway. I was so attracted to him, in fact, that I could hardly breathe; but I also wanted to know everything about him, what every day of his life was like from his childhood in Haiti to his nights at the hotel. I'd been married to Phil for six years and nothing like this had happened before—crushes, yes, an occasional passing attraction to someone else's husband at a summer barbecue after too much beer. But not this: a moment when you felt like your whole life could change.

I stood up. "I'll think about it," I said.

After he left, I lay down on the living room carpet and looked into Blister's eyes. Since the attack we'd had a special bond, and he tended to stick close to me almost all the time, as if he were still looking for the protection I had not, at the crucial instant, been able to offer.

"What am I going to do, Blister?" I asked him. "I'm in trouble with the Dutchman again."

Blister wagged his tail, once, and gave me no answer, which was understandable. Being in trouble with the Dutchman was my own personal code, one I shared with no one, not even Genevieve, my closest friend at work. I'd met the Dutchman just before Phil and I got engaged. I was in school for the summer session, and he was in one of my classes. I called him the Dutchman as a joke—he'd been born in this country, the same as I was—because his hair was so blond, his cheeks so round and red, that he looked like a grown-up version of that kid with his finger in the dike. His name was Albert, and when he sat down next to me in class, my whole skin registered his presence. I could feel when he was looking at me and when he wasn't, and at breaks, in the hallway, we talked and made jokes about the professor and the whole time were really talking about something else, we were talking about each other. Class met Mondays, Wednesdays, and Fridays, and for me it was as if the rest of the week didn't exist.

I wasn't even alive on those days. But when I saw Albert I was. He knew I had a boyfriend, but he could also tell how I felt, and so he was confused, and bided his time. And I was this close to cheating on Phil. I mean my body was already cheating. It had already made the decision to be attracted to someone else, and the rest of me was only postponing the inevitable.

At the end of July, before the inevitable happened, Phil proposed. I loved him then, as I do now, and I said yes. When Albert asked me out a few days later, I said, "I'm engaged," and we stopped talking in the hallways.

Ever since then, whenever I've fallen victim to these few passing crushes and summertime barbecue attractions, I've said jokingly to myself, *I'm in trouble with the Dutchman,* and remembering the romance of Phil's proposal, I've been able to shut it off with no problem, as easily as turning a faucet.

This was not like that at all.

We received a notice in the mail that a date had been set for the dangerous-dog trial. It was at city hall, with a judge and everything, and Phil offered to take a day off work to go with me, but I told him I was fine. Ever since the attack he'd been treating me like a delicate vase he was carrying from one room to another, something too decorative and valuable for everyday use, and it was driving me insane. I dressed with care, wearing loose pants that could be rolled up, if necessary, to show my ugly scar. I'd expected the trial to be in a regular courtroom, like on TV, but it was just a conference room full of tables, with the judge sitting behind one at the back of the room. She was a well-manicured woman in her late thirties, wearing a yellow wool suit. The animal-control officer was there, and Jean-Michel and his brother's wife and their daughter, and their lawyer. Jean-Michel's brown eyes flashed when he saw me, and I knew that whatever I was feeling, he was feeling it too.

The animal-control officer acted as the prosecutor. Jean-Michel's family, the Chevaliers, had hired a cheap lawyer from the look of his suit; he slouched there with his fedora on the table in front of him, next to his briefcase. The little girl, Mireille, glowered at me. The judge explained to all of us that the hearing would be held in confidence, and that we would have to leave the room when other people were testifying. They began with Mrs. Chevalier, Jean-Michel's sister-in-law, and the rest of us filed outside. Mireille put her small hand in Jean-Michel's.

The lobby was filled with prostitutes and petty criminals and drunk drivers in to pay their fines, still reeling and wasted from the look of it. Everybody's eyes were red and their clothing disheveled and too bright. It seemed natural that the three of us, being the only more or less normal people, would stick together. We sat together on a bench, and the girl looked at me and said evenly, "You are an ugly woman."

"Mireille, parles pas comme ça," Jean-Michel said. He picked her up and sat her in his lap, his long fingers at her hips. His shirtsleeves were rolled up to his elbows, revealing the fine dark hairs on his forearms, and I wanted to touch them, but didn't. "How is your leg?" he said.

"It's okay."

"My sister-in-law, she is very angry."

"Yeah, she looked pretty angry in there," I said.

Jean-Michel shook his head. "She hires this lawyer. But he is not a trial lawyer. He is an immigrant lawyer who helped her and my brother come into this country. He does not know anything about dangerous dogs."

"I see," I said.

"She also hired an expert witness. She will be here shortly."

"What kind of expert witness?"

"A dog psychologist."

"You're kidding," I said.

Jean-Michel laughed. "I wish, but no," he said. "She is going to testify that Sweetpea is not really a dangerous dog, only bored, and that with more activities she will not bite anybody ever again. My sister-in-law is going to arrange these activities."

"Activities?" I said. "Like Scrabble?"

He shrugged. "I don't know," he said.

In his lap, Mireille squirmed in my direction and scrunched up her face. "Is your dog dead?" she asked me.

"Blister? No, he's doing fine."

"Too bad," she said.

Jean-Michel apologized for his niece's behavior, then scooped her up and walked over to the other side of the room. It looked like he was giving her a good talking-to, which she certainly deserved. The door to the trial room opened and his sister-in-law came out, looking as if she'd like to hang me upside down by my toenails. The bailiff called my name.

I was put under oath and the animal-control officer asked me to explain, as simply as I could, what happened, which I did; then he asked me to show my leg to the court, and I did that, too. The scar was red and raised. "Ouch," the judge said. Then the immigration lawyer stood up. He was a mournful, thin man, wearing a pink shirt and an ugly tie. It made me feel sorry for the Chevaliers, that this was the best lawyer they could find to protect their dog.

"Ms. Grunwald, will you look at these two pictures for me?" he said. He held two color photographs in front of my face; one was of Sweetpea, the other of a dog I didn't know, around the same size and color. "Can you tell me which of these dogs attacked you?"

I pointed at Sweetpea.

"Is it possible you're confused? These dogs look quite alike, and one of them is Sweetpea, and the other dog lives two doors down."

I shook my head, and he looked disappointed. I saw that he'd hoped to stymie me with this line of questioning.

"Give your responses out loud, please," the judge said.

"That's Sweetpea on the left."

The lawyer put his photographs back on the table, next to his fedora. He looked defeated. Was that his best hope, the trick with the dog photos? It was pathetic.

"Ms. Grunwald, have the Chevaliers paid all your medical expenses and those of your dog?"

"Yes," I said.

"Do you really think they deserve further punishment?"

"Objection!" the animal-control officer said, and the judge rolled her eyes.

I leaned forward and looked into his mournful face. "No," I said.

As I left the room I saw the dog psychologist, a portly middle-aged woman in a green dress. All her accessories were canine: dog-shaped earrings, dog-tag necklace, a brooch in the shape of a bone. She was consulting some notes in a nervous manner. I looked over at Jean-Michel and shrugged to indicate, *I did the best I could.* He smiled, and driving home I kept thinking about that smile.

That evening, at work, I turned my thoughts over in my mind and scrutinized them, the same way I checked the chips for defects. Ellen Grunwald, I asked myself, can you love a man you don't even know? Do you think you could live with yourself if you had an affair? Would you ever leave Phil and go live with Jean-Michel in the house with the brother and sister-in-law and the horrible niece and the dog with jaws like a dinosaur's? To each of these questions the answer was no. And yet.

At breakfast the next day, Phil asked how the trial had gone, and I said I didn't know because I'd left after giving my testimony. I told him about the dog psychologist, though, and he laughed, and for a second I forgot about Jean-Michel altogether and laughed with him. Then he stood up and took his cereal bowl to the sink and said, "Well, let's hope those people pay."

"They aren't really all that bad," I said. "I mean, they're just people."

Phil just stared me for a second. "You're not serious," he said, and straightened his tie. "Blister still has scabs."

"They're almost gone. He doesn't even remember it ever happened."

Phil put on his suit jacket and shook his head. "What are you talking about? Whose side are you on, anyway?"

"You're right," I said quickly. "You're right."

But that afternoon, walking Blister, I went by Jean-Michel's house and he came outside right away, as if we'd planned it. Without speaking, we headed off in the direction of the park, our faces harassed by the cold spring wind. Blister licked Jean-Michel's gloved hand and nosed around his pants pockets for treats. Jean-Michel was wearing that same red Gore-Tex jacket, but the hood was down. His lips were chapped.

At the park I took Blister off the leash, and he bounded off to say hello to Chekhov. "So, what happened at the trial?"

"The judge said that she would waive the insurance requirement, since we had done so much to rectify the situation," he said. "But the dangerous-dog designation stays. She said, 'the law is the law.'"

"Well, that's true, isn't it?" I said.

Jean-Michel just looked at me. "Let's talk about something else," he suggested in his soft voice. "Tell me something about yourself that has nothing to do with dogs."

We sat down on a bench, watching the dogs wag their tails and sniff each other's butts and bark, and I told Jean-Michel about my job in the clean room: how the pink and blue geometry on the surface of chips reminded me of Navajo weavings; and about the sound of the air-filtration system in the middle of the night, how its mechanism was like the hushed breath of the sleeping world, which only I was awake to hear; and about how slowly I had to walk, like a person on the moon. He watched my face and nodded, and I felt everything I knew turn upside down. I didn't want time to pass but I couldn't stop it, and eventually I had to go to work. I called Blister and put him back on the leash. As I was leaving the park, Jean-Michel called out. I turned.

"I said, thank you for being kind, Ellen," he said. His voice made my name sound like two separate words.

I got off work at four a.m. and there he was in the parking lot, leaning against his car, still wearing the red Gore-Tex. It really was a stupid-looking jacket. I was overjoyed to see him, and scared, too. I thought, *This is really going to happen.* I was surrendering to the inevitable. I walked right up to him, and he looked as if he wanted to take me in his arms but couldn't. I'd seen that look before, on the Dutchman, when I told him I was engaged.

"You aren't wearing your suit," he said, gesturing up and down.

I laughed. "That's only in the clean room."

"I worry about you," he said. I had the feeling he was stalling for time. "I wonder what is in those chips that you have to wear the suit. What you are being exposed to."

This made me laugh again, and my laughter had an edge to it. "Jean-Michel," I said, "it's to protect the chips and keep them clean. It's not the chips that are dangerous. It's the humans. It's us." In the rawness of the night my eyes were watering. I wanted to kiss him badly, as badly as I've ever wanted anything, even Phil.

"Sweetpea is dead," he said.

"What?" I said, like an idiot.

"Your husband killed our dog, and my niece is very upset."

"What the fuck are you talking about, Jean-Michel?"

"I don't know so much how it started," Jean-Michel said. "I guess he gets the call from the animal-control officer, and he is very upset or something, because you know the insurance requirement is waived, and he comes over to the house, saying that the dog is very dangerous and must be insured for the sake of others it could injure, and he has a baseball bat with him, and he starts to hit the dog, and then kick it, and it is attacking him back and howling, and my niece is screaming holy murder, and he hits the dog on the head over and over and kicks it in the stomach also, until it lies quiet and dies."

The night was dark except for the pale yellow glow of a streetlight. On the other side of the parking lot an early-shift worker clambered out of her car, slow and groggy, and waved. I could not reconcile the Phil of this story with the Phil of my life, yet I didn't doubt that it was true.

"I thought maybe you already knew," Jean-Michel said.

I shook my head.

"He hasn't been here?"

I shook my head again.

"I'm supposed to be out looking for him, but I came here to see you instead," he said. "I wanted to see you."

"What will happen?" I asked him.

"I don't know," he said.

I thought of Phil on the day he found Blister, how he rolled around with the dog in our backyard, for all the world like two children, and I thought of him on our wedding day, too, how he cradled my face between his two hands and kissed me gently, too gently, and I said, "I won't break," and made him kiss me again, harder, in front of the minister and everybody. I thought that however much Phil loved Blister, which he did, he would not have exploded into violence over just the dog, and that this is what it means to live for six years with a person who loves you: if you take one step away from that person, even just one step, he knows. He can't stop it, but he knows. Another car pulled into the parking lot. Inside the building someone was stepping into the clean room and looking at the scanner, where the chips rose and presented themselves for inspection, each of them blue and pink and shining, containing in their beauty some remote, possible flaw.

The Tennis Partner

The first time my father played tennis with Frank McAllister, it was a cool, sunny, the-best-of-summer-is-yet-to-come afternoon in the middle of May. The McAllisters had moved to the neighborhood six months earlier, into a three-bedroom, split-level, single-car-garage ranch identical to ours, and joined the tennis club before it even got warm enough to play. As soon as my father saw Frank hitting practice balls in the frigid spring weather, he decided that he'd found a new and noteworthy opponent. Frank was a broad-chested man with short red hair, pale eyebrows and pale legs, and when he played his face turned as red and wide as a beefsteak tomato, the freckles standing out like seeds.

"That guy looks all right," my father told me, pointing at him unsubtlely with his racket. "Might even pose a challenge." The thing about my father was that he had no perspective whatsoever on his own game. He thought he was a fair player who compensated for his less-than-stellar fitness with a strong intellectual grasp of the sport. None of this was true, but it took me years to figure it out.

"Please don't ever play with that guy," is what I said to my father at the time. I recognized Mr. McAllister from a drug and alcohol presentation he'd made at my high school earlier that year. He was a drug counselor and made us all yell slogans back at him—"We're not sheep! We don't sleep!" which had something to do with peer pressure—and showed slides. It was the kind of forty-five minutes that made me dread going to school.

"I know what you're thinking," Mr. McAllister had said about the slide that showed a joint. "Peace and love, right? If they'd just put this stuff in the water, there would be no more war." We were supposed to laugh. Throughout the presentation I stared at his daughter, Ivy, who had enrolled at the start of the spring term. Like him she was redheaded, unlike him she was beautiful, and I had a furious crush on her.

"What's the matter with you, son?" my father said. He only called me *son* when we were playing tennis. The game brought out the patriarch in him. I told him the "there would be no more war" line, and he laughed.

"We'll have no rush to judgment," he said. "On the court he might be all right."

He walked up to Frank, welcomed him to the club—where my father considered himself an elder, as at a church—and invited him to play the following Saturday. Frank pumped my father's hand in his enthusiastic, drug-counselor way, and said, "Hey, that sounds *great!*" As the days wore on, my father kept mentioning the match and rubbing his hands in anticipation. His previous tennis partner had wrecked his left knee diving for a ball one day and, after an expensive operation, had elected to take up *water aerobics* instead, a phrase my father went around repeating, in a disgusted, wondering tone, for weeks after he heard the news. He'd been at loose ends ever since, with only me to play with; he just didn't have the heart, he said, to whip me.

When the afternoon finally came, I went down to the club to

watch. Mostly I was hoping that Ivy would be there, and we'd strike up a casual yet witty and flirtatious conversation about our fathers and their foibles, a conversation that would lead to a date, and then to another, and, eventually, though my vision here got cloudy, to sex. Of course she didn't show up. She was above watching her father play tennis on a Saturday afternoon. I, sadly, wasn't.

But it was pretty interesting to watch. Frank McAllister had a strong serve and a pretty good backhand, and for a solidly built guy he could cross the court fast. My father, who was neither fast nor solidly built, hung back, waiting for opportunities to show off his killer forehand, which was the centerpiece, and maybe the only piece, of his game. Frank kept coming up to the net, harassing my father with his backhand, and my father kept running back to the baseline as if it were home base and he'd be declared safe once he got there. It turned into a close contest. Both of them hit the ball with audible, satisfying thwacks, and it arced fast and clean across the net. The sound of the game was like music: their shoes made rhythmic, percussive sounds on the asphalt, and the ball hit and bounced in beats, the measured pace of a serve, the sustained pause of a lob, the staccato shock of an overhead smash. Soon they were sweating mightily, their foreheads dripping, their thinning middle-aged hair damp. By the time they were done their shirts were translucent. Frank beat my father in two sets, 6–4, 6–4.

My father shook his hand. "Get you next time," he said.

They took to playing regularly, once or twice a week in the evenings, and a longer match on weekends. The tennis club wasn't fancy—just a set of private courts with a changing room attached—but my father talked as if it were. "Going down to the

club, darling!" he'd announce to my mother as he left the house—
the only time he ever used the word *darling*—and for years I pictured the place as a gentlemen's establishment, with leather
armchairs and Oriental rugs and gin and tonics on the balcony.
The first time I went there with my father, I couldn't believe what
a letdown it was.

My father played up his own game in much the same way. He
claimed that tennis was a game of finesse, just like chess; that
he could minimize, through strategy, the number of calories
expended versus the number of points won; that a smart man
with a solid return could beat all the fancy footwork in the world.
Frank McAllister was his exact opposite, with a game like his
personality: messy, overfriendly, bombastic. My father said it
was like playing tennis with a Labrador retriever. Frank was
always chasing the ball, fixated on it, always bounding up to the
net, smashing his racket down like he was killing a fly. Sometimes he managed it and sometimes the maneuver failed him, but
he never changed his style. He was a risk-taker, a hand-pumper, a
winker at me as I watched on the sidelines. At the end of the
match he'd jog up to the net and shake my father's hand. He won
every time.

Whenever my father and Frank were playing, I'd hang out at the
club, sometimes playing Anil Chaudury, who was around my age
and skill level, sometimes practicing my serve against a back
wall of the building. I was fifteen and had a part-time job that
summer, bagging groceries, which I hated, and I had friends to
hang out with—skateboarding or playing basketball, both of
which were much cooler sports than tennis—but my secret focus,
the real target of my day, was spending time at the club, hoping
Ivy would come by. Sometimes she did. Even now, without the

slightest difficulty, I can summon up in my mind a complete, five-sensed portrait of Ivy McAllister at the age of fourteen. She had long red curly hair she never tied back and that she tossed around in a manner that would've seemed affected in another girl her age. But Ivy had no self-consciousness; she was like her father in that one respect. She knew she was pretty and saw no reason to hide it. When she played tennis, with a girlfriend or sometimes, under duress or the promise of shopping money, with her mother, she wore short white tennis skirts and tiny white socks and filling the space between them was all creamy, freckle-dusted leg. The tennis court was the best chance I had of seeing her, now that school was out, although I occasionally caught a glimpse of her in the park, at night, drinking peppermint schnapps with a bunch of eighteen-year-old guys who, I could tell, were also in love with her.

What I couldn't tell was whether Ivy really liked them or not. It didn't seem to matter to her what anybody thought, not her friends, not the eighteen-year-olds, and certainly not me, and in this respect she was unlike the other girls I knew. No other girl could match her ease, her self-confidence, or how calmly she inhabited herself, so completely comfortable inside her own skin. It's hard to explain what I mean by this. I've tried talking about it once or twice to friends and wound up clamming up after seeing their stares. Years later, a girl I knew at school said, in an angry blurt, "Jesus, Kyle, you love her because you never got to sleep with her and you know you never will. If she weren't gone you wouldn't think she was so great." I denied it, but maybe the girl was right. I really don't know.

A typical conversation with Ivy involved me stammering, try-ing to say her name, and her laughing, waving, and walking on. I'm not sure either of us ever got to the stage of actual words.

And to be honest, I didn't even mind her laughing at me. Her laughter wasn't mean; it was more like a basic acknowledgment of the gulf between her world and mine, a gulf that I did not dispute. I knew I didn't have a chance with her, and she knew it, so what else was there to say?

Meanwhile my father played tennis with Frank all that summer, and the next, and the next. He lost constantly, endlessly, cheerfully. Some matches were closer than others, but the final outcome was never really in question.

"Get you next time," he'd say to Frank at the end of every match.

"Sure thing, buddy!" Frank would say, and shake my father's hand. I think he liked knowing he could always win, and it wasn't so easy that he didn't have to try. As for my father, he'd been trying for years to put together a jigsaw puzzle he'd bought at a stoop sale in New York City: a 10,000-piece picture of a Jackson Pollock painting, each piece an identical dribble of red and brown and black. He'd never been deterred by lost causes.

Over the years and matches, my father and I transformed Frank McAllister, and my father's inability to beat him, into a legend. He never mentioned Frank without referring to him as his nemesis. One time, at Christmas, when we ran into him and his other daughter, Melissa, at the mall, my father greeted him by extending his arm, as if about to strike his killer forehand, and exclaiming loudly, "If it isn't my tennis nemesis, Frank McAllister!" Melissa, who was thirteen and by some accident of chin length or nose placement nowhere near as pretty as Ivy, scowled at me and snapped her gum. Her father laughed heartily—he was always laughing heartily—but I'm not sure he knew what a nemesis was, or if my father was joking, or whether the whole thing was good or bad. My father didn't care. He worked in advertising and was a coiner of words, an inventor of slogans, a singer of jingles, and once he'd decided that Frank was his neme-sis, his nemesis he stayed. We came to use "McAllister" as a code at home, a term referring to some long-desired but impossible goal. A McAllister was like a Pyrrhic victory or a Sisyphean task. It was a mythological situation.

"Going to get an A on that history paper, Kyle?" my father would say, only asking so I could answer him with the code.

"I'm hoping so, Dad, but I think it's a McAllister. Mr. Martin's a tough grader."

"Don't give up," he'd say, clapping me on the back. "Even McAllister will fall one day!"

Yet however large a place Frank McAllister assumed in our con-versations, however grand a figure he became, however tightly he was wound into our family lore, he and my father never social-ized off the court. It wasn't that they didn't get along, only that tennis was the single thing they had in common. Frank and his wife, Beth Ann, were younger than my parents and ran with a different crowd. Beth Ann was a professional caterer whose con-tributions to bake sales and potlucks were intimidatingly accom-plished, while my mother brought Pepperidge Farm cookies to everything. She was an archivist, and at school functions, while other mothers congregated around the food to gossip, she would corner the librarian and discuss acid-free paper.

I was an only child, and both my parents treated family life as an enjoyable, if time-consuming, hobby. I knew them as relaxed, imperturbable, and lazy, and both liked and loved them. I also loved that because my mother was sick of driving me around she encouraged me to get my driver's license as soon as possible and practically forced the car keys into my hand. I used to spend hours on the weekends cruising around the neat suburban streets in my mother's Toyota, passing parks and pools and tennis courts and strip malls while pretending I wasn't just making a big loop around Ivy McAllister's house.

One day when I was seventeen, I finally parked the car. Ivy came to the door wearing a pink tank top whose straps seemed almost to blend into the pale freckles on her shoulders. My courage failed me, and I didn't ask her out; I couldn't. Instead, I asked her to play tennis, which seemed less wildly implausible than asking her out on a date. She shrugged and said, "Sure." We were sort of friends by then, I guess—or at least we knew each other well in the way kids do who grow up in the same neighborhood, know the same people, see each other all the time without ever really talking to each other that much. At seventeen, Ivy still wore her hair long, but now she gathered it in a high ponytail that shook when she laughed, which was often, and that showed off her pretty, freckled cheeks. She agreed to play tennis with me, I found out, because she was on some kick involving exercise. She told me she had a new dream, of joining the youth tour in tennis, a dream I would've taken more seriously if she hadn't also taken up smoking.

The first time we played together, we hit the ball back and forth a few times for practice, then she told me to go ahead and serve. I watched her tuck a ball into the pocket of her short white skirt, bouncing my own ball against my racket a few times. I was torn between wanting to show her that I could play well and not wanting to beat her. Ivy crouched, an unusually serious look of concentration on her face, then nodded encouragingly, and I served. But instead of even trying to return it she straightened up, stood perfectly still, and watched the ball come to her, with a calm evaluating smile. The ball hit the court and then slapped against the fence behind her, all without her moving a muscle.

"Just checking out your technique," she said, and this completely unnerved me. She lost that first point, but it took me the next four to get any rhythm going.

I think the psychology of the contest was the only part that interested her. She'd had plenty of lessons and her strokes were decent, but after a few minutes her attention would wander, making her miss easy shots. Soon enough I found out why. The reason she was into playing tennis now was that she was in love with a guy named Patrick Goddard. He also played tennis, and he was as out of her league—he was twenty-one and home from school for the summer—as she was out of mine. Before long she started telling me about him as we sat under an oak tree in the park, drinking water (me) and smoking (her), after tennis. There is a very specific hell reserved for teenaged boys, and it involves hearing the closest confidences of a girl you're in love with, feeling her unburden herself to you, get close to you, all the while knowing that the reason she can talk to you so freely is that she'll never want to kiss you, that the thought *never even crosses her mind*. It's hell but an exquisite one, is all I can say about it.

"I'm like completely fed up with all this bullshit," is the kind of thing Ivy would say to me after tennis. She still said whatever she wanted, and didn't seem to care what other people thought, and now she swore a lot, too. The combination of her tennis outfits and her dirty mouth made me faint with desire. "I want to move on to bigger things. Don't you want to get the hell out of this suburban shithole?"

"I don't know. What are you talking about, exactly?"

"Hey, do you ever wonder if animals have souls?"

"Not really."

"Ha! Me either," she said, lying back on the grass and revealing an almost unbearable amount of thigh. "I'm so sick of stupid high-school stoners asking stupid questions like that when they get high, and thinking it's so deep. I want to have a real conversation with, like, an adult."

"Okay. What about?"

"I meant with Patrick."

"Oh."

"No offense."

"None taken," I'd say, which both was and wasn't a lie.

Every once in a while we'd run into Frank and my father at the club. That summer they'd sometimes play doubles with my mother and a woman named Eleanor MacElvoy, who was a guidance counselor at our school. Beth Ann's catering business had taken off, Frank said, so she was working nights and weekends, but there were rumors this was a cover-up. Ivy never said anything about it.

"It's the Big Macs!" Frank McAllister would cry out as he bounded onto the court. Eleanor MacElvoy was a strapping young Scottish woman with long blond hair she wore in a single braid. She'd told me I should consider medical school—I wanted to study history—because there was going to be a medical shortage in rural communities and I could get somebody else to pay for it. She was constantly doling out these harebrained ideas she apparently thought were helpful.

"That cow," Ivy said, watching her. "I told her I wanted to be a news anchor, and she told me I should consider being a certified public accountant because math was my highest grade last term. I told her to kiss my certified public ass."

Hellish as these long talks under shady trees were, I would have withstood them forever; but Ivy wasn't as content as I was to know when she was out of her league. And in a way she was right; there was no such thing as being out of her league. She was seventeen and gorgeous. She got Patrick Goddard to notice her, then to watch her, then to tease her and be teased back, then to ask her out. I watched all of it. I watched Patrick Goddard, who was a good-looking, callow asshole, charm the pants off Ivy—I mean literally, in his Stingray after tennis, right in the parking lot of the club. They drank together in his car, Ivy being too young to go to bars, and in the movies, and in the park, and Ivy, I noticed miserably, seemed happy.

Ivy and I still played every once in a while, but only, I think, because she didn't want to cut me off immediately after reaching her objective; she was trying to be polite, or sensitive, or something. The talks under the trees got shorter, though. During one of the last ones, I asked her—emboldened by my understanding that the talks were coming to an end—whether she was having real, adult conversations with Patrick Goddard. She just looked at me like she had no idea what I was talking about. Then she said, "Look, girls have to get experience somehow. And high school guys—no offense, but they don't know what the hell they're doing. The guys at school, they'll get drunk and feel me up and I'll be like, 'What the hell are you doing?' I feel like saying, 'Hey, what are you even trying to *accomplish* down there?' I almost feel bad for them, and that's not a good thing to have happen. You know why?"

I didn't.

"You wind up giving it away out of pity," she said flatly. "And pity, Kyle, is the worst."

But Ivy was wrong. It wasn't the worst, not at all, not even in the same neighborhood. The worst was that one morning I came down to find my parents standing in the kitchen. The phone had just rung. Generally my parents ignored me at breakfast, sitting at the kitchen table reading the newspaper and refusing to make any conversation whatsoever until they'd finished their first cups of coffee. On this day, though, my mother was actually cooking, frying eggs and sausages, and pouring glasses of juice. I sat down and started to eat without asking any questions.

After watching me for a few minutes, my father cleared his throat and spoke. "Ivy McAllister died last night in a car accident," he said. "She and Patrick Goddard were driving home at midnight and he lost control of the car. They hit the highway median and rolled over. Patrick's in critical condition but he's going to survive. We just heard from one of the neighbors."

I put my fork down. It was years before I ate eggs again. "He was drunk," I said.

"They didn't say anything about that," my father said in a measured tone.

My mother looked at me. "What makes you say that?"

"I just know," I said.

I left the house and drove around for hours, all that day and well into the night, passing through all the dark, safe, suburban streets, and when I got back at one in the morning my parents were sitting straight-backed on the couch, waiting for me to come home.

Neither my father nor I returned to the tennis club for the rest of the summer. He was obviously not going to play with Frank, and I planned never to go back to the tennis club ever in my life. My plan was to avoid all the places I had ever seen Ivy; that way, I reasoned, it wouldn't be so glaringly obvious she was gone. I was helped in this line of thought by the fact that I was leaving home at the end of August. I had another terrible summer job, packing boxes in a factory, and worked as much overtime as I could, exhausting myself day and night.

When my father drove me to college he tried to get me to talk about her—he knew how I felt, and I knew he knew—but I just wouldn't, or couldn't, and I never did. Even over the years, even after I went back to the club, I never talked about Ivy with my parents, and if the subject came up with people from school, people who'd also known her, I changed the subject or left the room. I only rarely talked about her, with people who'd never met her; it was as if she belonged to me, and couldn't be shared.

My father and I stopped using "McAllister" as a code word, and so far as I know he never played with Frank again. They lost touch, and anyway it wasn't as if they were ever really friends; they just played tennis together for three years. My father played with a rotating succession of partners and, when I was home in the summers, with me. We slipped into long, lazy matches in which we focused as much on maintaining long rallies as we did on hitting good shots; there was a harmony between us, on and off the court, that only increased the older I got. Though I'd been playing tennis all my life, it was in those later years, after I graduated from school, that I really fell in love with the game, its easy back and forth, the thud and twang of racket strings, the shadows of trees over an asphalt court on an otherwise sunny day. There was no more graceful moment, I came to see, than the finite silence of the ball before it hit and bounced, no more satisfying equation than a strong serve meeting a stronger return. It was like my father always said: it was a game of finesse.

Of course we saw the McAllisters from time to time, in the store or on the street, and news of them reached us now and then. What happened was that Frank, to no one's great surprise, left Beth Ann for Eleanor MacElvoy. Beth Ann kept the house and was given custody of Melissa. Frank had two more kids with Eleanor, strapping, poorly behaved blond children, according to my mother, who thought Beth Ann had gotten the short end of the marital stick. I couldn't help wondering if he would've gone through with leaving Beth Ann if it hadn't been for Ivy dying. But of course there was no telling. The world would have been different in a million ways if she hadn't died, and that was only one of them.

As I got older I came home less often—saddled by job commitments and, eventually, family ones as well—but always visited at least once in the summer, and my father and I always played tennis when I did. The game grew into a staged ritual for us, less sport than ceremony, a language each of us spoke best with the other. My father stood practically glued to the baseline with stiff knees, his old man's legs seeming too thin to support the rest of his body. He'd stretch his arms out far, then farther, to return my shots, with his feet unmoving, and if one made it past him, which happened all the time, he'd only shrug. He'd grown philosophical to an intense degree. Then, in his seventy-fifth year, he was diagnosed with cancer and soon became too sick from the treatments to play. Over a period of months he grew thinner, older, sicker, and a year later, philosophical even then, he said good-bye to us and died.

My mother and I shared the work that followed his death: arranging the funeral, settling the estate, selling the house. She was going to live with her sister out West, and I wasn't going to be coming home anymore, not to this home, anyway.

On a windless, quiet Sunday I went to hit a few last balls at the club with Anil Chaudury, who still lived in town. It was a cool July afternoon; a front had blown through the night before, and the air still held the wetness of it. We served a few balls, slowly, no hurry. On the next court over, a father was yelling instructions to his teenaged son, and I stared at them for a second, awash in memory, before realizing that the father was Frank McAllister. He'd grown stout in his middle years, his face rounder and redder, and his hair was almost gone; but he still ran back and forth to the net like a bounding Labrador, and was trying to teach his son to do the same. The boy was thin and freckled and had very blond hair. He looked around fifteen.

Does it make any sense to say that although I was grieving for my father—whom I had the joy of loving and of knowing well, as a friend and as a parent—it was at that moment, thinking about Ivy, that I thought my heart would break? All of a sudden I was fighting back tears. It seemed crazy to me that I had gone on living without her all these years, that the world had somehow kept functioning, that anyone had grown reconciled to the death of a seventeen-year-old girl. From the other side of the net, Anil asked if I was okay. I lifted my palm to him, asking for a pause, then walked over to Frank McAllister and said hello.

"Hey there!" he said right away, holding out his hand. "How are *you*?" He seemed so happy to see me that I didn't realize at first he had no idea who I was. He was just that kind of guy—a meeter and greeter—and he never turned it off.

"Kyle Hoffman," I said. "You used to play tennis with my dad."

"Is that a fact." He stood there nodding and grinning.

"Dean Hoffman," I said. "You were his nemesis."

"Nemesis!" Frank McAllister said, shaking his head in hearty amusement. He didn't have a clue what I was talking about.

"I was a friend of Ivy's," I said.

The smile never left his face. It had been false to begin with, and it stayed false. "Well, nice to see you," he said, and shook my hand again.

I saw that he didn't want to hear that I'd known Ivy or—which I'd almost said—that I'd loved her. He didn't want to talk about her any more than I wanted to talk about her with the people she and I had gone to high school with. He wanted her to belong to him, too.

"Dad," his son called from the other side of the net, "can I get a drink?"

"Sure thing, kiddo," Frank said.

"You want to hit a few balls?" I said.

"Hey, that sounds *great!*" Frank said. "I'm in the book. Give me a call."

"I meant right now," I said. "Unless you're too tired."

He watched his kid, who was talking to another teenager over by the Coke machine, and nodded. He looked winded from all his bounding, but I could tell he didn't want to admit it. "Sure thing," he said. "Why the hell not?"

I ran over and explained to Anil that I was going to play with my father's old partner for a few minutes. He hadn't kept up his game and looked relieved, wandering over to the sidelines.

I took my place at the baseline. Frank McAllister was bouncing the ball against his racket, getting ready to serve. As I crouched there, I began trembling with anger. I wanted to beat the shit out of Frank McAllister, humiliate him in front of his kid, make him feel tired and pathetic. I knew I could do it, too; he looked out of breath and old. I wanted to beat him not because he wouldn't talk about Ivy but because he didn't remember my father. We had mythologized the McAllisters, had loved them, and he didn't even know who we were, just as Ivy had never known who I was, not really, never cared to find out before she'd gone off and died. To the McAllisters we were nothing. The world, I thought then, is divided into sides just like a tennis court is: into winners and losers, into forgetters and forgotten.

I realized that my father had always known which side he was on, and he didn't care. He was even, I thought, proud. All around me was the sound of his game, of rubber soles and asphalt and the hiccup of a ball crashing into the net; and, beyond that, the sound of the suburbs on a summer afternoon, the lawn mowers and radios and family conversations. Across the court, Frank McAllister asked me if I was ready.

"Sure thing," I said, and prepared myself to lose.

An Analysis of Some Troublesome Recent Behavior

by H. G. Higginbottom, Ph.D.
Department of Biology, Western University

ABSTRACT

This paper will address the root causes and consequences of some troublesome recent behavior by Hank Higginbottom, Ph.D. Professor Higginbottom studies sexual selection in *Poecilia reticulata,* aka the Trinidadian guppy. In his office, on the sixth floor of a concrete building in the southwest corner of the university campus, his main enjoyment comes from the blue burble of the tanks and the swishing, distinctively orange-spotted bodies of *Poecilia reticulata* within them. It's a precarious enjoyment, a calm easily disturbed. It's most easily—and frequently—disturbed by Joseph Purdy, who studies sexual selection in the human male, whose office is located next door, whose research is more provocative and better funded than Hank's, and who therefore has a much nicer and larger lab, with windows, even though said research seems to take place mainly through the observation of pickup lines in bars and therefore does not even require much office space, and whose seemingly favorite activity during the day is to stroll into Hank's office wearing his cowboy boots and offer Hank some deer jerky from an animal he has personally shot himself. On the day in question Hank responded to this offer with a right hook to Joseph Purdy's angular jaw, landing Purdy in the hospital.

INTRODUCTION

In all honesty, the day did not begin well. It began as so many had lately—with Erica crying in bed in the silent fashion she had, without noises or sniffling, and what really got to Hank was how she could get up, turn off the alarm, start the coffee, and get dressed, all without ever acknowledging that she was crying, without so much as wiping away a single tear. She stayed stony-faced while tears ran in multiple streams down her cheeks, the snot swimming down from her nostrils; she wouldn't lift a hand to wipe the snot off her face, and Hank knew she did this to broadcast her suffering and his role in it, that *even her mucus* was a personal indictment of him and of their life together. Even Max, who was only five and not generally perceptive of adult behavior—in fact his own behavior was causing a lot of problems and costing Hank and Erica some serious money in child therapy bills—looked at his father and asked what was wrong with Mommy. Hank only shrugged—which he knew Erica hated, but still couldn't stop doing—and told Max to get dressed.

Then, as Hank drove him to kindergarten, Max threw a fit because he wouldn't pull over and buy him some ice cream, even though it was eight o'clock in the morning and Hank had explained the proper moments and places for the eating of ice cream time and time again. Obtuseness was the major facet of Max's personality—that and anger. No one knew where it came from, the anger, not Hank, not Erica, not the teachers or the therapists. They gave him crayons and he drew mushroom clouds and corpses with blood pooling around them in waxy, Razzmatazz Red streaks. They gave him toys at group playtime and he threw the toys at the other children, whose parents later (and understandably) requested that he be removed. Max, in general, hit people. He was a disturbed child. After a while the teachers and therapists who'd once nodded sympathetically in conversation with Hank and Erica began to look at them searchingly and then stare down at their own hands, as if there were questions in their minds they weren't quite sure how to phrase. Hank knew what those questions were. In fact it came down to only one question: *What kind of people are you, that you produced this child?*

He looked to work for relief from the problems of home. This was essentially the reason work was invented, as far as Hank was concerned. That and to pay the child therapy bills, since Erica had quit work to spend more time with Max, not that it was helping, which was another subject that had been gone over time and time again. In the office, crammed with fish tanks and filing cabinets and scientific journals and old posters for talks his graduate students had given at regional conferences, Hank felt at ease. He was working on a manuscript that summarized his recent research into sexual courtship and predator behavior in *Poecilia reticulata*. He had crunched the data into graphs and tables and believed that he could clearly demonstrate the truth of his hypothesis that the male guppy showed a constant interest in appropriate females regardless of the presence of potential predators. The male guppy was oriented to risk-reckless behavior, and Hank could prove it. It was a sheer joy to work quietly at the office all by himself; the place promoted a sense of relief so strong that it almost felt physical—like blushing, or being drunk—and that's why it was so extremely annoying when Purdy strolled in to his office yet again, without even knocking , his cowboy boots scuffling, his jaw working away at a stick of jerky, to say, "Hey, how's it going, dude?"

Purdy was from California. He was in his forties and used the word *dude* without irony. For this alone he couldn't be forgiven, in Hank's considered opinion.

He clenched the stick of jerky between his large white teeth—which Hank suspected were caps, incidentally—and offered Hank another one, wrapped in wax paper. "Got this baby myself," he said, for the umpteenth time. The deer were always *baby* to him. "It was a large buck, a handsome animal. I had it made into partly sausage and partly jerky. Jerky's great to take to work. They make it for me in a mom-and-pop place on the East Side. You want some?"

Hank said no thanks without looking up from his monitor, which he was pretty sure constituted the international sign for *leave me alone.* Didn't everybody know this? For someone who studied patterns of human interaction, Purdy could be pretty oblivious.

Instead of leaving, he strolled around Hank's small office, chewing audibly on his wizened piece of meat. "Hey there, buddies," he said to *Poecilia reticulata.* "You guys want some jerky?"

Hank put his hands on the sides of the chair. "You know not to feed them, right?" he said. There was, he couldn't help noticing, an undignified squeak in his voice.

"Relax, man." Purdy tapped the stick of jerky against the glass pane of a tank. "Give me some credit."

Hank clenched his teeth.

Purdy was the star of the department, with an endowed chair. He appeared on news shows and was the subject of feature articles in newspapers. He'd made a name for himself, in scientific circles and in larger ones, by stipulating that there was a biological basis for a lot of skanky male behavior. *Men Suck: Scientific Fact* was a typical headline for a piece about him. Dumping your girlfriend because she got fat, cheating on your girlfriend, lying to girls you met in bars, putting Rohypnol into their drinks—it was all just biology, Purdy said, steps on the quest to get ahead in this Darwinian world. Cultural critics said his work was a justification of the basest parts of human culture. Confronted by these remarks, Purdy smiled cagily at interviewers and said, "I just go where the science takes me." The controversy served him well; he brought in millions of research dollars to the school and had lunch with the dean once a month.

Ordinarily, Hank dealt with Purdy like everyone else in the department—by smiling to his face and making fun of him behind his back. But today Hank was a little more on edge than usual. Okay, a lot more. The week had been a swirling mess of anxiety and tears at home, of Erica refusing to talk and then talking in the middle of the night when Hank, needless to say, was not at his best in terms of providing the listening, the holding, the *reassuring* that Erica wanted. In fact he hadn't had a good night's sleep since Sunday night, when she told him, in a quiet, desperate-sounding blurt, that she was pregnant. He stared at her. Under the fluorescent light of the kitchen she looked haggard. Erica had once had a perfect complexion—an English rose, her parents had called her—but it was marred now by dark circles beneath her eyes and flakes on her dry skin. Max was aging her; life was aging her.

She was waiting to see what he would say. There was no right thing to say, he knew.

"Are you sure?" he said. She rolled her eyes. They had sex rarely enough these days that he thought he remembered the night it must have happened. They'd been fighting about Max—Erica wanted to put him in a special school, with other disturbed children, and Hank thought that this would be the end of him ever turning into a normal kid—and they'd gone to bed angry and drunk and resolved the fight with sex, drunk, blotchy-faced, no-eye-contact sex. At thirty-eight, Erica didn't bother with the diaphragm. Standing there in the kitchen, Hank thought sex like that shouldn't bring a child into the world. Then he told himself, *You are a scientist, and you know that has nothing to do with it.* As Purdy would say, sex was sex, whatever the circumstances. "Means to an end," he liked to say while presenting data on courtship rituals, smiling with his huge Californian teeth. Erica stood with her back to the kitchen counter, her hands clutching the marble rim of the top, and gazed emptily at the tile floor. Finally she said, "I don't want to keep it."

This hadn't even occurred to Hank as a possibility.

"Max is enough," she said. "He's more than enough. He's more than we can handle already."

Hank swallowed. His mouth was dry. He and Erica had met in college, in a stats class, and now he was a biologist and she was a bank teller who'd quit her job to take care of Max. She'd given up whatever career she might have had to follow him where he got work, and then to take care of their son. He never talked to her about *Poecilia reticulata.* The fact that they both wanted a family was what had kept them together so far.

"But," he said. He could see her hands tighten around the marble countertop. He wanted to say that maybe if they had another child and it was normal, that might dilute the effect Max was having on them. Which would make it sound as if he didn't love Max and was therefore the wrong thing to say. He also thought, but did not say, that he was amazed Erica didn't want to keep a child when they had a household and the opportunity to raise it. They weren't teenagers; they weren't poor. *What kind of woman are you?* If she could let this go so easily, he thought, there was no telling what she'd let go of next.

"But what?" Erica said.

He realized that she'd been standing there, waiting, for minutes. He opened his arms in a gesture of openness and defeat. "We'll do whatever you want," he said. Which apparently gave the impression that he didn't care what happened and was therefore, as it turned out, also the wrong thing to say.

MATERIALS AND METHODS

For three days Erica wouldn't talk about it. When he tried to bring it up she'd just shut down, literally; she'd leave the room or put a pillow over her head. In the middle of the night he'd wake up to hear her sniffling quietly in her pillow, or sometimes whispering, a string of soft muttered syllables, although it wasn't clear what she was saying or whom she was saying it to. Herself? Him? The fetus? He was a scientist. He tried to confront the situation scientifically. The evidence suggested that the idea of giving up the baby was making her sad. So he leaned closer to her in the bed, took her hand, and said, "You know, we could do this. We could have this child."

"Fuck you, Hank," she said.

"What? Why?"

"You get to go to the office all day and stare at your fucking fish. You're not here getting phone calls from teachers and therapists. You're not here when your own son kicks you in the shin because you won't let him play video games for three hours straight and the kicking hurts, it really actually hurts, and you want to *hit* him and you almost do but then stop yourself because he's your son, but you wonder how much longer it'll be before you give in and smack him across the face."

At the end of this speech there was silence and then a long, snot-filled intake of breath. She got out of bed to blow her nose, several times in a row, in the bathroom. She hadn't generated snot like this since her first trimester of pregnancy.

"It's okay. It's okay," he said when she got back into bed.

"No," she said, "it fucking isn't."

Also, during the next few days Max did them the favor of being his usual self, which is to say a terror, as if he wanted to remind them the whole situation wasn't going to get any better and they should stop pretending it would, as if he didn't want the situation to be clouded by cheap sentiment arising from his acting like a normal kid. He insisted, to the point of hysteria, on wearing his football helmet to bed, and in the middle of the night he woke them up by banging his helmeted head against the wall. One afternoon, while Erica was in the shower, he went into Hank's study and pulled down all the books from the shelves, then managed to pull the shelf itself down on himself, covering himself in scabs and bruises (though not, thankfully, breaking anything) that made him look like the victim of some horrible household abuse and was only going to earn them more doubting looks from all the various child-care professionals in his life. The doctors concluded that they needed to up his medication.

Hank escaped to the fish. Starting in college, fish had been his calm and his succor, and once he'd married Erica and had Max— both of whom he loved, and never wanted anybody to think otherwise for a single second, and he was grateful he had them and would die if anything happened to them, okay?—the fish had mattered even more, because they were *quiet*. They swam around quietly, they ate quietly, they developed patterns of sexual selection quietly. The occasional splash or ripple was all you ever heard, and you had to love them for that. When your home was full of falling bookshelves and indeterminate midnight whispering, the quiet of fish was a blessed thing.

What he'd been studying was the relationship between predator presence and sexual behavior in *Poecilia reticulata.* Purdy, he knew, thought of this as dating in the fish world: the males were trolling the aquarium for dates, their orange spots standing out like unbuttoned shirts and gold chains on chests. The females were hanging out at the bar, eyeballing the available options, waiting for the flashiest candidate to pick them up. To Purdy, fish were interesting only insofar as they provided corollaries to similar patterns of behavior in humans. Mere ammunition for his theories about sexual competition and male hierarchy, they provided the biological context that proved (so Purdy thought) that humans were exceptions to no rules.

Whereas Hank, not that he was some starry-eyed undergrad, thought the fish mattered in their own right. In fact, some wise-ass in the lab had plastered a bumper sticker to the side of a tank that said FISH MATTER. These were the kinds of jokes that made Erica dread department parties, and Hank couldn't blame her—but still. When Purdy, on the day in question, came in and tapped on the glass with his jerky, it obviously annoyed him. So Hank asked him, very politely, very calmly, if he could please not do that anymore, and then mentioned that he was trying to finish a paper for the upcoming meeting of the ichthyological society and it was going slowly and that he'd really appreciate some peace and quiet.

"You bet, guppy man," Purdy said, cheerfully as always. And this, for some reason, was the last thing Hank wanted to hear. *Guppy man.* He basically just could not stand those two words coming out of Joe Purdy's mouth. And Purdy, incredibly, was smiling at him as he said this, even waving his jerky good-bye as he started for the door, and Hank knew *guppy man* was code for a lot of things that weren't related to guppies at all. That, in sum, is why he stood up, crossed the room, and smacked Purdy square in the jaw, causing him to stagger backwards, hand on his chin, jerky flying across the room—though even in his expression of shock Hank couldn't help noticing that there remained a kind of smirk, as if yet another hypothesis about male dominance and hierarchical behavior had just been substantiated by real-world observations. Then Purdy, from the floor, said, "Whoa, Jesus, Hank," and blood streamed out of his nose, thick and red as if in a drawing by Max.

The next few minutes passed in a kind of a blur.

Hearing Purdy cry out and fall to the floor—actually, he fell against a filing cabinet, knocking off a stack of journals on top of it, and *then* fell to the floor with a clatter and violence that, admittedly, gave Hank no small amount of satisfaction—two of his grad students came in and took him away, apparently to the hospital, although it seemed unlikely to Hank that he personally could generate enough force to put someone in the hospital. He wasn't exactly brawny. But the grad students were shaking their heads and clucking almost maternally over their fallen leader and stage-whispering things like "What the hell's the *matter* with that guy?" and "We'd better get to the emergency room right away," which Hank, sitting back in his chair, acted like he couldn't hear. They left him alone in the office, the fish still swishing quietly, and he could hear mutters and whispers outside in the hall, and no doubt everybody in the department already knew about this behavior, which, though it might confirm Purdy's research, could still potentially get him fired. Which would mean no more escaping to the fish. Which would be the last thing he needed just now. Which is how he came to be alone in his office as day turned to night, afraid to go home and face Erica and Max, unwilling to face even the hallway outside; instead he was sitting there typing this analysis of some recent troublesome behavior.

RESULTS AND DISCUSSION

It is possible to think logically about all this. Like a female guppy responding to the brilliant orange spots on the male, which mimic the orange fruits that guppies like to eat, the subject's behavior arose in response to a clearly defined set of stimuli. If he were to defend himself to the chair of the department, or at the very least provide evidence of these stimuli, Hank would have no trouble providing the data. He could, for example, present the following data points:

TABLE 1. Annoying Behavior of Joseph Purdy

TYPE OF ANNOYING BEHAVIOR	NUMBER OF TIMES IN RECENT MEMORY
Starting conversations about grant funding merely in order to brag about the amount he has gotten	8
Mentioning expensive renovations done to house, clearly paid for by salary attached to said grant funding	6
Offering deer jerky and using offer as opportunity to brag about hunting exploits	5
Asking questions about fish, then not paying any attention to the answers	4
Tapping items (e.g., jerky) against aquarium glass and bothering fish, which even a behaviorally challenged five-year-old knows not to do	MORE TIMES THAN CAN BE COUNTED

This was not the only data. Ideally, for a complete discussion of the behavior in question, other figures would be designed and included—a graph, maybe, showing the relationship between these factors and the factors at home. An xy graph, where x would plot Purdy's annoying interruptions and y would plot Erica and Max, and the two would intersect in a jagged, mountainous line cresting at the peak point, which would represent the events of today.

Yes, a graph like that would certainly illuminate the subject.

CONCLUSION

Whether this troublesome behavior is a temporary aberration or a permanent feature of the animal's behavior cannot be determined at this time. Perhaps this paper will result in copious grant funding to pursue the crucial questions raised by the preliminary investigation. Or, perhaps not.

Cleaning up the journals that fell off the filing cabinet, Hank found lying next to a power outlet the stick of jerky that must have fallen from Purdy's mouth at the climactic moment. He clenched it in his hand, thinking again of Purdy's swagger, his large white teeth, his cheerfulness, and Hank's only wish was that he'd hit him harder. With these thoughts in mind, it is impossible for the author of this paper to express regret for any troublesome recent behavior by Hank Higginbottom, Ph.D.

But home is a different thing. At home Erica sits in the dark, crying or not crying, and Max is in his room—because he does not enjoy the company of other children or even, lately, his parents, and at this point you can't really blame him—either screaming or not screaming, but most likely screaming. And Hank is left to wonder what will happen when he gets there, whether Erica will have changed her mind or solidified it, and what he will say to her. He can't go home yet, because he can't stop thinking, among other things, about what the life inside her will look like when the doctor drains it: a potential human form stripped to some forever partial version of itself, a reduction, a piece of *jerky.* He pictures Erica's face and his inability to comfort her; he pictures Purdy nodding and chewing and saying, "Certain scientific facts may be hard for people to grasp." Men act according to biological imperatives. While your wife cries at home, you manufacture figures on a desktop computer in your office. *What kind of man are you?*

In the tanks the fish watch quietly, showing themselves off, selecting their partners. One mating of *Poecilia reticulata* can result in several batches of fry, spaced over an interval of months. If the newborn fish are not provided with cover or protection from their parents, they might be eaten by them. Yet they come nonetheless—batches at a time the guppies emerge, orange-spotted and oblivious of risks, swimming reckless and confused into the world.